THE
J.E. KRAFT
SURVIVORS

Editing by Kimberly Macasevich
Cover art by Adon Henrik Dizon

Contents

For Mom who believed I was a writer.

1

Cover

Rule #27 Never take anything from a vampire

The office line jarred Adrian from his reverie. He tossed the small paperback he'd been reading on his sleek, wooden coffee table and picked up the phone.

"Yes?"

"Sorry to disturb you, Mr. Russo, but your 11 o'clock is here early."

"Thank you, Vanessa. I'll be right down."

He crossed the wood floors of his stripped down penthouse suite and glanced in the cracked mirror beside the door. He hadn't fed recently, but the habit of checking his clothes for blood splatter had become automatic. Wavy black hair fell loose around his dark eyes. Even without sunbathing, his Italian skin had a subtle bronze color in the places it peeked out from his Brioni suit. Though Italian blood no longer ran through his veins, he'd never lost its pride. Another couple inches in height would've been nice, but the DNA had given him a nice vehicle at the very least. It was an asset he'd been unaware of when he was still human.

Probably the reason he wasn't still human.

Leaving the suite, he came to a short hall with an elevator. The building was old, but the elevator had been "enhanced" for him. It took no new calls after he pressed his button, and his coded access took him straight to whichever floor he wanted. Wouldn't do to have it opening up on a floor with windows.

Vanessa rose to greet him when he entered the sixth floor lobby. She was pretty, with a fake tan, fake breasts, and no desire to know anything she didn't have to. It lessened the chance of "accidents". Vanessa had been with him for several years. Ideally, she would be kept for ten or fifteen, just long enough not to notice his lack of aging.

His 11 o'clock, Eugene Shultz, wheeled himself over. Grey had long ago overtaken his hair, but despite the wheelchair, he looked strong. Ezekiel, a near carbon copy of his father, followed.

"Right this way, gentlemen." Adrian didn't have to fake his smile. With simple tastes and ample money, they were some of his favorites. They were perfect clients for getting rid of a few things.

After they were settled in his office, Adrian asked, "What are you looking for today, Mr. Shultz?"

"My daughter, Ellie, is coming up on a birthday, and I wanted to get her something unique."

Normally, Adrian would ask questions about the recipient and try to get an idea of their tastes. People spent more money that way, and every commission stashed away put him in a better position in the slow game he'd been playing with the company.

Today, however, he knew exactly what he wanted off his hands. He swept through a few pictures on his com and then handed it to Eugene.

"Found in an Indian market of all places. It's thought to be around four centuries old." He paused, watching. The slight twitch of Eugene's lips as he twisted the image on the com was all Adrian needed.

"It was likely crafted as wedding jewelry for some wealthy merchant. In Indian culture at the time, moonstone was considered sacred, while the garnets in the filigree holding the cabochon were said to be stones of passion. You can see the hand-wrought scroll work on the band. There is a skill level to it that is simply unmatched today."

Ezekiel shifted slightly in his seat to get a better view of the image.

"Do you think she'll like it?" Eugene asked him.

"It's hard to tell with her lately, but it is..." Ezekiel paused, trying not to show his already evident interest, "a nice piece."

"So, Adrian, how much for this 'nice piece'?"

This piece? He'd pay them to take the damned thing and its taint off his hands. He couldn't believe he'd let it linger under his name this long, even if it was at the show house.

"Given its age and quality, we'd like to see it go for fourteen."

Ezekiel snorted and Eugene sat back in his wheelchair. All part of the show.

"It is unique, I'll give you that. But I'm not giving you fourteen. I think five is a much more reasonable number for this."

"I'd lose my job if I let *that* go for five." Adrian sat back and feigned offense.

Eugene glanced down at the image on the com. "I've been coming to you for several years now, I'm sure your superiors won't mind giving an extra discount to a repeat customer. Can you do seven-five?"

"Half the asking price? I can meet you around eleven—"

"Ten."

Adrian shifted, trying to look uncomfortable in his seat. Finally, he looked toward the door, as though he were choosing them over the company bigwigs who might be lurking outside. He sighed.

"Alright, ten."

Eugene smiled and extended his hand. So easy to manipulate.

"When do you want the piece?" Adrian pulled up the bill of sale.

"I need it for the twenty-eighth. That's Ell's birthday."

Adrian frowned. That was the day of the council. The day he was planning on getting the thing.

"Will that be a problem?"

Adrian forced his face into a relaxed expression. "It should clear processing that day. It will still be at the Manor show house, but Mr. Kapur runs an exclusive restaurant there. Not only can I get you a table, but I will personally see to your tab and deliver the article at dinner."

"Then we have a deal," Eugene said. "Make our reservations for 7:30."

Adrian held the door while Ezekiel wheeled his father through, then went back to his desk to log in the reservation. He hated mixing business with, well, other business, but he'd be damned if he was going to make two trips. He closed his eyes and took a deep, needless breath.

2

Hell

Rule #22 Do not anger a vampire

T he week passed quickly. Too quickly. Visiting the manor was a slightly better fate than walking nude into the sun, but at least sunbathing could only happen once.

When the sun finally set, Adrian took the elevator down to the garage where his dark blue Harley Fat Boy waited for him. Its paint sparkled under the incandescent lights of his private stall. He ran a finger lightly over the finish. His baby would need waxed again soon.

Next to it was a company BMW, the motor likely seized from disuse. Adrian resisted the urge to kick the damn thing as he settled astride his bike. It wasn't the car's fault he refused to touch it. He revved his engine, the sound echoing in the enclosed space, and careened into the night.

The late summer air was fresh and alive with scents. They tempted him. He could let himself go, let the vampire rise, and read the smells like stories. He allowed the tingling vampiric changes to overtake him and breathed deeply… This house was having meatloaf. The reek of cats and a single middle-aged man flowed from another. There on the corner were some teens getting high. One of them was pregnant. The stories of humanity passed by with the streetlights.

Riding past a house with a For Sale sign, the unmistakable scent of blood assaulted him. Damn. Lots of blood. So much better than going to the mansion.

He whipped his motorcycle around and parked on the street. The smell called to him, diminished him to hunger and instincts, and he welcomed it. Adrian walked around to the back of the house, disturbing a mouse in the high, unmown grass. The heat of its coursing blood gave it a soft red gleam as it fled further into the yard. Closing his eyes, he drew in a deep breath. The air was rich with AB negative. An ocean of instinct surged in him, begging him to go deeper, drowning him.

He tried the back door. It swung open, and he was enveloped in the glory of the aroma. At the far side of the dark kitchen, a small stream glowed faintly with heat. He answered its begging and knelt, lapping it from the hardwood floor. The flavor was rich, low in serotonin and abundant in adrenaline. The blood still flowed to a soft drumbeat. His eyes followed the trickle along the uneven floor. A hand extended from behind a baseboard dividing the dining room and living room, blood leaking from a neat slice at the wrist.

With one final lick, he stood and followed the trail. A purple-haired girl lay on the floor. Her eyes were closed, and her breaths were soft and shallow. A backpack and knife were at her feet, and there was still plenty of blood in her. When Adrian grabbed her arm, her eyes shot open. Shit. He tensed for the scream. It didn't come, but her crashing heart made blood spurt from the wound.

Everything else dimmed. There was only bright, hot blood and the yearning. He placed his mouth over the cut and let it pump into his mouth, savoring the flavor and gritty feel of it. Each swallow was a slow gratification. Life seeped into his body: despondent, lonely, and beautiful. Oh god, it was so good. A moan escaped him, and he felt her body jolt.

Reverie broken, he looked at her. Blue eyes were open wide between strands of damp hair, but not with fear or disgust. He couldn't place the stormy emotion he saw there. The drumming of her heart was quick and light now. Without lifting her head, she whispered, "Are you going to take me to hell now?"

He could. She didn't have long to live otherwise.

"Would you like to go?" he said in a voice that had become deeper and gravelly from his vampiric changes.

"Yes."

"Then we'd better hurry."

Adrian grabbed her bag and scooped her into his arms. She slipped out of consciousness as he ran through back alleyways and side streets, but they weren't going far. She wouldn't suffer permanent damage if the staff were quick. Five minutes later, he was close and let smell guide him more than memory. When the sign came in view, he pushed the vampire back down into hiding. The girl's eyes fluttered briefly when he wiped his mouth on her shirt and again in the glaring lights as he burst with his back through the double doors.

"Somebody help," he shouted.

Everyone in the emergency room turned to look.

"Please! She's bleeding. I think she tried to kill herself."

Several nurses came running, another made a frantic call on the little red phone at the front desk. Adrian staggered, bending his knees as if she was heavy. He was soon surrounded. The head nurse barked orders and questions.

"Get her on the gurney!"

She was lifted from his arms. Gauze came from nowhere and was pressed over her wrist.

"What's her name?"

"I don't know. I just found her," Adrian said, keeping his face down so his wavy hair would shield it from the security cameras.

"Get her back there now!"

The gurney sped away. People were standing, staring.

"Where did you find her?"

"In a yard not far from here." Adrian put on his best concerned face. "Is she going to be all right?"

"Please come with me."

"Just a moment, let me get my wife from the car."

The nurse nodded, and Adrian jogged out of the E.R..

Adrian hurried through the old stone corridors of the mansion avoiding the eyes of his kind which glowed cat-like in the darkness. His little detour with the girl had cost him time, and of course, Siri had been waiting for him when he arrived. Getting past that *troia* was never easy. Leaving the mansion had been his way of getting away from her, but there was no way to avoid her entirely.

And now, he was an hour late. That was unacceptable by all but the most forgiving, and his world was not forgiving.

At the entrance to the business wing, he took off his long, leather duster. Aside from being a great biking jacket, it kept the inevitable blood spills off his clothes. It didn't matter how smooth of a transaction he was pulling, a little blood on the lapel was a put-off. He checked the mirror—there were always mirrors at the transitions—and smoothed down his black dress shirt before opening the door.

The glow of candlelight spread into the hall as he stepped out onto the balcony of the ballroom-turned-restaurant. Like everything at the mansion, it was a bit overdone. An expansive crystal chandelier hung over white marble walls and floors trimmed out with gold. Tables were clothed in deep red silk and lit by candles, a display of power and waste that suited the Solifugae as much as the wealthy.

Before Adrian could scan the tables for the Shultzes, an odd glow caught his eye. It felt dangerous, like the sun, but it was a sun that could be turned off, that begged to be turned off. And it was coming from the woman at his table.

Shit.

The dim candlelight might hide the vampiric eyes of a trainee who was losing control, but it wouldn't do much about wanton slaughtering.

He took the stairs as fast as he could without attracting attention and turned through the doors of the kitchen. It was a cacophony. Servers were hustling about, trying to keep up with the dinner rush. The chef, who was the size and build of a bison, was screaming at his prep cooks in abbreviated gibberish that they echoed back to him in apology. Stainless steel utensils clanked on the grill, and plates seemed to be tossed about with abandon. Of all the hobbies a vampire might choose, working with food had to be the most idiotic.

Adrian grabbed the server nearest him in the chaos.

"That table, the one with the light-bearer, who has it?"

"I do." A different server smirked. "You want to follow her home? I know we aren't supposed to play with the patrons, but that glow is…" his fingers twitched, "provoking."

There were a couple of snickers.

The little thrip hadn't seen provoking yet. Adrian took a deep breath, steadying his body's response to the rising anger.

"How have they been treated?"

"Well, let's see. They were sat about an hour ago, and I managed to get drinks out. Yeah, that's about it. The younger gentleman looks quite irate." The server grinned. "It's kinda hard with that glow, ya know? We're taking bets on how long it takes for them to walk out and then on who's going to follow her home. Want in?"

Adrian ran his tongue over his teeth, and the volume in the room dropped. The smile on the server's face faltered.

"Not only are those business clients," his quiet voice that carried throughout the kitchen, "they are *my* clients." Adrian reached out and straightened the server's tie before continuing. "And if I lose my clients tonight, I will make sure I'm not the only one at a fucking loss."

Adrian left the kitchen and threaded his way through the tables. Dammit. That glow was agitating. Maybe it was a good thing the server had stayed away. Even so, he could see Eugene scowling and Ezekiel's stiff body language from the moment he left the kitchen.

The woman was seated with her back to him. A light clung to her, freeing her from shadow but otherwise unobtrusive. It lit the blond hair that fell past her shoulders and illustrated subtle curves wrapped in a black dress. She seemed to be studying the tapestries and trimmings of the room.

As Adrian approached the table, Ezekiel stood up red faced.

9

"Where have you been?" he said in a whispered yell. "We've been here an hour with no food and no word from you!"

There went his easiest clients.

The woman put her hand on her brother's arm.

"Calm down, Zeke."

"I'm very sorry." Adrian said bowing his head slightly. "The item took longer to clear than was expected."

"That wouldn't have mattered if we'd had any food. I haven't seen our server since we gave him our orders. This is supposed to be an exclusive establishment. He should be fired for ruining Ell's birthday!"

Adrian was about to speak when Ellie said, "Woah, calm down there big boy. No heads are going to roll on my account."

Actually, heads rolling seemed rather appropriate.

"Ell—"

"I said, it's fine. Now, sit down."

Zeke thrust himself back in his chair but didn't look placated.

"I apologize for the server." Adrian said. "I'll send someone else to your table immediately, and you can be assured that your first waiter won't be with us in the morning."

"Thank you," Zeke said.

"That's really unnecessary—" Ellie said, and when Ezekiel tried to interrupt, she held up her hand. "No, it's not, and it's my birthday, that means I win." She turned toward Adrian. "Right?"

She placed her hand on the table, her fingers brushing his, and it spread fire through them. He closed his eyes, fighting the urge to jerk it away, and opened them on Ell. Her brown eyes looked pointedly at him.

"Um. Absolutely." The fire from his hand was slowly climbing through his arm, warring with his instincts. He was only vaguely aware of the ongoing conversation. It would be so easy to douse that light. He twitched his arm away, and logic returned as the heat dissipated.

Zeke tossed his own hands in the air and turned to his father, but Eugene's scowl broke into a smile.

"You always have known how to get your way, just like your mother did."

He looked to Adrian. "And now, the present."

Right. That. Adrian pulled the carved box from his pocket. He handed it to Eugene, who peeked under the lid, eyes twinkling.

"I'll go check on your food."

Adrian backed away, bumping into the table behind him. He apologized to its startled inhabitants and wound his way back to the kitchen. They needed to get their food and get the hell out before there was an accident. At the sight of the server watching through the window in the kitchen door, the edges of his vision shimmered. *Pezzo di merda!* Adrian pushed back the vampiric change. He had to keep eyes normal, at least until he got in the kitchen. Mustn't alarm all the little sheep having dinner.

He burst through the doors.

"I'm sorry Adrian. I stayed away because I was having trouble keeping the change back. I swear! Please let me—"

The kitchen light became harsh as his pupils dilated, engulfing his irises in black. Adrian grabbed him by the throat and threw him against a dish rack. The sound of breaking glass filled the room like angry, sharp rain.

"The woman wants you to keep serving them. Get their food. Now." He turned to look at the rest, paused in mid-activity. "And no one touches my clients!"

The kitchen became conspicuously busy as he strode through to the other side of the mansion.

Adrian wound his way up to the rooftop. No point in suffering through the company of his people. Bunch of assholes, all of them. He would wait up here until Council began. Besides, it was a good vantage point to make sure no one followed his clients when they left.

As he exited a window onto the roof, a warm wind whipped his clothing. Storm clouds roiled in the sky. A shiver went through his body as it reset from the changes brought on by his anger. Adrian lay down next to a gargoyle and let his legs dangle over the three-story drop. He smiled and listened to the thunder cracking in the distance.

There was the sound of the window opening, and Adrian's smile faded.

"Good evening, Adrian."

Ah, and the king of the assholes had arrived. It would be Lachlan. Adrian sat up, but didn't say anything.

"Still like your old haunts, I see. I heard you had a bit of a spat in the kitchen. Fight with the missus made you irritable, hm?" He hadn't lost his sing-song Irish brogue despite centuries in America. Dressed in his usual white, Lachlan practically shone against the storm clouds. The bastard sat down next to Adrian, and the wind whipped strands of long, blond hair into Adrian's face. Daring him.

Lachlan put his arm around him. Adrian swallowed. The piece of shit was trying to goad him into a fight because they both knew who would win. Lachlan was far older and more powerful. Adrian didn't move, didn't look at the vampire's preserved, boyish face. Instead, he focused on the lightning strikes in the distance.

"One of these days, Siri will grow bored with you. And that day, laddie, you will die." The storm was nearing. "It surprised me when she made you. There's no accounting for desire, I suppose, but you never have grown up. You're still the impulsive little thrip you were when she turned you." Lachlan leaned in, whispering against his ear, "And it's a shame you're too much of a coward to woo. I'd love to see her disappointment after you tried to satisfy her."

The lighting was lost to the image of Siri pressing against him, asking him to give himself to her.

Dagger points grazed his neck, jolting him from the memory. Bloodlust roared through him setting off the cascade changes. He wrenched Lachlan's arm out of its socket and off his shoulders.

"Don't *ever* set your fucking teeth on me again." Adrian was on his feet.

Lachlan stood up, snapping his shoulder back into place with a smile. Placid blue eyes stared into Adrian's vampiric ones. One way or another, Lachlan always won. And the bastard knew it.

"That wasn't good for you?" He sighed dramatically. "Shame. Well, enjoy the rain, Adrian. I'll see you at Council." And he swept back into the house.

Adrian stared off into the night, grinding his fangs together. There wasn't a damn thing he could do about the sadistic bastard. Yet.

Adrian sank onto the ledge of the small balcony, gravel crumbling where his fingers dug into the stone. He watched the rocks tumble down the face of the building. Then, a sudden light caught his attention. It glared against his sensitive eyes.

Ellie walked next to Zeke as he pushed Eugene the short distance from the colonnades to their car. Their clothes writhed around them in the wind, but the light that engulfed the woman didn't even flicker. As her scarf blew in and out of its clinging glow, it splashed bright red, then muted, then red again. The glow hid her pulsating veins, even with the vampiric change.

Adrian leaned over the balcony to get a better view. In nearly two centuries of existence, he'd never seen anything like it. Ellie slid into the car on the far side while Zeke bent to lift Eugene into the seat. The wind caught the blanket from his chair. It lunged and flipped through the air like a soul free of its anchor.

It was dark. He could have a little fun.

Adrian leaned forward and pushed off the ledge. The wind ripped at his clothing. He met the blanket halfway through his descent, grabbed it, and landed lightly. Damn, that was good. He allowed a measured run to the car as he shook off the change. The door was still open, and Ellie was leaning over her father, telling Zeke to forget the blanket. The storm was moving in too fast.

"Wait!"

Zeke turned and Ellie glanced out the door. The glow was so much more obvious in the dark, an alluring threat. Shit. It was good none of his people were out tonight.

"I believe," he forced an exaggerated breath, "you dropped this." Another breath.

Her mouth opened a little in surprise as Adrian held out the blanket, but Eugene grabbed it. "Thank you, Adrian."

The rain arrived in torrents, and Zeke shut the passenger door. The golden light cast shadows on the tinted windows. Zeke ducked in the car with a wave of thanks.

As the car pulled away, the sky lit and thunder boomed overhead. The rain was pelting, plastering his hair and clothes to his body, and the air turned cold. Good weather for a tornado. One of these days he'd have to hunt one down.

Then, there was a tug on the chains that bound his soul. Dammit. Time for the Council.

3

Survivors' Handbook

Rule #17 Never search or blog about vampires on a computer traceable to you

*S*ome *members of this underground culture are easy to spot. They wear spiked collars and wrist guards and never cut their hair short or expose their skin. Hands, feet, and head are covered in tattoos. The most cautious have tattoos laced with trace amounts of silver over all the main arteries.*

Others are harder to find. They think that extreme measures are a taunt and asking for trouble. They keep the main arteries covered by collared shirts with long sleeves and pants. Women keep their hair past their necks, and men keep their top button fastened. In the end, the vampire will kill whomever it wants, but the less exposed skin, the better. None of them go to the beach in swimsuits, and all the women take measures so as not to menstruate.

Clare stared at the notes on her com and sighed. The day she'd spent trying to find the fanatics had been bizarre. The overt ones were easy enough to spot but were all zeal and speculation. It was the normal looking ones who were unsettling. They seemed intelligent, had jobs and families, but could a sane person believe in vampires?

Several of them had tried to give her *The Survivors' Handbook*. She already had one, thanks. None of them claimed to have been a victim of a direct attack, like those in the *Handbook*, but many had second-hand accounts. And of course, it was completely understandable that all the contributors to the *Handbook* were anonymous. They didn't want the vampires to come and finish the job.

Right.

She rubbed her temples. That look. She could still see it when she closed her eyes. They all had the same look. By the end of the day, she could tell a true believer by their fidgety, haunted eyes, like a gazelle that knows the lion is nearby but can't see it.

Clare glanced at the clock: 9:37. She'd been at it too long today. There were four names to follow up with tomorrow. That was enough. But...

She loaded up the search engine one more time. None of the obvious words had given her any good leads, but perhaps she was coming at it by the wrong angle. She tapped the keyboard a few times, then began to type in any phrase she could think of associated with the sun. Too vague. She narrowed the search to omit tanning. A pop-up asked if she was shopping for sun lamps.

Sun lamps? Do they come in flashlights?

Another search, and she found it. The site not only sold "Sun Flares" but also metal and spiked collars, body odor masking cologne, and her personal favorite, chlorophyll eye drops to enhance night vision. No mention was made as to why a person would want these things. It was just assumed that the people who found them would know what to do with them. The site had no billing address or phone number and recommended that people made their purchases with a generic prepaid card, once again with no explanation. The "About Us" page said that they sold novelty items for people with varied interests. There had to be a way in. She clicked on all the items and all the links. Nothing. No place for questions or a casual, "Hey your site sucks." There were no leads there.

She typed "buy sun flare" in the search bar. Her screen flickered as the results came up. Clare didn't even glance at the corner of her screen to see which program was updating. She was finally getting somewhere. She visited several stores, but none of them were any more helpful than the first.

Maybe an actual purchase?

Clare went back to the first site, *A Little Light*. It seemed the most professional. Rummaging through her purse, she found a company credit card. The purchase was for business purposes after all. She entered her card number and pressed "continue". A window opened asking if she would like the item shipped to a local post office for pick up by tracking number or directly to her location (not recommended). These people were committed to their paranoia. Clare entered the company's address and finished the order.

Nothing happened. There were no fireworks, no congratulations for joining the ranks of the delusional, and no further contact information. She sighed. It had been a long shot anyway.

She logged off and swept her com and paper notes into her red Aleksio briefcase. The clock hands pointed to 10:51, and she would not still be in this building at eleven. It just wasn't right. She scanned her lanyard to unlock the door and smacked the light switch on her way out.

The halls were empty, and the building had that surreal feeling that settles on them when all the people are gone. Clare thought about an old horror movie she'd seen as a girl where the house had been alive and killed anyone who moved into it. She reached the elevator and paused. She could always take the stairs. It was only five floors.

"Girl, get a hold of yourself. The elevator isn't going to kill you."

She jabbed at the down button and the elevator grinned open. Clare grinned back, then giggled and shook her head. It was getting late, and apparently paranoia was contagious. She stepped in and punched the L. The elevator hummed comfortably down and deposited her on the ground floor. Alex, the night guard, looked up from his book and waved to her.

"Working late tonight. Got a deadline coming up?"

"Just chasing leads."

"Hey, if you're going to be late tomorrow night, let me know and I can order you in some Chinese."

Clare smiled and shrugged, hoping to come across as non-committal without actually saying anything.

She stopped at the door waiting for him to buzz it open.

"Umm."

He continued to smile at her.

"The door, Alex?"

He jumped, apparently startled out of his cozy little universe where they ate dinner together on late nights.

"Oh! Right. Sorry."

The door buzzed, and the lock slid out with a satisfying clunk. Clare walked through without looking back, in effort to spare the man some dignity. If he was quick, he'd take the hint without requiring her to explain that she had neither the time nor the desire for relationships of any kind. She hated doing that. Guys either got pouty—which did nothing to scrape their self-respect off the floor—or occasionally did the psycho stalker thing. Mr. Puppy Dog Eyes the night guard probably wasn't the stalker type, but she'd rather not have to find out.

The air outside was cool and smelled of wet concrete. Clare buttoned up her long coat and hurried to the parking garage. Waiting patiently on deck two was her red Mini Cooper. Her father had gotten her an auto-driving electric car when she turned 18, and she should have been grateful, but she wasn't at college for more than a semester before she sold the personalityless hunk of metal for her Mini. She patted its vintage roof and chirped it open. Opening the door a crack, she checked the back seats in the glow of the dome light. She didn't believe in vampires but neither did she believe in being stupid. Satisfied, she got in and started home. Tomorrow was going to be another long day.

4

Solifugae

Rule #16 They are always watching

A drian grabbed the spare set of clothes from the saddlebag on his bike and changed out of his dripping wet ones before going to the council room. He usually arrived before anyone else to claim his favorite seat on the far side of the long dining table. It had the best view of the room and was conveniently far from Siri. Despite being a good defensive position, his seat was empty, along with the two directly next to it. Lachlan must not be the only one who'd heard about the incident in the kitchen. All the better.

Adrian sat down and watched the first small group arrive. With appraising glances, lip biting and toothy smiles, they vied for seating closer to the head of the table. Adrian had fought his way up that chain years ago, not for better positioning but for the right to be left alone. Only pain and use were respected here.

Lachlan glided in next. Very few even looked at him. His position had been won before most of them were made and even perceived slights were carefully avoided by those under him. He took the seat to the left of the high-backed chair at the head of the table. Siri would sit in the one on the right.

A vampire with tousled mousy hair that Adrian had never seen entered, and he came in alone. He stopped in the doorway, taking in the room. Interesting. The council chamber was the most decadent one in the mansion, but the decor was rarely a vampire's focus upon entering any space with more of their kind. True, crystal chandeliers graced the ceiling, illuminating scenes of the family history in Sistine Chapel style, but what was that when there was position to be gained and kept?

It was the walls that seemed to capture the new vampire's attention the most. He paused under each painting, reading the name plates: Jan Vermeyen's *Portrait of Mulay Ahmad*, Raphael's *Portrait of a Young Man*, Jacques-Louis David's *Lepeletier on his death-bed*, and other lost classics. In the far corner stood Michelangelo's bronze *David*. The young man gasped, reached for it, then pulled his hands back to himself, looking around.

The other Solifugae, busy with posturing and seating, took no notice of his odd behavior. He must be very young to have so little sense of self preservation, but even the young tend to have better instincts. His eyes met Adrian's gaze, and he froze. Well, he had some instincts then. Adrian sighed and motioned with his eyes to an empty chair across the table from him. What was one so fresh doing in the council room?

The taint of Siri's presence distracted him from pursuing that thought any further. Before the new vampire's ogling eyes announced that she had entered, Adrian could feel her pull on his soul like the moon's tug on the ocean. She wore a simple red dress that hugged her torso before lightly flaring to the floor, accented by large gold jewelry. She made a point of slinking down the length of the table and trailing a honey brown hand across Adrian's back as she made her way to her seat. The familiar lust and revulsion rose in his throat, and Adrian shoved down the growl that tried to rise with it.

The young vampire's eyes flickered from Siri to Adrian, incredulous, and for just a moment all Adrian's impotent anger transfixed on a new target, one mannerless thrip whose loss of existence would only serve as a valuable teachable moment to any other vampires who lacked a good sense of self preservation.

A murmur broke the spell.

"I'm sorry. What did you say, my lord?" Adrian said.

In his distraction, he hadn't noticed Deval enter. Siri's father may well have been a shade. In the rainbow of browns that come from India, his skin was among the darkest. That, coupled with his choice of dark suits and quiet demeanor, made him easy to overlook in the twilight. Few errors could be more fatal.

"I see you've met Jonathan." Deval gestured to the new vampire. "He'll be working with us on a project."

This was surely a mistake. The only thing this mannerless, immature thrip could possibly be good for was to amuse the elders by being torn apart.

Adrian opened his mouth, but Deval continued to his place at the head of the table. Jonathan gave Adrian an awkward half wave and smile.

Deval took his seat and pressed a button on the com at the head of the table. A contingent of lesser-made vampires, who had the sense to know their place, brought in crystal goblets and decanters. The clean smell of O negative filled the room. With resignation, Adrian let the layers of change ripple through him.

The room shimmered and brightened as new colors emerged from the infrared spectrum with the enlarging of his pupils. That vampiric faculty could at least be beautiful at times. The slight sting of his canines protruding, however, brought only longing as the waft of blood became distinct and loud. He took a sip, and the rush of fresh life filtered into him and joined the glut already circulating inside him. He should be satisfied, but there was never any quenching that desire. No matter how much he had, every drink was a mix of satisfaction and desire for more. There was only thirsty and more thirsty.

He could feel Lachlan's stare without looking up. Lach could hold back his vampiric changes even while drinking blood, and although the display of control was lost on none of the others, it was always pointed at Adrian. The game was ridiculous. Siri only wanted Adrian because he would not have her, and Lachlan hated him for the position and safety her attraction bestowed. It would be laughable if a misstep with either of them didn't mean death.

21

The lesser vampires, made from vamps with little power to give and who had yet to build their own, took their leave as soon as all were served. They might posture and fight with each other, but it was best not to linger with the old and truly ill-tempered. Once the door closed behind them, Deval took a deep draught then stood to convene the council.

The hum of conversation quieted. He looked at them, each one, betraying nothing in his perfect, flat expression. Then, he tossed a small paperback book on the table. Big block letters adorned the cover with the words *The Survivors' Handbook*. After a ripple of shock, Adrian let disinterest flood him and glanced around the table. Lachlan wrinkled his nose. Some leaned in closer to see, and a few looked down or away. Only Jonathan looked unaffected by its presence.

"Whose fault is this?" Deval's voice was calm and slow.

No one answered.

"Lachlan, have any of your experiments in Research and Development gotten out of hand?" That would be the day hell froze over.

Lachlan met his gaze. "No, my lord. I personally oversee every trial, and *I* dispose of them. They are all accounted for."

Adrian squelched a tiny spark of disappointment and picked at some lint on his shirt. The light bits stood out so much more when the eyes changed.

Deval continued. "Tyrone, I want the names of your brutes whom you trust the least."

"Brian and Serge, sir," Tyrone answered in a deep bass. "They are often late from the field, and they're sloppy with their reports."

Sure. Those two vacuous thugs were probably out there just spreading dissent like poppy seeds.

"Track their movements," Deval said. "If they are anything other than lazy, report to me. Otherwise, discipline them as you see fit. Crystal, the social websites and chat rooms?"

"I turn any suspicious activity over to Justin for tracking, my lord."

Adrian allowed his disinterest to drop and focus. He remembered Justin's rise in the mansion. The vamp's instincts had won him enough space to acquire skills valuable to Deval, but in their interactions, Adrian had not found him particularly thorough. That defect was about to cost him.

"Justin."

"Yes?" Justin looked up from the book.

"Why didn't you bring this book to my attention? Were you unaware?"

"No, not unaware. I just didn't think it was that important. I mean, books about vampires are published every day and-"

"I see." Deval walked around the table, continuing in his soft voice as he went. "You didn't think it was important that there were survivors? Perhaps you didn't *think* it important that they were convening together or that they had published very accurate material about how we operate. Did you *think* to check with the listening algorithms to see if there was an uptick in talk about our people?"

Justin shook his head and stammered but produced no answer. Deval stood behind him, resting a hand on his shoulder.

"I *think*, my son, that you have outgrown your usefulness to me."

An unforgivable sin. Deval would feed, shelter, and tolerate all manner of destructive behaviors within the manor so long as one was useful. That and remaining invisible to humans were the only commandments in his world. Both had just been broken.

Justin looked over his shoulder at Deval. His words were strained. "No, my lord."

Deval's nod was almost imperceptible. "Lachlan, do you have any use for him?"

Given to the devil himself to play with. Shit. Deval must be truly enraged under that quiet demeanor.

Justin's pleading stare jumped from Deval to Lachlan.

"I do, indeed." Lachlan's smooth voice was practically a purr.

"Please. Just kill me, lord."

"See if you can get any other information from him."

The fresh blood in Adrian's system seemed to congeal at the thought. Lachlan's natural sadism made him particularly effective at creative interrogation. Death was fair. This was excessive. Justin would be inventing information before it was over just to get Lachlan to stop.

Lachlan smiled. "Thank you, my lord!"

"Please! I don't have any more information!" Justin thrashed in his chair under Deval's age-strengthened hand. Red began seeping through his clothes where Deval's fingers were fixed.

"Tyrone, please escort this young man to R&D." Turning to Lachlan he added, "You may be dismissed as well."

Tyrone was hefting Justin out of his chair before Deval had finished speaking. There was no getting out of Tyrone's grip, but Justin screamed and pleaded and fought, nonetheless. Adrian turned his eyes on the table to hide his aversion as Lachlan flowed out of the room with the blissful look of a lover going to a tryst. Besides power, pain was the only thing Lachlan truly loved, and Adrian didn't have to see the glance the sick bastard threw his way to know he'd enjoy nothing more than having Adrian released to R&D.

When the commotion had faded down the hall, Deval turned back to the council.

"Jonathan, you brought this," he waved at the book like he was trying to wipe its presence from the room, "to my attention, and I know you have been searching for the authors. I would like you to head up Media in place of Justin, but I want this to be your pet project. Jen in Tech and Adrian in Human Resources will be at your disposal toward that end. I trust you won't disappoint me."

"No, uh. No, I won't. Thank you, my lord."

Adrian ground his fangs. Fantastic. Now he was strapped with the idiot most likely to get killed next. The night could hardly get better.

Adrian finally escaped the mansion to find that the storm had passed during the two hours sucked away by the rest of the meeting. He picked his way around branches and debris as he strolled down the drive toward freedom. He'd tucked his bike between the corner hedge and a monstrous oak this time. As he neared the tree, however, it was as though a string vibrated deep within him. Closing his eyes against the disgust, he waited until he was in control again, then rounded the oak. Siri was perched sideways on his Harley, the wind tugging and playing with her long raven hair.

"I see you've been tweaking the engine," she said. "Care to take me for a ride?" She blinked her wide almond eyes at him. Their innocent expression had lured him once, but he knew the harpy that was behind it now.

"No."

She tsk'ed at him, like he was a stubborn child. "I thought we could finish our conversation from earlier."

"We did finish." Adrian uncurled a hand that had fisted of its own accord. No amount of money or position could possibly be enough to tempt him to live back inside that hellhole again. He should tell her what he'd sold tonight. That ought to convey the idea. Of course, it also might get him killed, but the look on her face would be worth it.

Before he could say anything, she gave him a roguish smile, then hiked up her dark red dress and swung fully astride the bike. Her long legs were beautifully crafted instruments of torment. His inability to check the reaction they roused in him was a worse torture than anything else that had happened that night. He closed his eyes for a moment and swallowed his rage.

"Get off my bike."

"Come on. Take me for a ride."

"I'd rather watch the sunrise."

She leaned forward on her hands, supplying a view of her ample cleavage. "You can't run forever. You could try, but we both know you wouldn't get very far."

As if toying with him sexually wasn't enough, the implied threat of her control over him as his maker caused him to lose what little grip he still maintained on himself. He could feel her presence even more as the vampire rose to the surface, could feel her satisfaction at making him lose control. He knew that's what she was after. She had a way of getting what she wanted, but even if he couldn't keep his emotions or body from reacting to her, he would deny her anything else as long as there was life in his body.

"Get. Off. My. Bike."

She sprang off the Harley and landed in front of him with ease. The scent of incense rose from her skin. She kissed his stiff lips, forcing her tongue in and running it across his fangs.

"Don't stay gone so long next time."

Madonna santa. What he wouldn't give to kill her.

She walked away without looking back. Even if she wasn't so much older and stronger, he would never be a threat to her. She had made him. Her life essence gave him life, and she could summon him, manipulate his life-force, or kill him with a thought. It would be another fifty years at least before Adrian's well of power was strong enough to break free of her hold. Until then, only his usefulness to her father gave him freedom from her. It was a hell like none any religion could dream up.

Adrian peeled out of the drive in the direction of the storm.

5

Hunting

Rule #4 If going out at night, travel in groups

drian rode toward the mountains. The sounds of the pavement beneath him and the roaring engine massaged his nerves. He watched the sky break with lightning more and more frequently as he approached the storm. Speeding up, he chased the rain, and caught it on the foothills. By the time he turned off onto a dirt mountain road, the rain was coming down in thrashing sheets. He thought of the water pouring off of him and imagined it as blood, thought of the smell of A positive rising off of his skin, and his vision sharpened. The pine trees grew close here and their needles kept the ground from turning to mire, but the dark road was still covered in dips and bumps that were lost to human eyes at night. He navigated his bike for a few miles before pulling it off the road. Careful not to scratch the dark blue finish, he maneuvered the bike to a semi-dry spot under the trees. He pulled a cover from the saddlebag to keep the sap and needles off, gave it a parting pat, and set off on foot.

Away from humans and his own kind, it was like stepping out of a cage. He had no part to play, no rules to follow. He let his instincts drive him through the dense forest. The storm created an interesting challenge, obscuring scents and limiting vision. The mud ran in torrents and, after slipping twice, Adrian felt almost human for a moment. It would be a good night for a hunt.

The weather rarely offered such a challenge. Lighting struck nearby, and the sound of its thunder ripped through him. It would be a damn good night.

He climbed the pathless terrain with care, looking for a print, a bent leaf, a scent, anything the rain might have missed. Even with enhanced senses, he found nothing. The downpour had erased everything physical, so Adrian stood still in the rain. As the heavy drops poured over his hair and skin, he pushed against the boundary of his body until some part of him, his soul perhaps, slipped past it. Adrian began to *stretch*.

The world unfolded without sight into a perceived reality much richer than the one which contained his five senses. Space was tricky, and Adrian had to orient himself by the strength of the mountain below to keep distance from losing its meaning. The feeling of rain on his body became muted against the backdrop of the green and beating life of the forest. He *stretched*, his physical body unmoving, and the soft lives of smaller things revealed themselves to him along the strands of webbing that made up the essence of the mountain. Dips and ridges made little difference, but the swollen rushing of a stream crackled against his perception, probably what gave rise to the myth about vampires not crossing running water. While it took a moment to *stretch* past the disturbance, it was nothing more than an annoyance.

Not far past the other side, Adrian felt a ripple along the strand he moved on. Shit. There were Watchers. Granted, there was less danger from them here, away from humans—the ones that guarded humans could be seriously aggressive—but aggressive or not, Watchers were still nothing to toy with. They only operated in this shadow side of reality, not on the side of the living, but while Adrian *stretched*, he was vulnerable to them. As he slipped away down the strand, he could feel their eyes snap to him and a cold sneer press against his consciousness, but these particular Watchers didn't seem inclined to give chase. Relief spread through Adrian, and he grabbed a different strand that flowed up and in the other direction. There was no need to give them a reason to change their minds.

There! In the cover of a tangle of green life, something quivered. Lighting struck, and he could feel its fear. He brushed against the outline of its soul, snapping it into focus. It was a yearling doe, and though Adrian was not corporeal in the shadow realm, his touch startled her. She bolted up and stood, stamping her feet. He pressed more firmly, and she began to relax under his hold.

"Come."

She refused to move her long, thin legs toward him. In that cold place where he had no hands and she had no body, Adrian stroked the deer. He lied to it with peace.

"Come."

It took effort to hold the *stretch* and draw the doe, more than it should have, but the city was too full of people and their Watchers to practice *stretching* safely. He was out of shape, and the ache of a muscle too little used permeated his essence. The deer came, slowly.

A new smell carried by the wind teased the edge of his senses, and he fought to keep his focus. Against the sound of the rain, a twig snapped. Adrian's hold slipped, and the *stretch* recoiled like a rubber band snapping back into shape. Distantly, he heard the deer bound away.

"What—" A massive weight rammed him into the mud.

"Who said you could hunt on my grounds," a low voice growled.

Adrian swung his legs up under his attacker and launched the man off him. He flipped up to his feet and looked the intruder over. A full beard overshadowed the man's short, copper hair. In red flannel and khakis, he was the epitome of a mountain man, except that two average sized adults could probably fit inside his ill-chosen clothes.

Time for some fun.

"You lost me dinner," Adrian said, wiping the mud from his leather trench coat, "and you will pay for it."

Thunder pealed.

The man's hazel eyes laughed, but his face remained stoic. "I'll bury you in the mud." And then he lunged.

Not today. Adrian lowered his body at the last minute to catch the man by the middle and flip him over. But as Adrian lifted, he felt an iron grip close on his own waist. The mountaineer had anticipated his move and grabbed hold, carrying them both to the ground with the momentum. More mud.

With a sudden twist, Adrian broke free and sprang. He rammed his fingers deep into the slick bark of a tree trunk. He gripped and jumped again, just snagging a higher branch. Pushing wet hair from his face, he looked down at the soiled man with a sneer.

"Coward," the man bellowed at him. "I had you!"

"It doesn't look that way from here, asshole. Better luck next time."

"You bastard! You can't stay up there forever! The sun will chase you down sooner or later."

"Admit it, Perry. I win."

"You cheat! You know I don't do trees." Perry tried to frown, but his grimace wavered into a grin that turned into a laugh. "Fine, fine, you win this time. Now, come down before I shake you out."

Triumph conceded, Adrian swung down and dropped. Once on the ground, he found himself in a crushing, muddy squeeze. Despite the wet dog smell and his protesting ribs, he smiled.

"It's good to see you," Perry said, finishing the hug with a sound smack on the back. "It's been a while."

Adrian nodded. "Too long. In-town hunts and business."

"We have a lot to catch up on."

Perry's tone was carefree, but he glanced away. There was something hidden behind his words. Adrian waited, but the mutt didn't offer anything further, so imitating the same light tone, Adrian said, "You owe me a hunt first."

Perry snorted. "That was your own fault. You should have come by before you went hunting. Besides, you were being careless. I could have killed you before you realized I was there."

Adrian waved the comment away. "I smelled you a little ways off. I just didn't want to lose the deer."

"Right. Sure you did. That's why you ended up on the ground," Perry flashed a lopsided victory grin. "Well, since I owe you, let's see what we can scare up."

The hulk of a man disappeared into the woods and Adrian followed. They could talk later. Watching Perry hunt was like watching bottled lighting looking for a place to strike, and the enthusiasm was contagious.

The storm was spent by the time they began to make their way back to Perry's den. Adrian was so full he felt sloshy, and Perry, looking a little rounder in the middle himself, picked at his teeth with a bone fragment from the buck. It should have been a relaxed action, but despite having gorged, he didn't look relaxed. The closer they got to his home, the more he glanced around. He took in the scent of the air even though the wind came from their backs.

That was enough. Time for the idiot to spill what he was worried about. "What's up with you tonight?"

Perry glanced at Adrian and sighed. He looked up into the trees as though words might fall from them and opened his mouth to speak but then stopped. His eyes were on a patch of night visible through the leaves. The black of the sky was hinting toward dark blue.

"Let's get you inside before dawn. We can talk about it then."

Adrian studied his friend for a moment longer. He didn't seem distressed as much as distracted, and there was no telling what had grabbed Perry's attention this time. The cur hadn't come out of that cave for six weeks when he was studying telomeres. So be it. Whatever it was could wait. Adrian quickened his pace.

A long ago shake of the earth had slid a blanket of boulders from high up the forested mountain down its side. In the process, it had covered the mouth of an expansive system of caves. How Perry had found the caves was anyone's guess since his story was different every time he was asked. It was probably something inglorious like twisting his ankle and literally stumbling into them. But Perry had called them home for many years now.

They were coming down and around the slope of boulders when a scent, expanding on the night air, met them.

Human.

Female.

Adrian motioned Perry to stop. His eyes grew wide, but Adrian didn't wait to explain before jumping from an outcropping boulder into a treetop below. It would save time on descending and give him the advantage of high ground. The intruder was almost at the cave entrance. She was probably just some wandering hippie type, but if she found the caves, she might decide to bring her hippie type friends to see the new cool place she'd discovered for them to have a drum circle.

She needed to forget she'd ever been there.

6

Beginnings

Rule #31 Let those you trust know about the danger

Adrian jumped two more trees and pulled a syringe full of Zeta Inhibiting Peptide from his duster. The Z.I.P. shot was formulated to make every neuron that fired lose its connections. Any neuron that was sparked by the cave or seeing a vampire would promptly forget everything tied to those subjects.

Perry was tearing down the slope behind him, but he needn't worry. Adrian could see her now. The woman was well built, in both senses of the phrase, with smooth brown skin and short African hair. She was wearing a pair of tactical boots but not much else. Long naked legs emerged from... one of Perry's giant, flannel shirts.

And the picture became clear.

Her gaze darted up the slope, eyes widening in the predawn light. There was no way she could miss the commotion of their descent. That was fine. He nearly had her and—dammit. She slid back between the rocks hiding the cave entrance. No matter. She'd have no way past him now.

So long as he got to her before Perry did. Obviously, the idiot wasn't thinking clearly.

Adrian dropped at the entrance, making no effort to appear human. Whoever she was, she would never remember tonight. Ignoring Perry's shouts, Adrian turned sideways and slid between the rocks a few feet. The crevice to his left, normally dark, was glowing. There was a thump on the ground outside. Perry must have jumped as well. He was running out of time.

Adrian slipped through the fracture and into a room-sized cave that Perry affectionately called the "foyer". A lantern lay on its side casting long shadows against the rocks, and the woman was waiting. To his vampiric eyes, she thrummed and glowed with the beating of blood. Heat waved off a brandished knife she must have been carrying somehow next to her body. Her mouth opened into an "O", and there was a crash of heartbeat. The taste of her fear wafted through the stale air, and the smell of adrenaline came to him like a challenge. He raised the Z.I.P.—

And Perry burst through the entrance. He thrust his heaving body between them. His eyes blazed yellow instead of their normal hazel green, but he made no other motion toward Adrian.

"Move." The vampiric change turned Adrian's voice into a feral snarl. "This is for your own good."

"Adrian..." Perry's voice was quiet, but the growl was unmistakable. Adrian couldn't tell if Perry was having trouble maintaining his human phase or if it was a warning. Anger was inciting his own instincts, making it harder to see his friend over the smell of an ancient enmity. Adrian pushed back at the bloodlust.

"Perry?" a low, feminine voice questioned.

"It's fine. He won't hurt you." Perry's eyes bore into him. "This is my *friend*, Adrian."

"Is he like you?"

Perry hesitated. "No."

Adrian hissed. "Like you? She knows?! What the hell are you thinking!"

Perry ignored him. "What were you doing out at this hour?" He spoke with forced lightness.

The intruder opened her mouth, but Adrian cut her off. "What is she doing here?"

"Miriam, go back to the bedroom," Perry said without looking back.

For the first time, her eyes left Adrian. She narrowed them at Perry. "If *you* can't handle this thing, I'm sure as hell not safe back in the bedroom."

He didn't relax his stance, but a grin tugged at Perry's left cheek. Finally, unable to contain it, a smile broke over his face. It was disarming. He rubbed a hand over his chin and beard.

"Come on, put the Z.I.P. away, dumbass. And Mary, you can put the knife back. It wouldn't do you any good anyway."

Miriam did not look convinced.

"Mmm-hmmm," She said, eyebrows raised and looking Adrian up and down, "And just what is he?"

"He's a vampire."

Miriam's grip on the knife tightened. "No he isn't. Here? In your home? Are you *crazy*?"

At least *she* had some sense even if Perry had lost his. What was he thinking? He knew how dangerous human exposure was, and it was no longer pitchforks and torches. Guns or laboratories would be the consequences. There was no way Adrian could Z.I.P. her now without risking a real fight. He'd have to wait until the dumb mutt dropped his guard. Adrian took a deep breath and let the changes go out with it. As his vision returned to a human level, the light he could see dimmed, and her body no longer danced with the heat of blood.

She blinked at him. "And if you could do that the whole time," she said, waving her knife in his direction, "why'd you come crashing into your friend's house all ugly? That's just rude."

Adrian smiled, in spite of himself, and Perry laughed. She looked from one to the other and shook her head.

"Adrian, meet Miriam Elizabeth."

Adrian tucked the Z.I.P. back in his coat and stretched out his hand. Miriam pursed her lips.

"So, I'm supposed to just shake hands with you like you didn't just try and eat me?" She slid the knife into a pocket on her boot but made no other move. Perry reached toward her, like he was going to give her a hug, but she held her hand up.

"Don't you try and touch me either. You're covered in mud and I don't even want to know what else."

She scooped up the lantern from the floor and stalked down the worn, gravelly path toward Perry's living area, "My brother always said I had horrible taste in men. I cannot believe I got myself into this." The tirade faded to a distant mutter punctuated by occasional profanity.

Perry looked down, scuffing the ground with his foot, the very picture of a scolded dog. It was about time someone got under his skin, but a human?

"*Ma quanto sei coglione.*"

Perry snorted. "Still less of an ass than you."

Adrian rolled his eyes and followed the retreating light down into the natural cave system that made-up Perry's home. The dirt path gradually gave way to rough rock as they descended. When Miriam's lantern was extinguished around a corner, Perry unsnapped a pocket and pulled out a small LED light. Despite its size, the beam was bright, and the walls sparkled with calcite. Fissures opened occasionally, but Adrian and Perry didn't turn until they came to the fourth on their left. Even without his perceptions being heightened, Adrian could detect Miriam's feminine scent against the dusty smell of the cave air.

This particular passage followed an incline for several feet before opening into a roomy chamber that had been converted into an apartment of sorts, furnished with rustic wood furniture. From an adjoining room, Miriam's irate monologue carried over the walls and floor which were polished smooth from holding water long ago.

He and Perry passed through the main living area and ducked into a lower chamber that contained the bathroom and laundry. The apartment was near enough to the side of the mountain that Perry had been able to install basic plumbing and ventilation after only a few years of back-breaking work. Motion activated lights cast a soft glow from their hiding places in crevices and behind rocks. The floor was smooth, but the walls were rough where Perry had chipped away stone to widen the space. The changes to the cave would cause any speleologist to have an apoplectic fit.

Adrian loved it.

He stripped and stepped into the alcove that housed the shower while Perry grabbed a spare set of clothes for him from his "linen closet". Adrian had been coming here as often as he could sneak away for decades. Should anything go bad quickly, everything Adrian would need was already here.

"You know this is a terrible idea, right?" Adrian asked, watching the caked on dirt and blood swirl down the drain.

"Yep." Perry's voice sounded tired over the water.

When he was as clean as he would get, Adrian reached out and snagged a towel off a flat-ish stalagmite. Fresh clothes were set on the ground nearby, and his dirty clothes had already been whisked away...

"Where's my duster?"

"Bite me, vampire boy." Perry took off his muddy shirt and tossed it on the floor, revealing his barrel-shaped, hirsute chest. "I'm not stupid. You'll get your Z.I.P.s back when you leave."

Adrian tried to snarl in response, but there was no real threat in it. "*A fanabla.*"

When they were no longer covered in mud and gore, he and Perry made their way back up to the main living area. Miriam was in the connecting kitchenette, her long legs now covered by a pair of black sweatpants. She banged a copper cup onto the wooden counter as they entered. Perry's eyes lingered on her as she got a drink of water from the small refrigerator. Adrian had never seen Perry like this. As good natured as he was, Perry had avoided romance on principle. Watching him look at Miriam like that was like seeing a whole different person.

"When—no, better,—*how* did this happen?" Adrian said.

"She's been doing a wildlife survey on the other side of the mountain." A big dopey grin spread over Perry's face. "Pulled a gun on me, and that was all I needed to know."

Adrian's brows rose. "A gun?"

"That's because he was rude," Miriam snapped. "Strange mountain man following me in the middle of nowhere."

"Hey, I saved your life."

37

"Don't even play. I could've handled that bear, and she was fine until you came lumbering around."

Adrian shook his head trying to clear the tangle of conversation threads. "A bear? Really? Is this the basis of all your long term attachments?"

Perry shrugged as he found his way to the couch. "It's clearly a winning strategy." He patted the spot next to him, and Miriam glared at him in response. She settled on the far end of the sofa. "Besides, you know Bertha's deaf in one ear. She startles easy."

Ah. Adrian nodded as he moved a stack of Perry's research binders from a side chair to the floor and sat down. Bertha was the resident matriarch, and no matter what they did with her suitors, at least she garnered their respect. Not that either of them would ever admit to thinking bear cubs were cute.

"*He* was following me," she said, pointing her finger at him, as though that trumped bears.

"I was." Perry said, inching a little toward Miriam on the couch. "Had been for a week, watching where she was setting up camp, what she was doing."

"Making sure she didn't find your den," Adrian interjected.

"Stalking," Miriam said.

"Exactly," Perry said, eyes twinkling. He was decidedly closer to her now. Miriam glared at him. "So this day, she was surveying in Bertha's territory, and the bear was out with this year's cubs."

"That bear was fine until *you* showed up making noise."

"*I* was trying to scare her off for you."

Miriam clicked her tongue at him. "Made her defensive is what you did. Mama bear hears something and rears up. Next thing I know, he comes busting out of those snapping pant things he wears, turning all fuzzy, and roaring at this bear. I felt sorry for the bear."

"And then she shot me."

"She shot you?" Adrian couldn't keep the smirk from his voice. Damn it all, it was a good story. It'd be a shame to make her forget something so hilarious. Especially at Perry's expense.

Miriam's cheeks reddened slightly, deepening her chocolate color, but

BEGINNINGS

she held her head high as she said, "Of course I shot him! If the bear was running away from him, I figured I needed to be running too! When it actually dropped him though, I was terrified. I hadn't meant to hit him, just let him know I wasn't some helpless Snow White chick lost in the forest. So, I holster my weapon and go over there. The whole time I'm thinking I've just killed some innocent, hairy hermit for scaring a bear away. Probably just some dude with hypertrichosis, you know?"

Adrian snorted. Werewolf syndrome was a great cover for Therians.

"He was on his stomach when I got to him, and I didn't really want to touch him but," she shrugged, "he wasn't responsive. I got down—all the time telling myself it's always the brother or sister that dies in these movies. This wasn't a movie though, right? This was a real guy I might have killed and his airways might be blocked with leaves... So I rolled him over."

Perry leaned back on the couch, grinning. "I was mid-change."

"About as ugly as you were too." Miriam jerked her chin at Adrian. "Face all misshapen and those creepy yellow eyes half open. He was bleeding from his chest."

Perry snorted. "I was dazed, but that woman's got a set of lungs that could wake the dead."

"He grabbed me!"

"I didn't have any Z.I.P.s on me, and I was thinking I had to get her back here before she shot me again. Healing one bullet wound is hard enough. But all of a sudden, I'm getting pummeled! She's kicking me and punching me with her free hand, screaming like a banshee."

Miriam folded her arms. "I was not going gentle into that good night."

Perry drew her in to himself. "Rage, girl. Rage against the dying of the light."

She held her body stiff for a moment, but Perry was undaunted and nuzzled her neck. A smile hinted on her lips. Looking at each other, they fell silent.

Adrian cleared his throat. "I hate to interrupt a moment by Dylan Thomas. He is one of my favorites, but I was rather enjoying hearing about you getting your jewels handed to you."

Perry grinned. "Especially since you've never managed it."

39

"Do you need another lesson?" Adrian asked, running his tongue over his teeth.

"Anytime," Perry said, cracking his knuckles in turn. Miriam rolled her eyes.

"You two need a room?" she said.

Perry didn't miss a beat. "I'll take you in a room."

"Little boy, please. Don't act like you can handle me."

A hungry, wolfish look came over Perry's face. Miriam ignored him and continued.

"So, I reach for my gun, and he grabs hold of my arm. Then, he has the nerve to tell me to calm down. Calm down!"

"I've never had a more colorful or creative telling off in my life," Perry said. "Gran would have been taking notes."

"Does she know?" Adrian asked.

The smile melted off Perry's face.

"That would be a no, then."

"If she wiped Miriam…" Perry's voice was almost a growl. "If *anyone* wiped her…"

Adrian held his friend's gaze, which was sharper and harder than he had ever seen it. If that's what Miriam meant to him, then so be it.

"I get it. She's perfect for you." The tacit threat in Perry's eyes began to fade. Adrian forced a shrug. "A little like your grandmother, if I'm being honest."

Perry blinked, a faint flash of horror crossing his face.

Adrian swallowed a chuckle. "So, how long has this been going on?"

"Since late spring," Perry recovered himself. "She does research for her mom's department."

"My mom's a herpetologist," Miriam added. "Dad's a historian down at Wilmington University. The university gets all kinds of grants for field study since the mountains are in its backyard and it's not difficult to get on a detail. I still have to go back and write the papers when I'm done though." She looked at Perry and brushed her fingers along his arm.

Obviously reminded that her time was short, Perry leaned in and breathed deeply. "'Maybe you think that you can hide, but I can smell your scent for miles.'"

Adrian shook his head. "She gives you Thomas, you give her Maroon Five?"

"Artistry takes more forms than you skulking in your tower writing bad poetry." Perry grinned. "Don't worry, I'm saving Duran Duran for a special occasion."

They all chuckled, and for a moment, the room and company felt safe. Miriam needed to realize that it wasn't. Time to switch tactics. He wouldn't Z.I.P. her, but maybe once she realized what was at stake… Well, she'd have to be a damned fool to stay. "You're playing a dangerous game, Perry."

"It's worth it," he said, looking at Miriam. She nodded her assent.

"Does she know what happened to your parents?"

The raised eyebrow she turned on Perry told Adrian all he needed to know.

"Uh, — I…"

She put a hand to her hip and raised both her eyebrows at him.

"Oh, you better believe you're going to be telling me about that," she said. "And I want to hear about you and Ugly here."

"Adrian," Adrian said.

"You're Ugly until you prove that you're not."

Adrian cocked a brow.

"You," Miriam pointed a finger at Perry, "have been sparse enough with information." Perry opened his mouth, but she cut him off. "Yeah, yeah. The less I know, the safer you think I am, but when your 'friend' shows up for dinner, I'd like to know I'm not on the menu."

Perry was a full blown idiot, but Adrian had to admit that this woman had more than her fair share of intelligence. It shouldn't be too hard to make her see reason.

"I don't know how much Perry has told you about immortals," Adrian said. "Therians—shape-shifters—and vampires are ancient enemies. All the while you humans go about your little lives, there is a war raging in the background." Adrian could see the slight twitch of Perry's lip. This was dangerous territory.

Good.

"Perry is, himself, a sort of rarity among us. Most immortals are made. One way or another, we lose most of our human blood and are briefly dead. Ever after, we borrow our life from the blood we consume. But your Perry, well, he's a natural born. His gran has some cock and bull story about his lineage, but that doesn't change anything. What matters is that, unlike other Therians, Perry has living blood. His blood is a prize in this war that can bestow strength and abilities that vampires will go to tremendous lengths to obtain. They certainly wouldn't think twice about killing a human to win it."

A shiver went through Perry. He was struggling to keep his anger at bay. Miriam, however, didn't react as Adrian had expected her to. There was no tirade this time. She grew very still and her eyes darted back and forth while she took in the information. Finally, she looked at Perry.

"Is this true?"

"Mary, you don't have to worry—"

"That's not what I asked." She pushed away from him. "Is this true?"

Perry opened his mouth but didn't say anything.

"She can see through your bull. I like her," Adrian said.

She sat for a moment, and then her eyes narrowed.

"I can see through your bull too, Ugly. I think you're so twisted up with hate inside that you can't remember what love feels like." She stood, suddenly. "I'm going to bed."

Perry started to stand, but Miriam put her hand out. "Just don't."

7

Favors

Rule #19 Do not associate with other immortals

A screaming noise broke the morning silence.

Clare swung at her alarm clock, knocking it off the nightstand, unplugging it in the process. She smiled, rolled over, and then remembered that the snooze button didn't work when the alarm was unplugged. With a moan, she kicked the covers off and plopped her feet on the floor. A strand of blond hair fell into her face.

Coffee. She needed coffee.

An hour and two cups of coffee later, Clare zipped out of her little house with a bagel in her mouth and purse and keys in either hand. The thought wisped through her mind that if she switched to an autonomous car, it would give her more work time, but after she threw the Cooper in gear and zipped out of the driveway, the thought was obliterated in the victory of weaving around the more sentient vehicles.

She did the math in her head as she drove. A half hour to work would put her there around 8:50. She'd have two hours to follow up on leads, file paperwork, and beg David to do some light hacking before lunch, and then she would write the rest of the afternoon. It was doable.

She wiped at some crumbs on her cheek, then turned up the radio. The karaoke diva in her would handle the rest of the commute.

Clare triumphantly clocked in at the office at 8:49 and began a blitz of paperwork. She looked up a half hour later when David straggled through the door. His jeans and Galaxy Fight t-shirt were wrinkled and with his rumpled bed-head hair, it could have been on purpose. Some people put a lot of time into cultivating an "I don't care look". David, on the other hand, actually *didn't* care.

"Hey David," she said.

"No."

"But I—"

"No"

"You didn't even—"

"No. I did not come in on Saturday morning to be your sirrah." He walked past her, without looking, on his way to the cubicle.

"I can get you an early copy of *Zombie Eater 3*."

David stopped and sighed, then turned with hand extended. Clare held out her list. As he moved to grab it, she jerked it back.

"*Zombie Eater's* worth two favors."

His eyes narrowed, but he snatched the paper and began scanning the list of websites and chat rooms she'd scribbled down. "What do you need from these?"

"Information. I want to know who created them, who visits them, anything really. It's kind of a hard society to break into."

"And I'm sure snooping into their sites and databases will garner you all sorts of trust."

"Do you want the game or what?"

David shrugged. "What's your other favor?"

"I don't know yet, but it's worth two."

He ran a hand through already disheveled hair and looked at the list again. "I'll see what I can find."

"Great! Thanks, David."

"Yeah, sure," he said with the enthusiasm of a man going to jury duty, and continued on to his cubicle.

Clare set to work. Several hours later, her desk phone rang, startling her out of focus. No one called on Saturdays. That was the whole point of going in: to be left alone.

"*You Know It* magazine," she said. "This is Clare speaking."

"Some friends said you were asking questions for an article," a soft female voice spoke. "I might be able to help."

"Fantastic, let me just pull up my notes here."

"I'd rather not discuss this over the phone."

Well, this one was definitely a believer.

"Where would you like to meet?"

"Can you be at the courthouse by 11:30?"

Clare looked at the clock. It was 11:04.

"Absolutely!"

"Buy a hotdog from the vendor and then sit on the third bench to the right. That way I'll know it's you."

"Okay, sounds good. May I have a name, so I'll know you."

"It's Meg."

"Just Meg?"

"Meg E."

"All right, Meg, I'll meet you there."

There was no response.

"Meg?"

Clare shrugged and hung up the phone.

At 11:15 she breezed out of the office and merged into the trickle of people for the five block walk. When she arrived at the courthouse, she found the hotdog vendor and bought lunch. She looked around. There weren't many people and none of them seemed particularly paranoid. Finally, she settled on the benches that flanked the courthouse fountain and began to nibble at her mystery meat.

"Clarity Zetler?"

She looked up and blinked away her surprise. "Meg E.?"

Meg gave a knowing smile. "You were expecting someone younger."

Younger and crazier. The elderly woman with white hair past her shoulders lowered herself on to the bench. Meg looked the perfect picture of a grandmother, right down to her blouse and skirt, which had been major designer labels about fifty years ago. There was no hint of the haunted believer Clare was used to dealing with.

"You wouldn't be the first to make that mistake. They send me out when people start asking questions since I'm less of a risk. But you, now you're different. You're not interested for yourself. They said you're a reporter."

"Journalist."

"Journalist, then. You can ask your questions, and I'll answer as many as I can. It will help our cause, but I should warn you: what you're doing, young lady, is quite foolish."

Clare nodded gravely for the woman as she pulled out a button-sized dome recorder the company had just bought. It was supposed to supply a 180 degree viewing angle with focus and zoom available during the editing phase. It would be handy, when she got used to it.

"No. No video please."

"Oh, um, ok." She fumbled with the electronic device trying to turn it off, then gave up and dropped it back in its case.

"Do you mind if I script this?"

"Not at all. I just don't want to give them my image, if I can help it."

And there was the crazy.

Clare rummaged through her red briefcase and pulled out her trusty com. It wasn't the new kind that was flexible like a paper notebook—that would probably turn out to be a fad anyway—but it had everything she needed. She swiped through the programs until she found the one that recorded and scripted audio and laid the com on the bench between them.

"You said you were less of a risk. Why?"

"The elderly would seem an easy target, but apparently we tend to be unpalatable from all the medications we take. There is something to garlic repelling them you know, but it's not in the wearing of it. If you eat enough, it flavors the blood."

"So, you eat a lot of Italian." Clare smiled.

The woman shook her head and opened a vintage Gucci purse. The bag probably cost more than Clare made in a month, and it was being used to store... Yep. That was a jar of garlic pills.

"Most of us just take a supplement," Meg said.

"I see. So...can you tell me why you believe in vampires?"

Her informant put the garlic back in her purse and stared off. Clare was beginning to wonder if she should repeat the question when Meg spoke.

"I was a nurse." She looked down at her floral print skirt and tugged a few wrinkles smooth. "One night they brought a man into the ER. He was crazed, mumbling, covered in bruises and cuts. Kept saying 'Sarah.'"

The thought of the ER made Clare's mind wander for a moment. She hadn't been in one since the car accident when she was eight, and she could still remember the smell. Still remember...she shook herself. Meg was speaking again.

"My initial thought was that he was just another crackhead—his eyes were so wild—but the tox screen came back clean. We sedated him. Had to, in order to dress his wounds. I was wrapping a slash on his hand," Meg traced a diagonal from one side of her palm to the other, "when he turned his head and looked at me."

Meg looked up into Clare's eyes. "He said it ate her and that he couldn't stop it. Then he started to cry—not sob, mind you. He was too sedated for that."

"I knew I shouldn't say anything, shouldn't add to the delusion, but I couldn't help myself. I asked him what he thought he saw. He looked at me funny, like *I* wasn't right in the head, and said, 'the vampire.'"

The older woman shook her head. "Well, I finished dressing his wounds and recommended to the doctor that he be transferred to the psychiatric ward. But when we went back to get him, he was gone. Completely gone. He wasn't on any of our surveillance recordings for the evening. There was no chart, no blood work. Just gone."

Meg rubbed a stubborn crease over a yellow flower.

While a man disappearing was interesting, there were endless possibilities that didn't end with Dracula. Still, it would make for an entertaining read. Clare tried to look sympathetic and patted the woman's hands. "Do you mind if I use your story in my article?"

"I wouldn't have told you if I did. Is there anything else you'd like to ask?"

This woman was a dream!

"Many of the rules in the *Handbook* seem to be based on a single experience. Is that all you have to go on?"

"Most of what we know is speculation drawn from the survivors' experiences, but it's logical speculation. If you had just given blood the day before and were attacked by someone who said that they had to have another taste, you would find it logical to assume that vampires frequent blood banks."

"But with our technology—and the *Handbook* asserts that theirs is more advanced—we can clone blood. So, why wouldn't they?"

"I'm sure they do, but how much do you know about blood?"

"I know that there are different blood types…"

"Right. Each blood type has different proteins, different flavors, but less than half of your blood is blood cells. Most of it is plasma, which, among other things, carries hormones like estrogen, testosterone, oxytocin, and adrenaline. The combinations of these are unique to an individual, even unique to a situation or a moment. It's the spice of life. Cloned blood would be bland by comparison."

Made sense. Clare nodded and moved on to her next question.

"I have the *Handbook*, so I understand about the logistics of keeping safe. Those rules are common sense," if you believe in blood-sucking, light-hating immortals. "But is there anything you can tell me that I wouldn't find in the *Handbook*?"

"Well, the survivors say—"

"Is there any way I can meet *them*?"

"No! Who knows what careless things you've done. The vampires may be tracking you already." Meg softened her tone. "I'm all you get."

"Oh. Okay, I just figured I'd ask."

Meg nodded and continued her previous thought.

"They say that the vampire appears human until it feeds. The pupils dilate until they fill the whole eye, and the canines elongate. There is no begging or pleading. They don't remember being human, or if they do, they have no

48

sympathy, no regard for our lives."

Seemed a bit much to assume what a vampire did or did not remember, but then again, these people believed in all this whackadoo nonsense. Clare gave a sympathetic "Mmm," as Meg continued.

"The only hope is to make as much noise as possible because we have no way of fighting them off. Even if there were something to drive through their heart, they'd see it coming. They're too strong and too fast. But they don't like attention. Their operations thrive on the fact that no one believes in them. That's why the survivors made the book, not so much to protect others, but to bring vampires into the light." Meg stopped and chuckled at her own quip. "That is what they hate most. Well, that and the Therians."

"Therians?"

Meg gave her a crooked smile, "Shape shifters, Therianthropes"

Clare scrambled to cover the incredulous look she knew was all over her face. She looked down at her com and pretended to highlight the word. When her facade was secure again, she continued.

"You mean like werewolves?"

"Yes, the Lycans—werewolves—are the largest of the group, but there are more. Berserkers are bears. Kumiho are foxes. Tsavo are the big cats. There are others too, but these are the ones that we know fight."

"Wait, so… are there survivors from the werewolves too?"

"Goodness, no child. They're the ones who brought the survivors together. It's their new strategy against the vampires."

Clare blinked. It was the only safe response.

"You see, people are more ready to believe in vampires than Therians. Even you have a harder time accepting werewolves, despite the fact that the *Handbook* refers to them. So the Lycans considered it a safe move to expose the vampires. Not that we deal with them either, mind you. They can be… unpredictable. We prefer to deal indirectly. It's best to stay away from them anyway. The vampires are always hunting for them. That's the reason for rule #10 in the *Handbook*."

"I see," Clare said. She cleared her throat of the laugh she'd been stifling and looked over her notes. There it was, rule #10: Do not associate with other immortals.

No explanation followed that one. It seemed an interesting trail to follow.

"You said the Therians and the vampires fight. Do you know why?"

"That's a long story, and I haven't got the time for all of it. Let's just say that their ways are contrary to each other."

The older woman was starting to fidget, but Clare was far from done. "So, is it that the Therians are friends of the humans, and they don't like vampires eating them?"

"As far as either of them are concerned, we are cattle or, at best, dogs," Meg snorted. "We just happen to be useful to the Therians."

"Then, do the Therians drink blood as well?"

"You really know nothing." She sighed and shook her head. "Not that it's your fault. I just thought that—well, it's not important what I thought. They are immortals. They don't get that way by doing things the way you do them. Life is in the blood, and when they run out of their own, they take it from others. Vampires drink ours, and Therians usually get theirs from other animals because they don't lose their memories of being human."

Clare was tempted to ask how Meg became the source of all this 'immortal' knowledge, but instead just said, "Usually?"

"The... flavor of the life gives its attributes to the one who drinks it. Apparently, animal life doesn't compare to what they get from us. Once they get a taste for human meat, they don't lose it. However, I think the other Therians kill them when that happens." Meg shrugged. "Like I said, they are unpredictable, but we share a common enemy."

Before Clare could get another question out, the older woman had pushed herself up off the bench.

"Well, I suppose that's enough for your article. Watch yourself now, because they'll be watching you."

Clare scrambled for more time.

"But wouldn't killing me just further the proof of their existence?"

"It would if they did it outright, but they're not stupid. And if it won't suit them to kill you, they have ways of making you forget."

"How do you know that?"

FAVORS

"Goodbye now. I look forward to seeing that article." Meg shuffled to the curb.

"Wait, I just have a few more questions!"

A white Lincoln pulled to the side, and a black clad driver got out and opened the door. The old woman eased herself into the back seat. She turned and looked back at Clare while the car drove away, as though she were considering something. It was only when the car was out of sight that Clare realized she'd forgotten to check the license plate. She resisted the urge to smack her forehead. Clare turned to go back to work and ran right into someone.

"Oh. Excuse me."

The man was short with greasy hair falling into his face and wearing what looked to be a janitor's uniform. Everything about him seemed to shrink away from her. Clare bent to pick a small container that he'd dropped but drew her hand back when she realized it was full of bugs. He snatched it up from the ground.

"I'm sorry. I didn't mean to…" Clare trailed off at the intense look he shot her before he walked away entirely. She shook her head and made her way back to work. The people of this town were weirding her out today.

Clare dropped her briefcase on her desk and headed over to David's cubical.

"Please tell me you found something good."

He glanced up from his screen.

"Not really."

"Come on, David." She dragged a neighboring chair into his cubicle and plopped down. "These people are killing me. I can't get anywhere with them."

He held his palms up. "I've got nothing, literally. Public databases don't even register that those sites exist. The one site I could trace is accessed in the city, but by public ports, different ones every time. One of the recent logins was in a library, so I tied into the surveillance, and the user is a brown left sleeve. Everything else was out of the camera's range."

David ran a hand through his unruly hair. "Oh, and I got *my* computer

51

hacked while doing your dirty work."

"You got hacked?"

"You're quick today. Yeah, I got hacked. It was subtle. If I'd been surfing on the page's front side, I wouldn't have seen it, but I was looking at code. When the code jumped lines, I knew there was an intrusion. I nabbed the program and tried to trace to it, but it disintegrated. I have no idea where it originated, but I don't think it was from the site."

"So... what? Does that mean someone is monitoring the site?" She twisted the ring on her middle finger.

"I don't know, Clare. Probably." David ran his hand up into his hair. "Probably hacked your computer too. Do you have any sensitive material on it?"

Clare's eyes widened. She ran to her desk and pulled the com from her briefcase. She hurried back and thrust it at David.

"Here. Check it for me."

He plugged it into his screen. Clare watched his fingers fly over the type pad. Her screen changed from a picture of ocean fish to icons she'd never seen before and then to some mysterious language that David seemed to understand. He grunted, more typing, and the screen changed again.

"Well?"

"They're good. The computer was accessed, but I can't find any residual programs. Several of your files were opened during the time of the breech."

"Which ones?"

"These." He highlighted a list of files opened within a ten minute window.

Her article notes were first. That was to be expected considering what site she was on when they hacked her. Then they hit her internet history, recent documents, employee inbox, and address book.

Clare picked at her top lip.

"Can you tell me if they took any particular address or if they just looked at it?"

David looked surprised. "Clare, all these files, they didn't look at them. They copied them. Grab and go."

Clare looked up from the computer screen and stared at David, fingers still pulling slightly at her lip.

"They copied my address book?"

"Yeah."

"They copied my address book."

"I said that."

Clare bit down on her thumb. "Can you find 'them'?"

David shook his head. "Nothing to be done there. Unless..." his voice trailed off.

"Yeah?"

"Well, there's no guarantee, but I can write a program to try to track them. Then you'll just have to go on the site again and wait for the program to access your computer."

"But there's no guarantee?"

"No. They wrote an amazing program to begin with. I'm sure it's got all kinds of failsafes."

It sounded like he was talking about a hot blond in a bar, not a viral computer code. She rolled her eyes. "No thanks. I'll pass on letting them get a second look at my info."

David shrugged and handed her back her com.

"And that's why you're supposed to have separate coms for work and personal use."

Clare scrunched her nose at him. "I thought that's why I paid a month's rent on a security program, so I could use the same com for everything."

David raised his eyebrows. "Which one did you get?"

"A Lyon 595."

His eyes got dreamy again. "If I could write a program that could get past a Lyon, I'd be a rich man."

"That's helpful David. Maybe I should set you up on a date with our mystery hacker."

"I don't think James would appreciate that."

Clare's eyebrows shot up before she could contain her surprise. "James? Like James from Layout, the one with the—" she motioned like she was pulling something out of a suit pocket, where James always kept a pressed hankie.

"Please, Clare. I hope you think more of me than that. No, James is an online interest."

That made more sense.

"By the way," he continued, "you should be able to get a refund on your Lyon. It has a warranty."

"Oh. Thanks."

"That's your only freebie. The next bit of advice counts as your second favor."

Clare smiled because she knew he meant it.

"Alright. I'll get out of your way. Thanks for the help."

"It's not charity. *Zombie Eater 3* comes out in four months," David said as he turned back to his computer screen.

"You'll have it in a week."

"Then you're welcome," he said, his fingers already busy on some inscrutable task.

8

Heliophiles and Hobbyists

Rule #1 Operate during the day

The sub-culture of Helios may be eye-catching, but it
has a nasty privacy invading side...kjdoifnapenfoiaskdlkafs-
dlkdlilapoiew3nlkvioashjfevp98v noiasefijo.........

Clare tapped out her frustration on the keyboard. She took a breath, tried
to smother her irritation, and focus. The magazine's fashion and current
events were supposed to target the ages of late teens all the way through
midlife. It was a wide margin in which the story should fit easily. The angle
was what was eluding her. She drummed her fingers some more before
deciding to try coming at it from the fashion side. Clare looked over her
outline and notes one last time. Receiving no inspiration, she started typing.

*When we first saw this new trend, we thought it was simply a revival of the gothic
style seen decades ago. Many, though not all, sport spiked collars and wristbands;
however, the Helios have emerged not as a fashion fad but more of a cult, following*
The Survivors' Handbook *as their Bible. After receiving question after question
from our readers,* You Know It *went out into the field to get the answers that
you want to know. The answers were cryptic and few, and then my computer got
hacked. Lovely.*

Clare deleted the last two sentences, read over it, and cringed. It sounded sappy and precocious. Her boss would probably love it. Maybe that was the sign she needed a new job. She sighed and tried again.

In a time when there has been renewed interest in both science and spiritualism, it should come as no surprise that there has also been a renewal of superstition. You Know It has received many queries from our readers, most a little afraid to ask the people themselves, wondering what is going on with the self-proclaimed Heliophiles. They wear unusual clothing and have silver laced tattoos, but most importantly, they believe in vampires. You Know It got the answers you want to know.

Still sappy but better. At least this time there were no passive aggressive bits slipping through.

Though they don't like to draw attention to themselves individually (none of them would give a full name), their purpose is to draw attention to their cause: the awareness of vampires and the prevention of further attacks. They live by rules set out in The Survivors' Handbook, *a collection of stories from the supposed survivors of vampire attacks. These rules span everything from donating blood, staying inside after sunset, and, the rule most commonly broken in my experience, not talking to strangers about vampires. While it would seem that vampire attacks are rare, given the lack of a medical record for any such event, following these rules purportedly lessens one's chances of becoming a victim.*

The Helios order their lives around an absolute certainty that vampires exist and are the top predator in the food chain, so they have taken on the evasion mentality of prey. Not only do they keep all main arteries covered, but they often wear cologne specifically designed to hide their scent, rather like other people use mosquito repellant. They operate only during daylight hours and often block Internet access in their residences. They believe that vampires keep surveillance on everything and have influence in all institutions. How they achieve this while being nocturnal is up for speculation.

When asked why they believed in vampires, the responses varied, but their faith never wavered. The most detailed response came from an elderly woman who went by the moniker Meg E. She claimed to have been a nurse working a night shift when a slashed and crazed man was brought into the Emergency Room. While being bandaged, he told Meg that a vampire had attacked him. As a rational person, she requested that he be transferred to the psychiatric ward, but when she returned, he was gone, along with all records of him. She has believed in vampires ever since.

Clare stopped typing. Something about Meg's story was bothering her. She synced to her recorder and pulled up the file. Meg's voice sounded strong, confident. That's what it was: her confidence. Other survivors told their stories in hushed tones and gave out sparse information, but not Meg. She said things that Clare hadn't heard from anyone and said them like they were absolute facts. Who was this woman?

Clare shook her head and chuckled. This assignment was getting to her. Meg was just a paranoid old woman with a creative imagination.

Simply by writing this article, I am breaking one of their rules. I am drawing the vampires' attention to myself, and while it may not end in my death, I have been assured that they will be watching me. One thing is certain, if they're right, I'm screwed.

Clare snorted. Their paranoia might be catchy, but that's all it was. Still, the article would never be approved by Janice with its mocking tone. She glanced at the clock. It was 4:21, it was Saturday, and her brain hurt. Time to go home.

* * *

Leroy Satterfield clutched the specimen container as he unlocked his basement apartment. His morning's work was almost lost when that clumsy woman bumped into him earlier. No consideration. And yet it was his babies that were considered the pests! He entered his sanctuary, a mossy sort of smell greeting him. Leroy took a deep breath, set his burden down, and turned on the light. Containers and tanks filled the small living space.

He was a hobbyist, really, but he did have an impressive collection: over a hundred local species that he hunted for, managed, and replenished himself. His favorites were on either side of his bed, gracing his nightstands. Argiope was common but huge. Her bloated yellow and black body sat in the middle of a zigzagged orb web in her twenty gallon tank. In a much smaller collection tank on the other side was Latrodectus Mactans. Though not as deadly as people assumed, the pain she inflicted from a bite was excruciating. He often daydreamed about using her to ward off robbers or assailants. Who wouldn't flee a Black Widow?

He gently stroked her box on his way to feed her neighbor, Parasteatoda Tepidariorum, the American House Spider. Hardly a good candidate for a favorite, but she was his first and an ant killer. Stupid ants. They were pests and always into everything. Many spiders avoided ants and with good reason. He'd seen spiders set them free rather than face their bite and even watched an ant kill a spider, but his tiny girl wasn't afraid. She'd already lived much longer than she should. Perhaps he could keep her alive indefinitely.

He smiled and plucked an ant out from this morning's collection, dropping it into the web.

The pest caught, then spun as it tugged at the webbing attached to its legs. Trying to bite its way free only gummed up its mandibles. Parasteatoda rushed in and attached more webbing to the legs. The ant thrashed, trying to bite the spider, but she was deft, moving in and out faster than Leroy could keep track. Finally, with the ant safely tied, she bit. He took a deep sigh and watched the ant's feeble thrashing and spasms in reaction to the poison. When its movement stopped, the spider settled over her meal and drank.

Leroy fed his others with less ceremony but no less satisfaction, all but one. He had plans for his darling, Argiope. Orb Weavers had been rendered innocuous by starring in the ridiculous book *Charlotte's Web*. While he would use that fact to draw people, he planned on rectifying the damage once they were there.

9

Advice

Rule #12 Carry styptic powder at all times

A drian heard the door open, but he was still asleep. Such a nice sleep. The yelling and screaming had been far off. It was getting louder. He smiled. There was a thud. The screaming was deposited in his room, and then the door closed. Banging on the door now accompanied the screaming. The room smelt so good. He rolled over and moaned, a happy, sleepy moan. The noise stopped. Tentative footsteps brought the luscious aroma closer. He could hear a distant drumming.

"Adrian?"

He opened his eyes. The light from flickering oil lamps danced across the bed canopy to the drumming sound.

"Adrian!"

He rolled his head over and looked at the noise. It was beautiful. It drummed and pulsed for him. Its eyes grew round, and the drum crashed faster. It moved away from him, backing up around a low table.

"What did they do to you?"

It was getting farther. It should not move away. He sprang off the bed. The thing jumped back against the wall. He smiled. It had nowhere to go. It had to stay and play with him.

"You're one of them!"

Its throaty whisper was enticing. Adrian slid his head from side to side looking at the bright pulsing that traced its body. He wanted it. The thing brought its hands up through short hair and left them on its neck, covering the brightest areas. It shouldn't do that. He growled. The thing's head snapped up. Its eyes locked onto his.

"No. You are not this." The drums began to slow.

Its eyes, blue ocean eyes, he knew them. Ocean? He could see it before him, water crashing without end. The smell of salt filled the cool air, and sunlight played on the distant waves. Then the blue eyes were there again, and the ocean was—a memory. A tremor tore through him, and when it was gone, it seemed to have taken something with it. The pulsing light dissipated, and he could see them more clearly.

"Your eyes... Do you know me now?"

He opened his mouth, then shut it again.

"It's me, Adrian. It's me!"

Adrian.

"I am Adrian." As he said it, he could feel it burning into his mind, ready to release a thousand ghosts.

"Yes! You are Adrian." The thing dropped his hands from around his neck. "And it's me, Paul."

A ghost solidified. A man with ink black hair and tanned skin was standing on the wharf next to a creaking moored ship. This man. He and Adrian were laughing, a large wooden barrel between them, the sun on their strong backs.

"I know you." The man's face was not crinkled with mirth. His hair was wild, and his tanned skin was darkened with black and red in places, but this was the same man. Terror and hope were in those blue eyes.

"Yes!" The man took a step forward, but with his eyes still locked on Adrian, he snagged his foot on the deep floor rug and fell. He flung his arms out to catch himself, but one arm caught on the table and the other missed. His head hit the edge of the table, taking the brunt of the fall. He rolled to the floor dazed, blood flowing from his nose and a gash on his forehead.

Adrian was drawn under a current of sensations that flooded over him.

Pain pricked at his mouth, a dry ache in his throat. His vision expanded, and the pulsing lights engulfed the man, drowning out the features of his face in their dance. Drumming crashed against Adrian. It called him like a siren's song. He was there kneeling over the man without knowing that he moved. The ocean was stormy. He cradled the man to himself and heard a gasp as the liquid life began to flow and soothe the ache in his throat. The body in his arms thrashed and screamed so beautifully. He drank in the ocean, the wind, the laughter, his brother.

Paul.

Adrian looked down at the man. The ocean had gone dark.

"Paul. I know you." He shook him. "Paul!"

The ghosts released.

Adrian sat up gasping in the cool cave air. It had been a while since he'd that dream. He swallowed and pushed his hair back from his forehead. Probably his subconscious sounding an alarm about Miriam. Thanks. Already figured that shit was trouble though. He got up feeling strong from feeding, and his access to that strength let him know the sun had set while he slept.

He made his way from the spare room to the living area. There was no sign of Miriam except for her faint scent still hanging in the air. Here and there were little reminders that she had inserted herself into Perry's life: extra plates on the counter, a new toothbrush by the sink, a bra over his bedpost. Perry's form was sprawled out on the couch, lit by dim sleeping lights. Dumbass dog.

Adrian grabbed a pillow off the side chair and threw it at Perry's face. He didn't even startle, just gave a sleepy chuckle and left it where it landed on his head.

"Where's your lady love?"

Perry's muffled voice came from under the pillow. "She said your ugly was tainting the cave and she'd be back in a few days."

"If she has a brain, she won't be back at all."

"If you can't stay away, how do you expect a mere mortal to resist the draw of my awe-inspiring presence."

"That girl could get us both killed."

"She is something else." Even from underneath the pillow, Adrian could hear the smile in Perry's voice. Adrian shook his head and clicked on a lamp. That reminded him.

"Have you ever seen a light-bearer?"

Perry plucked the pillow off his face and lobbed it back at Adrian, who sidestepped the missile. It hit a wall shelf behind him, knocking off several books and at least one pile of scrap electronics.

"I swear you're a child."

"It's your dumb fault for waking me."

"You're nocturnal!"

Perry shrugged. "My internal rhythm got thrown off trying to clean up the mess with Miriam." He scrubbed at his face and yawned. "And no. I haven't seen a light-bearer. I think that's a vampire thing. They can't harm us, so we never evolved the ability to single them out. Come to think of it, that would be useful." Perry sat up.

Adrian raised an eyebrow at him. Perry had lost his sleepy expression and was shifting into science mode.

"You know, use their blood against your kind?" Perry stared past Adrian at a blank space of wall and began running his fingers through his beard.

"I don't think it's potent enough for mass use."

"But if we isolate the compound that makes it toxic and use that..."

Adrian frowned. "Light. Light makes it toxic."

Perry cocked his head to the side. "But it can't be light, or it would be visible to everyone." He got up and started pacing the room. When his foot kicked against the pile of research binders on the floor, Perry snatched one. He grabbed a pen from the debris that had fallen off the bookshelf and flipped to the first clean page.

"There's got to be something else, and if it's measurable, it might be duplicated."

Perry was scribbling things down and gesturing with the pen still in his hand.

"Even if it can't be used directly against your kind, what if it could be used as a sort of vaccine? We could end the war so easily. Every human could be inoculated." Perry stopped and spun around to face Adrian. "Why haven't you mentioned this before?" He pointed the pen to Adrian's chest.

Adrian held up his hands to ward off the onslaught of enthusiasm. "I'd never seen one. They're very rare, and my people kill them. Quickly. The light calls to our instincts."

"'Had never'? So you have now?"

"Last night before I came, but she's off limits. Client's daughter."

Perry shrugged. "Why do you care?"

Adrian opened his mouth. Then shut it again. Stupid mutt had a point. Why did that matter? His clients were off limits to other vampires, but Perry wasn't Lachlan after all. He wouldn't kill her. Drug her, draw some blood. No worse than Adrian himself would do. *Madonna santa.* He ran a hand down his chin.

"Fine. How would we do it? And it would have to be off the record."

Perry turned, his eyes lit by a broad grin. "Isn't everything?"

After that, most of the weekend was spent discussing possibilities. Adrian didn't bother much with the science side of things. It usually bored him, but for the first time in a long time, he felt some sort of hope. If Perry was right, this could turn the tide of the war, and maybe with Paul's death avenged, he could finally be free of this existence.

The touch of light was fading from the world above, and with the coming dark, the well of power inside him grew. Adrian said his goodbyes and made his way back to his bike. He removed the cover, popped the kickstand, and walked it back to the road.

The highway was empty, and the night air was calm. He turned on his player. Beethoven's "Moonlight Sonata" was playing, and Adrian began to weave through the reflectors to the music. His playlist moved down from Classical to Classics. "Kryptonite" began playing. Adrian opened it up, pushing the bike as fast as it would go while still slaloming. The music, the bike, and the wind played off one another, and Adrian found himself laughing as he pulled out of a lean that took him a little too close to the pavement.

And then the blue lights. Adrian smiled. What the hell? It'd been a while since he last had some fun, and he was still sated from dinner the other night, enough to permit a little playing without the danger of going overboard. Besides, he really didn't need another traffic violation on his record. Time to let another survivor loose into the world.

He whipped his bike around to keep the tag out of view and skidded to a stop. Adrian made a show of stumbling off the bike and lurched down the shoulder while the patrol car caught up.

"Stay where you are and put your hands in the air," the police car announced.

Adrian put his hands up, took an unsteady step, and tripped over nothing in particular, falling face down onto the asphalt. He listened as the officer radioed dispatch about a ten fifty-five. The radio fuzzed back asking if he wanted back up. Nah. This one shouldn't be too much trouble. There was a clang as the car door shut and the slow crunching of boots on the gravel.

"Stay right there, sir, and put your hands behind your head."

Adrian let a little sound escape his lips but didn't move. The cop repeated his command. This time, Adrian was silent. He could feel the tension, smell the adrenaline, and then came a crescendo of drumming. His throat was suddenly dry, and every long breath ushered in the smell of moist flesh. The man nudged him with his boot, nudged again, then finally, knelt down and turned Adrian over.

Adrian avoided the neck. The bleeding there would be harder to control. Instead, he grabbed the arm still resting on his shoulder, bit through the jacket, and began to feed all before the man's scream could exit his throat. Adrian flipped his body on top of the officer, pinning him with his legs and free arm.

The blood was smooth, an O positive, and the life was strong. It seeped through his throat and into his body with a delicious tingle. The screaming, that was still annoying though, not the sound but the damning pleasure it gave him.

He allowed himself only a few minutes before squeezing down on the vein.

65

It throbbed underneath his thumb as he released his bite. The screaming stopped. Adrian looked at the man. His eyes were wide, and his mouth was making silent words. His hand jerked downward toward his holstered weapon but made no more progress against Adrian's grip than if it were pinned under a house.

Adrian released pressure on his vein. He was precise and hadn't mauled it too badly. The cop shouldn't be in danger of bleeding out. Adrian pulled the sleeve back from the man's arm and slashed his skin with a tooth, just erasing the round puncture marks. The man let out another scream, thrashing with renewed vigor.

"Give it a rest! I'm not going to kill you."

The man looked unconvinced, but he stopped flailing. Now for the tricky part.

"I'll let you go in a moment. We are going to get up and walk back to your car. Trust me when I say that I will kill you if you try anything. Do you understand?"

The officer bobbed his head.

The radio in his belt crackled. "Five-twenty advise your status".

Adrian grabbed the radio and held it to the man's mouth.

"Tell them ten twenty-two. Motorist was just getting tired." Adrian said. "Make it convincing, or I *will* kill you."

Adrian pressed the button.

"Uh, that's a uh ten twenty-two, dispatch. Drowsy motorist."

The radio chirped back, "Ten-four, five-twenty."

Adrian slipped the radio back on the belt and relieved the man of his gun.

"Perfect." He eased off the man and motioned him up with the barrel of the gun. Free of Adrian's weight, the officer grabbed his arm and held it close. Then he kicked at the ground to distance himself.

"Come on. On your feet." Adrian could see himself reflected in the man's eyes by the light of the high beams. There was still some blood around his mouth. He licked at it, and the man made a choking noise. Silent tears began to stream down his face.

Adrian's stomach soured.

"I said on your feet!"

The man got up, then tripped. Probably light-headed. Adrian grabbed his arm to steady him, and the officer made a noise through his teeth. He raised his grip above the wound before jerking him back toward the vehicle.

"You know, you should have radioed for backup." He opened the door, pulled a small pack from his inner jacket pocket, and withdrew a pen-shaped object. Adrian leaned in, touching it to the back of the dash cam—there was a soft beep—and then to his body cam. It beeped again. He put the pen back and released the officer into his seat.

"Put your hands on the wheel." The man's hands were trembling. He placed them on the steering wheel, shaking his head while doing so. Adrian slipped his gun back into its holster. The man looked down at it, then back at Adrian, his head still shaking back and forth. He glanced to his lit dash and began gulping in air. Adrian followed his eyes to a picture of two brown haired girls on his dash.

Damn it. He really was getting soft. Reaching back into the pack, he pulled out a Z.I.P shot.

"Tell me," he said. "What am I?"

The officer's voice was a whisper; his head was still shaking a little, but he focused his eyes on Adrian. "Vampire."

"Very good," Adrian said as he thrust the small needle into the officer's external jugular vein. The man drew a sharp breath and then relaxed as the small dose of peptide ripped through his mind. His head finally stopped shaking. Adrian closed the man's eyes and waited. When the man finally opened his eyes, there Adrian was, reflected in calm eyes, simply another biker in a leather jacket.

"Are you all right, officer?" he asked him.

"I'm sorry?"

"I was nodding off on the road. You stopped me and were telling me to get some coffee when you passed out. I think you cut yourself on some glass when you fell. You got low blood sugar or something?"

The man looked sleepily at his slashed arm. His eyes seemed to center on it.

"Not that I know of."

"You gonna be alright? Maybe you should radio for some help."

"Yeah, maybe."

"Can I go? Or do you want me to wait around until someone gets here?"

The man looked up at him, his forehead knitting together. "Nah, just go ahead and get you some coffee. I'll be alright to wait."

"Thanks, man," he said. "Take care of yourself. And you oughta call for back up when you're way out here in the middle of nowhere. People are crazy, you know?"

The man gave Adrian a patronizing smile. "Will do."

Adrian listened as he walked away.

"Dispatch, this is car five-twenty." The man paused. "I think I need some assistance."

Adrian mounted his bike and headed home, keeping the player off.

10

Origin

Rule #10 Eat meals containing heavy seasonings like curries or take
supplements

I t was 9:05 Monday morning, and Clare was at the library. She'd clocked in to work at 8:46 and headed right back out. As much as she hated to admit it, there was still something missing from her story, and she'd already scoured the Internet and conducted personal interviews. So, it was the library or bust.

She was the first patron, and her pumps cracked the silence with every step. A trim, razor-eyed woman looked up from the check-out desk as she passed. Clare ignored her and headed straight for the catalogue computer. She was a grown woman, and she could find it herself. She sure as hell wasn't about to ask where the "vampire section" was.

The computer was compliant without any judgmental staring. There were several titles on vampires in the 200s. Clare grabbed them all and found an oversized chair facing a window. Flipping through the titles, she settled on *The International Vampire: A Chronicle of Vampires Around the World.*

The book was a hefty tome detailing vampires of different cultures as well as "documented" sightings, attacks, etc. She skimmed the different legends, taking notes. Some of the oldest stories arose in the Middle East and told of demons drinking the blood of infants to nourish them. As time went on, the story became a beautiful, childless woman. This woman drank blood, and once she chose a lover, would never let him go. Yep, because that's all that single women wanted, men and babies.

Finally, one story grabbed her.

It is said in India that in matters of family and daily needs, one should seek Kali. So, every night after his masters retired, a servant walked to the cremation grounds to go to the dwelling of Kali and pray. He went with no thought to the weather or his own health, praying sometimes until he fell asleep from exhaustion. After many years, Kali became intrigued and ordered her priests to bring the man to her chambers. She was, much as the paintings depicted, dark black with a tiger skin about her waist and wild hair falling over her breasts. She told the man she had seen his faithfulness and inquired as to the boon he sought from her.

The man spoke to her of his master. Despite his master's wealth and prayers, he and his wife had no children. So his mistress came to him, and he could deny her nothing. He lay with his mistress, though the master would kill them both if he were to learn of it. She conceived and bore a girl-child, and every day since her birth, he came to pray. Never had he loved so much or had such great pain. His daughter would never know him.

"It is a just punishment for my sin, but I cannot bear it. I have nothing, but I would pay with my life for my daughter."

Kali was moved by the man's request and agreed to grant his boon, but warned him that the price would be high. His life would not be enough, and his soul would belong to her. The servant was overjoyed, and Kali took his life as he knelt before her. She gave him a drop of her blood to seal him as her own, and then she sent the priests for his mistress and child.

When the servant awoke, Kali presented him with his mistress and told him that to have his daughter, he must dance the dance of death over his lover, as Kali had done over hers. His mistress pleaded for her life, and great was his anguish. He begged of Kali another way. She reminded him about her warning of the cost; however, she told him that while he asked for the child, he might choose the mother instead and kill the child. So, the man drank the blood of his child's mother, and Kali kept the girl in her dwelling until the man was strong enough to kill her and seal her with his own blood. Thus she would be his daughter forever.

Clare looked up from the book and stared out of the window. Cars passed by on the busy street outside, and she felt her throat tighten. It was her fault. If she'd never been born, there wouldn't have been a choice of who to pull from the car. She bit at her thumb, vision blurred, and pushed down at the images threatening the edge of her consciousness.

Clare snapped the book shut and left it on the pile of other books by the chair. She'd had enough research. Grabbing her bag, she rushed out of the library, her shoes echoing their exit. The morning air was still cool, stinging her salty eyes. She took a deep wavering breath and exhaled slowly.

"You're fine, girl. Just take a little walk," she told herself.

Clare pulled at her jacket, trying to straighten the signs of her emotional leakage. Pushing down the feelings, she walked head up in the general direction of work. But when she saw her building, she just couldn't do it and veered down a different road. This was silly. There was no reason to be emotional. Must be getting close to that time of the month. She swallowed hard against the lump in her throat, but it refused to budge. It was just a ridiculous story, dammit. Nothing to get worked up about. Vampires aren't real, and people just die. Accidents happen.

Clare found herself walking past the backside of her building's parking garage and stopped. She pulled out her phone: 10:49. Close enough to lunch. She didn't feel like eating, but the gym was only five minutes away. She walked up the ramp to her car. Being anal retentive had its benefits. Her gym bag was always waiting in her backseat for whatever spare moment might appear, and it looked like this week's spare moment had arrived.

The smell of rubber mats and antiseptic cleaner meet her at the doors. After signing in, Clare changed but didn't bother with her wraps, heading for the 80 lb training bag. One-Two. One-Two. One-Two-Three, Kick. Her body moved with the rhythm, leaning in and back. Again. And again until the lump in her throat disappeared. Then, she kept going.

"You're pretty good."

Clare jumped. She hadn't noticed the attendant walk in. The bag swayed from her last hit as he came over to her and took her fist in his hand.

"But if you don't put some gloves or a wrap on, you'll bust a knuckle the way you're going at it."

Clare pulled her hand from his light grasp. "I'm fine. Thank you." One-Two. One-Two.

"Take any lessons?"

The interruption broke her rhythm. Again. The bag swung in a small arc, waiting for her.

"When I was younger. But look, I just want to have some time with the bag." She gave it a pat. "Just us two."

"Sure. That's fine. But at least let me get you some wraps. Your knuckles are already looking rough."

Clare grabbed the bag to stop its motion. Now that she'd quit, her hands began to sting from the abuse.

"I'm good, thanks. I was about to cool down anyway."

"No problem. Let me know if I can help you. The name's Brayden." He flashed her a smile.

Right. And those toned muscles and too white teeth were all it would take to have her panting at his feet. Had she forgotten to turn on her giant, neon "Back Off!" sign this morning or something? She sighed. Men were impossible.

"Will do," she lied, and she headed out toward the track.

Two laps and a quick shower later, Monday was starting to look a little better. Then she looked at the clock. It was 11:51, and her stomach reminded her that it had needs too. It was either the disgusting yellow arches on the way to work or the health crazed cardboard at the gym café. On second thought, Mondays just didn't want to be liked. That was all there was to it.

At 12:04, Clare marched back into the office holding a greasy brown bag. Her father's voice echoed in her head as she wound her way to her desk. "Early is on time, on time is late, and late is in trouble." Her boss wouldn't care, but father continued anyway. "It will be hard enough to succeed in the workplace as a woman, but being late will just confirm to everyone that you are not to be taken seriously. Are you listening to me?" She shook her head and sat down to lunch.

Clare was reviewing her notes when a hand reached into her peripheral toward her fry pile. She smacked it without taking her eyes from the screen.

"Stealing fries from a woman is a capital offense, David."

"Would you like it to be your second favor that I never try to pilfer food from you again?"

"Not a chance."

"Worth a shot." He shrugged and headed back toward his desk. Clare smiled. David was just as impossible as Mondays, but he knew when her neon sign was on. Perhaps there was hope for the gender.

That reminded her, she owed him a game.

To: EZ@senterprises.com
Cc:
Subject: Pretty Please With a Cherry on Top
From: Clare@youknowit.com

Hey Z, I was wondering if you could get me the press release copy of *Zombie Eater 3*. Thanks!

She shook out her tender knuckles and had just stuffed a few more French fries in her mouth when her email chimed a new message.

To: Clare@youknowit.com
Cc:
Subject: Re: Pretty Please With a Cherry on Top
From: EZ@senerprise.com

No problem. I'll leave an extra at the house tonight. Swing by whenever you get a moment.

Tonight. Clare frowned. Might as well it get it over with. With that out of the way, the week could only get better.

11

Glitch

Rule #30 Be sure you know someone before trusting them

A drian woke a little after noon feeling strong and rested. The floor of his bedroom was cool under his feet. His sanctuary was sparsely furnished, but each piece was quality. The Brazilian rosewood armoire that stood in the corner of his room still carried a distinct pepper and floral scent. All his suits were saturated with it. Who needed cologne when your clothes smelled of the outdoors?

He dressed and ran a comb through his hair. A glance in the mirror showed bright eyes and a healthy flush to his olive skin. Despite himself, Adrian was looking forward to going to work. Today brought with it the possibility of a new weapon in the war.

He caught himself smiling as he headed down to the sixth floor. Vanessa rose to greet him when he entered.

"Corporate sent a man named Jonathan over. He's waiting in your office, sir."

Shit. He'd forgotten all about that little thrip. This was not how he wanted to start the week. He supposed he couldn't just rip his throat out. Even Vanessa might notice that. And he was not about to get blood on a Canali suit.

Adrian jerked a nod to his secretary and strode into the office. He half expected to find the intruder in his desk chair, but the little nuisance was seated on one of the leather patron chairs studying a com. Light brown hair hid his eyes and nose, but his mouth was a tight line. Jonathan jerked his head up and stood with his hand extended as Adrian walked in. It was an odd gesture for a vampire, especially a young one. Human social niceties had to be relearned and were usually relegated to human interactions.

Adrian shook it, then sat down and waited. He wasn't about to make this easy on Deval's new darling.

Jonathan sat and cleared his throat—another strange behavior. Curious

"I am sorry for coming so early," Jonathan began. "I had to be here before the sun, and I didn't want to disturb you—your sleep, so I waited.

"You could have called to let me know you were coming. My number is listed with the other department heads."

Adrian cocked his head to the side and ran his tongue over his teeth. A vampiric gesture, and one Jonathan seemed to understand since he ducked his gaze for a moment.

"I'm very sorry. I didn't think of that until last night, and I wasn't sure what time you turned in. They warned me that you slept sometimes at night because you work dayshift."

"Hm." Adrian just stared at him.

Jonathan started rubbing the corner of his com with his thumb.

"What is it you want?" Adrian said.

"As you know," the nuisance cleared his throat again. It was getting annoying. "I was tasked with solving the problem of *The Survivors' Handbook.*" He looked up. "You've read it haven't you?"

Adrian smirked. Sure. Let's call it that.

"I've perused it."

"Okay. Well, um, it is rather specific about vampires. Humans couldn't just come up with it on their own—not all of it anyway. So either, this generation doesn't know how to clean up after dinner and use Z.I.P. pens, or..."

"Or?" Adrian began tapping a finger on the desk. One. Two. Three. Jonathan stared at it a moment, swallowing.

"Or someone's a loose end, which would have to be purposeful. But..."

that would be suicidal." He took a useless breath forcing his gaze up and away from the tapping finger. "I've gone through the employee e-mails and folders from Tech. All our people are clean there. Whatever the problem is, they aren't dumb enough to talk about it. So, I was hoping to get your thoughts on any of your staff."

Tap. Tap... Tap.

"All my staff are human."

Adrian narrowed his eyes. The sooner the little thrip realized there was nothing to be found here and quit wasting his time, the better.

"Yes, well, I know, but have they asked any questions? Have there been any security violations on digital or written systems? That sort of thing."

"Jonathan?"

"Yes, sir?"

"Do you always talk this much?"

"Only when I'm nervous, sir."

"And why," Adrian resumed tapping, "would you be nervous?"

Jonathan somehow managed to go a shade whiter. "This isn't my thing. Well, that, and I was told that you, um," his eyes flicked back to the tapping finger, "don't play well with others."

Adrian indulged in a toothy smile. It was good to know his reputation was still intact.

"I don't. Especially the young. How old are you?"

"I'm twenty-three."

Adrian's finger stilled. Oh, hell.

Jonathan flinched. "Sorry. Habit. I've been a vampire a little over ten months."

New vampires didn't have habits. Their habits and memories were wiped away in the crossover. The only thing new vampires had were personality and instincts.

Fuck. That explained things.

"You have an engram—some human memory?" Adrian said.

Jonathan nodded. "It was purposeful. They wanted my skills."

Purposeful? Adrian's hand clamped down on the edge of his desk. There was only one vampire who would do that.

"Who made you?"

Jonathan looked away.

Adrian could feel his whole body stiffen. If it had been night, he would be fighting back the change. The little thrip knew the answer was dangerous. He took a deep breath. Deval would definitely notice if he killed this one. That didn't mean he couldn't find other ways to dispose of him if needed. Adrian leveled him with his stare and spoke slowly.

"Who?"

The answer was almost whispered. "Lachlan."

Adrian felt the wood crack under his grip. "And he glitched you?"

"Yes, sir."

"Those with engrams rarely live long." Adrian leaned forward. "Why would he do that?"

"Like I said, they wanted my skills."

"Which are?" Adrian growled.

Jonathan fidgeted in the chair. "I was a computer programmer with an interest in arts and antiques, and I have an eidetic memory."

The little shit.

"So he wanted you for *my* job?"

Jonathan licked his lips and swallowed. From any normal vampire, it would have been a threat. The *coglione*! It was a miracle he was still alive. He couldn't possibly socialize much with those his age. They would have killed him before the night was over.

Maybe that's what needed to be arranged.

"I don't know." Jonathan's voice sounded hoarse. "They're skills the company can use, and Lachlan wanted to see if I would glitch without a blood prompt."

Now *that* made sense.

Lachlan had been interested in the engram for as long Adrian could recall. Lach had devoted himself to figuring out the details of the vampiric crossover. He was the one who discovered that the neurons which restructured during change were still somewhat plastic until the first feed.

His theory was that if there was a strong enough stimulus or prompt, the vampire would retain an engram of some of their old connections. So far, the only known stimuli strong enough to cause that was the blood of a loved one since it carried the essence of the person. But Lachlan would find someone with a photographic memory an irresistible test of that theory.

"Did you? Without a blood prompt?" Adrian said.

Jonathan looked at his hands. Reading it as human, it was a gesture of helplessness.

"I did."

Helplessness was dangerous.

"What did you agree to," Adrian asked.

"I don't know what you mean."

Bullshit.

Adrian was on his feet and around the desk before the younger vampire could blink.

"Don't play with me boy." Adrian whispered, leaning in. "You won't cross over unless you say yes. Now, what did you say yes to?"

Jonathan shrank back in his chair, but his grey eyes turned steely, and he said nothing.

Adrian straightened. "Something he still holds over you. That's unwise of him, but now," he sneered, "you get to be his little pet."

Jonathan's pupils dilated, but the sun's sway still held back a full change. He clenched his jaw, and his eyes narrowed until none of their whites showed through.

"I am not his pet."

Adrian purred. "Do the others know that? It might color Deval's favor of you heading this project since it makes you biased against, well, whatever Lachlan tells you to be biased against."

Jonathan closed his eyes. "I know how this looks to you. Everyone knows you and Lachlan hate each other. But I really just need that information." His imploring tone caused a sympathetic twinge in Adrian that annoyed him almost more than anything the thrip had yet done.

"There's nothing particularly suspicious, per se" Adrian said, tapping a finger on his head in mock thought. "But you know, you have more reason to be a loose end than anyone I can think of."

"You hate me, don't you?" Jonathan said.

Fuck. The stupid human expression on his stupid hopeless face. My god. Perry was right: Adrian was soft. Stupid. Stupid. Stupid.

Adrian held his hand out for Jonathan's com. Jonathan wrinkled his brow but handed it over to him. After several moments of tapping, Adrian handed it back.

"You are now networked into Human Resources' databases. I don't know what you're looking for. You probably don't know either, but happy hunting." Adrian returned to his seat and began very deliberately signing papers. "And If I were you, I'd focus on having Media clean up the mess. If they'd done their job, that book would have never made it to publishing. I doubt you'll find only one 'loose end'."

"Thank you." Jonathan stood. The hopeless look receded a little, and he extended his hand.

"We don't do that," Adrian flicked his pen toward the other vamp's hand. "If it's a human ritual, Glitch, chances are we don't do it."

"Oh. Thanks." Jonathan looked blankly at the outstretched appendage for a moment before letting it fall. "You know, I would rather work here than in Media. When this project is over—"

"We don't have any openings."

"Right."

"You can go now."

"O-kay." Jonathan retreated.

Adrian sat back as the door closed, leaving him alone.

Lachlan had taken his plans to the next level. As long as Adrian was useful to Deval, Lachlan couldn't touch him, but his idea in making Jonathan was all too clear. Still, Lach couldn't risk Siri's wrath. As much as Adrian was disgusted by her interest in him, it did have certain benefits. She didn't care about her father's business, and she would kill Lach if he harmed Adrian. Whether or not her father liked it.

Adrian shook his head to clear it. He had other things to worry about.

He'd looked up the Shultz's file before the kid had even left the office. Adrian had only dealt with the father and son. There was nothing in the file on the girl, and he couldn't search for her on his computer while Jonathan had access. But he did have the father's address. It was a place to start. Now, he just needed to wait for night to come.

* * *

Leroy Satterfield had his beauties set up and labeled as part of a special exhibit called *Our Local Ecosystem*. There were various other local organizations present. A petting zoo just outside the museum started the experience with dirty mammals. Once inside, children were met with Area Aquatics. Those showoffs had built a mountain river set up with Plexiglass sides to better display the swimming fish. Young Herpetologists had an impressive array of snakes, frogs, and lizards. Leroy steered clear of that one. *The Entomology and You* display was by far his favorite, other than his own. He would love to feed his babies all those gorgeous insects, starting with the ant farm.

Standing by an informative poster he'd titled *Arachnids and Us*, Leroy answered questions from the snot-faced throng. Even though they pawed around him like ants around a bread crumb, he tried to better their appreciation, or least respect, for the genus. After about an hour, though, he was tired of the interactions. Time for some real entertainment.

He waited until there was a swell in the crowd, especially in the number of young girls, then began to explain the painful process of spider digestion. There was a satisfying amount of "ewws" as he spoke of the internal organs liquefying into a nutritious soup. Finally, he brought out a small container. Inside, a bright yellow and black butterfly fed on an orange slice.

"Hey, cool! He's going to feed it," a young male voice called from the back.

A chorus of excitement erupted from the boys, who began jostling to get a closer look. Leroy hadn't really expected that. He did expect the pouty faces that appeared on some of the girls, but not even all of them were put off. Some were pushing forward to see with as much vigor as the boys.

At least the arachnids were getting some respect.

Opening a small hatch on the back of Argiope's housing, he inserted the butterfly container, removed its top, and then closed the hatch. The butterfly flew right out and into the spider's web. There were gasps and "oohs" as the spider struck fast as a heartbeat. After spinning her struggling meal into a neat little pill, she hefted it up to the side of her web and left it there to digest.

"And *that,* children, is insect population control," Leroy said with a smile.

The crowd dispersed slowly, parading past the display with mutters of awe or disgust, and occasionally both. But even after his display, they just didn't seem to appreciate the skill and deadliness of Argiope. It was only another curiosity in their visit. He shouldn't have expected anything else. Let them scurry on to their blind lives.

When there was a break in the onslaught, Leroy made a side trip to the bathroom. He hadn't really thought through lunch, and chili was not a good choice on a day where breaks would be indeterminate.

The crowd was still sparse as he made his way back to his exposé. He walked up to his centerpiece to see how dinner was coming and felt his stomach twist. The habitat was empty, the web torn. A muscle spasmed below his eye.

Argiope was gone.

With a certainty of understanding, he forced his eyes to floor. By the bottom corner of the table a smear of gore met his gaze. He sank down, drawn by some horrid need for a closer look.

It was her. The beautiful yellow and black patterning was still quite visible, despite the blood. A leg twitched, and he could look no more.

"Who did this?" His words came out loud but strained.

The other presenters looked up from their displays.

"Who killed my spider?!"

There was a snicker from down the hall. Leroy saw a small group of boys hurry to join the rest of the masses, and the forgiving colony hid them in its arms!

Well then. They were all guilty.

12

Intrusion

Rule #14 Own a pet, preferably a dog

There was a lingering fringe of purple on the horizon when Adrian left for fieldwork, and even the air in the underground parking garage tasted like freedom. As much as he loved living away from the mansion, staying in Nidhi Towers still felt like a prison. It and everything in it belonged to them. The growl of his bike was his anthem, and he burst from under the shadow of the building to its song.

The address he'd downloaded from the Shultz's file took him to a wealthy subdivision at the edge of town. Adrian found a house marked "For Sale" a few blocks shy of his target and parked there. A dark character with menacing eyes stared over a trench coat at him from a neighborhood watch sign. He looked down at his own coat and smiled. Apparently long, dark coats were a portent of ill will. They were also rather convenient for hiding syringes, lock picks, and a variety of other useful tools.

The Shultz's house was tucked in the back of the subdivision. With two wings and several dormer windows, it was more like a mansion. A fountain stood in the center of the circular drive. Lights illuminated a four column entrance and manicured garden beds that curved along both wings of the house. In the house's backyard was a helpful expanse of trees. Most importantly, there were few visible surveillance cameras, and they all pointed downward.

Adrian glanced up and down the street before striding alongside the wrought iron property fence and into the trees. There was no neighboring house behind, only trees stretching for acres, with several standing close to the mini-mansion. Very helpful indeed.

Taking off his shoes and coat, Adrian hoisted himself up an elm with a conveniently thick branch hanging a couple yards above the roof. He stretched out on the branch and listened.

No sound came from below. Sliding his body down and hanging from the branch for a moment, he dropped onto the roof with a soft thud. Adrian waited. Still silence. A smile crept over his face. He'd missed this kind of thing. There was nothing that compared with the thrill of a hunt.

With unnatural quiet, he padded along the backside of the roof toward the center of the house. He was beginning to catch wafts of conversation, male voices backdropped to classical music. They were probably down there on plush chairs sipping red wine. Adrian moved to the other wing of the house. There was a satisfying silence below that part of the house. He slipped to the front of the roof. It faced south, and he was betting on his light-bearer liking the sun. If there was any such thing as luck, the window would be unlocked, because this place surely had an alarm system.

Keeping as low as he could, he crept to the dormer and pushed the screen up. He shook out his fingers, as if that might help the outcome, and then pushed up on the window. It slid with the ease and quiet that only too much money could afford. Ah, luck. The only lady he loved.

Moonlight spilled through the window, casting a cool glow around a room much simpler than he'd expected. Walls that looked green-grey in the pale light, a neatly made bed with a worn teddy bear, and an old oak dresser. Three pictures hung on the walls, the largest of which was the first piece he'd ever sold to Eugene: a brilliant expanse of trees and a river with stunning chiaroscuro worked across the forest floor. He smiled. Clearly, Eugene wasn't the only one in the Shultz family with excellent taste.

Pulling himself from the painting, Adrian focused. Her smell was here. Faintly. This probably had been her room at one time, but not anymore.

Adrian began to rummage. The drawers contained some clothes and a few other oddments but were mostly empty. The closet was also barren of anything useful.

He was about to creep out into the hall when an engine hummed up the drive. He stepped back to the window, keeping just far enough back enough to see a small car park and his quarry step out. Even having witnessed it before, the nimbus of light surrounding the girl was still fascinating. He'd had unending years to see what few knew existed, but this was unusual even among his kind.

She slipped from view, blocked by the roof line. He heard the gonging of a doorbell, shuffling feet, and then happy greetings. Lady luck must be feeling seductive tonight because she was all over him. Adrian slipped out the window and padded back along the roof to the overhanging elm. Ignoring any handholds the tree might have provided, he dropped to the ground, using his hands to soften his landing. There was no need to be careless and leave imprints in the lawn. He retrieved his shoes and coat and skulked around to the front to glance at the license plate.

He couldn't risk following her. She was too important to lose or spook. Providing she was observant at all, a lone motorcycle constantly appearing as she turned down the next street would scream crazy stalker. No, he would have to run her plate to get her address. Work coms were too risky, and this needed to be off the record from the Therian database too. If he wanted it done tonight, that left the library. He still had time to make it and get her information before the place closed at 9:30.

Adrian always sat at the same computer station. It was just out of view of the ubiquitous cameras. Tricky as it was hacking into the police database from a public computer, it was too important to risk using his own com. In a little under an hour, he had the woman's address. The property was listed under another name, but that could be a roommate or landlord. A roommate would make things a little more interesting, but still doable.

The librarian had been making announcements about the building closing for twenty minutes. He jogged out of the library, incurring a scowl from her for his tardiness. He smiled back, and her scowl turned murderous. Adrian had to stifle a laugh. He needed to get out of the office more often. He felt... felt good. Maybe this was what it would be like when he was free, when he was no longer tethered to Siri and could do whatever the hell he wanted.

Breaking into the light-bearer's small house had been easy. There was no roommate or alarm system to be cautious of, not even a pet to sound concern in the night. Adrian had waited until an hour after every light in the neighborhood had gone dark. If there was any trouble, people in a deep sleep would be slower to respond to a disturbance. Then, he'd crept around to the back door. It never ceased to surprise him how often front doors had deadbolts or slide locks in place and back doors, while often equipped with the same, were left with only the knob locked to defend the house against assailants. It wasn't even a challenging lock to pick.

He crept through the house, quietly getting his bearings. Her room was off the living room, the door leading to it slightly ajar. It was dark, save for the soft glow that clung close to her body. He let his human facade fall away so he could study her light with better eyes.

Damn. The light was intense on vampiric vision. It didn't seem to rise and fall with her gentle breathing, but rather flowed like currents. With measured movements, he dipped his fingers into it.

Nothing.

He brought his fingers to his face and wiggled them. There was no change, and nothing lingered on him. He'd felt pain when she touched him, but perhaps he was going about this the wrong way. Adrian took a deep breath, closed his eyes, and *stretched* toward her.

The pain was immediate. He jerked back to himself and heard her stir. Opening his eyes, he watched a shiver run through her. Had she felt that? He braced himself for the pain and tried again, this time keeping his eyes open. His vision blurred as his mind tried to reconcile the two competing streams of information. Without moving, he pushed, *stretched* himself out of his body and touched her. The light rippled. Her face scrunched, and her heart began to race in unison with the flicker of pain he felt.

Then he felt a different kind of ripple—a pull. A Watcher. And it radiated fury. Adrian fled into himself and took an involuntary step back. The blur in his vision tamed, and he found himself looking around, as if he could see the creature. But no, he was here, in the physical realm, and it could not touch him.

He tried to shake off the lingering feel of its hot anger. Of course one would be here. Who knew what else she might attract. Just because the Lycans couldn't detect it, didn't mean vampires were the only creatures to notice the glow. His mistake was in thinking that it was physical. It was something other, like the Watchers themselves.

He ran his hand through his hair. Perry would have a heyday with this. He'd still want a blood sample, but did it matter if the attribute wasn't physical? Adrian sighed. It would to Perry. He'd want to rule out everything himself.

Adrian closed his eyes against the irritation of her glow. Everything about this felt dangerous, and his instincts were growling to be freed. He just needed to do this and get out of here... Except now he couldn't use a *stretch* to calm and keep her asleep. A chemical tranq would taint the blood sample and possibly harm her, and her physical touch would burn him.

Fan-fucking-tastic.

He reached back in his coat to ready a Z.I.P. shot. This was going to be interesting.

13

Night Terrors

Rule #3 Never speak to strangers at night

Clare was dreaming, dreaming of cold darkness. It was chasing her. She was running, but her fastest run was a slow walk. The darkness enveloped her, reached and touched her. She cried out against the burning cold, and for a moment, it fled. In its place, a warm calm descended, and with the calm came a whispered command, *"Wake up."* She opened her eyes.

And the nightmare was still there.

There was a man in her room. He wasn't looking at her but fumbling in his long coat for something. Her eyes flicked to the nightstand. The alarm clock read 2:43, but time brought her no sense of control. There was no way she could open the drawer and get her handgun before he grabbed her. He was too close. Her eyes pulled back to him. In the faint glow of the alarm clock, he held something up.

A syringe reflected in the dim light, and her heart seemed to skip a beat. His head snapped up as if… as if he could hear the sound. Clare swallowed, and the man's eyes seemed to follow the motion, glowing cat-like in the dark.

Her mind numbed with shock, and her body froze. She wanted it to move, to get away from the man with the demon eyes, or even just look away.

But it did none of those things. There was an odd detachment as he bent forward. This was not happening to her. Some other woman was about to be assaulted by an impossible man. This woman should run, or fight, or scream for help, but she just lay there. His movements were fluid as he continued to stare with those unbearable eyes. Clare shut hers against them.

A sudden pain pricked her arm, her eyes flew open, and her body woke up. Her knee shot up and caught the man squarely in the head as he bent over her arm. He staggered, and she brought a strong left to bear in the same spot. They were solid hits and should have taken him down but only seemed to knock him off balance. Good enough.

She lunged for the nightstand, ripped open the drawer and pulled out her .38 revolver, turning it on him. He'd already regained his footing. She pulled back the hammer. The metal click didn't ring out like it did at the range, but fell soft in the small space. His lips curled in a smile, like it amused him.

"I didn't take you for a fighter. Had you pegged for the sweet and innocent type."

His voice was a growl, low and primal and striking the primitive parts of her with the assurance that this was a predator. It was like his eyes, not human. Not... human...

Oh God.

The realization must have shown, either in her eyes or the shaking of her gun, because he... it smiled wider, revealing sharp canines.

Clare squeezed the trigger.

Its smile disappeared, and the syringe dropped as its stomach took the impact. She tried to squeeze the trigger again, but the gun was wrenched out of her grasp and turned on her.

"Don't move." The command was a snarl.

Keeping the gun—*her* gun—aimed on her, the creature dug in the wound with its free hand. Time seemed to crawl, and the squishing sounds of its probing fingers made her stomach turn. With a final sickening squelch, it pulled the bullet through the wet hole in its shirt.

Bitter acid rose in her throat. She covered her mouth and gagged. The creature held the slug in its fingers like the bullet was a mere curiosity.

Clearly, this was not the first time someone had shot it. Tucking the bullet into its pocket, the thing spoke again.

"There. Now that we understand each other, sit up and put your arm on the nightstand."

"What are you going to do with me?" Her voice cracked as she spoke.

It tilted its head to the side, eyes running over her body. "I just need a little of your blood."

Her blood. It wanted her blood. Clare choked on the rising hysteria and tried to think. Meg had warned her. What had Meg said?

"They might not kill me, just make me forget," she mumbled through renegade tears.

There was a sharp intake of breath, and then it was in her face.

"Who told you that?"

Its hands were braced on either side of her on the bed, one of them still wielding the gun. She pushed herself up against the wall, but it leaned in after her so that the distance between them never lessened. The iron rich smell of its breath hung in the air.

"Who told you?!"

A cry escaped her, and she turned her head away from its demonic eyes.

"An old woman." The tears were flowing freely now. "She—she said her name was Meg."

Abruptly, it straightened. Glowing eyes widened, then narrowed. "Shit."

That small gift of space allowed Clare's mind to work again, and her thoughts raced. Why was it asking that? It knew already if it was following her. Didn't it? She should have listened to Meg. Or any of the other people she interviewed. Even the stupid *Handbook*—

"Why would *she* be talking to you, Ms. Shultz?"

That name stole the breath from her. It was as impossible as those eyes. The thing lowered its face back down to hers, the thing that knew the name she had buried.

"Why would you call me that?"

"That is your name, is it not, Ms. Eleora Shultz?" it said in a hush while she shook her head. "You know, you really shouldn't lie to me."

She found her breath. "It's not a lie! I— I had my name changed years ago."

It cocked its head. "With such a beautiful name, I can't help but wonder why you would want to do that?"

"I'm a journalist. I took on my pen name to keep my family's privacy."

The creature studied her for a long moment.

"Close enough. Well, then, what name do you go by?"

"Clare." She swallowed. "Clarity Zetler."

"Alright Clare, how about you tell me why you were talking to Meg." It spoke inches away from her face, and nothing but the truth seemed plausible under its scrutiny.

"She— she let me interview her." Clare took a breath, trying to think. The creature's wound fouled the air with a thick blood smell. "For, um, for the article I'm writing." Its eyes seemed to collect the green clock light. "About *The Survivors' Handbook* and the, um— the— the Heliophiles."

It backed away, and finding she could breathe again, her mind came back into focus.

"Isn't... isn't that why you're here?"

It laughed, if you could call such a hoarse and grating sound laughter.

"No. But it is rather lucky, don't you think?"

God in heaven. It looked pleased. Actually pleased.

Clare's gut twisted. It was going to kill her, drink her blood until she died. She looked at its teeth. They seemed so white, even in the dim light, and so sharp. How long would it take to die? Would it hurt much? Would it matter if she struggled? The Handbook said to make noise, but if she did, it might just shoot her and then eat her.

Maybe that would be better.

She opened her mouth to take a deep breath, and it was back in her face, stagnating the air around her. Her nascent scream turned into a cough. Bile and anger sloshed in her stomach.

"I want you to do me a favor," it purred.

No. No more. It was going to kill her anyway, and she'd probably already said too much.

"I'd rather die."

92

"Would you? Because I was planning on letting you live." It turned its head, serpentine, to the side.

"Why? Why me? Why are you here? What do you want?" Clare's voice climbed higher and higher. It sounded strange, squeaky, girly. She was going to hate herself in the morning. If she lived that long. …There was that detached feeling again. Probably some mental coping method for dealing with vampires trying to eat you.

The creature was looking at her but not at her face like a person might. Its eyes ran along the edges of her body, like it was studying something there. Something she couldn't see.

"Because you're useful, even more so than I thought. And I already told you what I want: just a little blood. Now, if you would be so kind. Put your arm on that nightstand." It pulled a sealed needle from his jacket. "I'm going to draw a couple vials."

"You… just want to… draw my blood?"

It smiled softly, seeming to appreciate the irony. "Only a little."

"I'm dreaming," she said, but she propped her arm up for him.

"This would have been easier if you were a heavy sleeper."

A small laugh caught in her throat and died.

It continued, "I'm going to set the gun down now and trust that you are smart enough to sit there calmly for me."

Clare felt her head bobbing up and down. She didn't know if she was smart enough, but she would try.

Kneeling by the nightstand, the nightmare took her arm. Though its touch was light, she flinched. But so did it. At least, she thought it did. The movement was subtle.

She felt a momentary cold as it swabbed her the inside of her elbow, but it was mercifully quick and sure with the needle. Without tying off, it hit the vein, pushed the vial onto the needle, and when that was full, it traded out for another procured from its pocket. Finally, it pulled the needle out and pressed a piece of gauze, from the same magical pocket, onto the puncture.

"That's all I— " The sentence broke off with a hiss that made her flinch. Snatching its hand from the gauze, it wiped it on its coat.

"You'll want to hold pressure on that for a few moments," It... he... the thing nodded toward her arm.

Clare looked down at the gauze. Blood was beginning to seep through. Blood the creature wasn't drinking. She pressed her hand over the spot and watched the thing stand. It was shaking out its fingers as if... as if they pained it. Giving the offending digits a final look, it turned to go.

The immediate danger past, Clare's inner journalist began overtook her.

"That's it? Why *my* blood? Did it hurt you?"

The nightmare standing in her bedroom turned those eyes back on her, and her inner journalist had nothing more to say. She flinched away. When she looked up again, it was gone.

Clare lay in bed and waited for the sound of a door, the creak of a footstep, anything. When nothing came, she grabbed the gun from the floor and crept through the house turning on all the lights. There was no sign of how the creature had gotten in.

Finally, she went back to her room. It looked warm, despite the darkness outside the window, like it was unaware of what had just happened. Maybe it was all a dream. But why wouldn't her hands stop shaking. She padded across the soft, white beige carpet, and a glint caught her eye. There was a syringe on the floor. With trembling hands, she picked it up. A clear fluid moved inside it. Clare took a shuddering breath and set it down on the nightstand.

What if he came back for it?

It was 4:00 am. She sat on the edge of her bed and looked at the gun. Her father had gone through a lot of trouble to get her one when she got a place by herself. Lot of good it had done. But she didn't put it away. Next time she'd aim for the heart or the head. Next time...

Clare rolled onto her side and sobbed.

14

Shedding Light

Rule #2 If possible, stay in the light

Clare slipped into the lobby at work at 6:11, and Alex, the night guard, was just getting off his shift. He'd been talking with his dayshift replacement, but his little puppy dog eyes went round when he saw her. The makeup must not be cutting it. She ducked her head and walked quicker.

"Clare!"

A mess of emotions churned, barely checked, inside her stomach. It was easy to stop walking. She looked at him without saying anything. She couldn't say anything.

"Are you okay?"

She didn't think she would ever be okay again.

"Long night." Longest night of her life. "Insomnia, you know. Figured I'd just come on in to work since I was awake anyway."

"Uh-huh." He didn't seem terribly convinced.

Unbidden, a gravelly voice echoed through her mind. *You shouldn't lie to me.* She felt her eye twitch.

"Well, you look like you could use some coffee. Do you want to get a cup and maybe a bagel or something?"

The emotions were burning their way up her throat, threatening to spill out.

"Umm, no. I'm good. Thanks."

She mustered up what she hoped was a smile before fleeing to the elevator. With the doors safely closed, she rubbed the palms of her hands in her eyes, and then through her hair. She was fine. It was fine. She was here, safe. It was almost day. She was fine.

Clare didn't realize she was pacing until the elevator arrived and she had to stop to get out. When she grabbed her lanyard from her purse to swipe into the office, it shook in her hand. The small light by the lock remained red. She glanced around at the shadows in the hall. There was nothing. She tried the lock again and stood exposed in the hallway while it thought about letting her pass. Finally, the light turned green, and the door unlocked.

Despite the lightening sky outside, the office was pitch black. She stood there with the door open, unmoving. Closing her eyes, she took several deep breaths, and then plunged her arm in to flick the switch. Glorious light flooded the empty office. She hurried to her desk, feeling vulnerable despite the light. Next to her article notes was *The Survivors' Handbook*. Grabbing onto it like a safety rope, Clare began reading in earnest.

"Clare." David's voice roused her from sleep.

She peeled her face from a page of the book, a guilty wet stain marking her spot, and squinted at the clock: 11:58.

"It's lunch hour, Sleeping Beauty."

She groaned. "How long have I been out?"

"Since I got here, but nobody's ratted you out to Janice. Yet." He grinned. "They probably figure you were working here all night."

She wiped the sleep from her eyes. "Not too far off."

"Overachiever."

A faint smile teased at her lips, like the promise of dawn after a long night. Bantering with David felt ordinary... safe.

"Hey, and I got your copy of *Zombie Eater 3*." Clare pulled the game out of her briefcase with a flourish.

"Now you're just showing off," David snatched the game from her and tore it open to begin perusing the instruction manual. "And you got mail," he jerked his head to the brown box perched on the corner of her desk, his eyes never leaving the game booklet.

Clare's own eyes settled on the package like an alien had sprouted from her desk. She pulled it toward her slowly until she spotted the return address: A Little Light. A half laugh, half sob choked in her throat. Her "sun flare" had arrived.

As she ripped through the tape and packaging, David glanced up from his manual with a creased brow. Clare gripped the light in her trembling hands. The sturdy metal frame made it heavier than it looked, but other than that, it seemed like a normal flashlight. She toggled the switch several times and frowned at the absence of light. Batteries not included. Of course not.

David was no longer even pretending to look at the manual. He was looking at her. Really looking. She swallowed.

"Clare...?"

His mouth hovered open for a moment, then closed. Apparently, there was no good way to ask why she looked like she'd been attacked by a vampire in the night. And that was not a conversation she wanted to have. Why yes, David. She *was* attacked in her home last night by a mythical bloodsucking creature. Thanks for inquiring.

Clare had to stifle a giggle and wondered if this was how hysteria started. She had to get a hold on herself. Clearing her throat, she held up the light.

"This is called a sun flare. It's a sort of UV blended light that mimics sunlight in order to stop a vampire. It's like a gun, since guns don't hurt them." David's brow furrowed deeper, but Clare rushed on. "I don't know if it stops them or kills them though. The sites are really cryptic."

"If it *supposedly* stops them or kills them."

"Right. That's what I said."

"Nooo," he drew out the word carefully. "You said you weren't *sure* if it stops them or kills them."

She forced herself to meet his eyes. "Same difference."

"Uh huh. Right." He let his eyes hold hers for a moment longer. She looked away from his concern and started writing nonsense on her com. He just needed to go. There was no safety anymore, and she couldn't do this with him.

When she looked back up, David was gone. Clare took a breath and tried to center her thoughts. They wandered to the slightly tender spot in the crook of her elbow. She'd scrubbed it with alcohol and put a bandaid on before coming in, but she should have cleaned it sooner. Who knew what kind of diseases those creatures might carry.

Batteries. She needed batteries. What kind of batteries? She rummaged through the box of packing and pulled out a sheet of care instructions. Two C batteries. There should be C batteries in the office storeroom, and this *was* research for the magazine.

Clare wove her way through the cubicles to the oversized closet at the back of the office and jerked open the door. Her prize was waiting for her on the bottom shelf. After depositing two batteries into the flashlight, she took a steadying breath. Then, she shut the door and turned off the overhead light. In the darkness that swallowed her, she could almost smell the suffocating scent of the monster and hear its growling voice. The memory of green flashing eyes invaded the darkness. Her heart pounded as she fumbled with the switch on the sun flare.

The beam of light scattered broadly, or at least it seemed to in the storage room. Long shadows danced as she swept the light around the closet. Clare squinted and took a deep breath. She was okay, and she was safe.

But she wasn't.

A scream and a sob both fought to get out. Monsters were real, and the only thing she had was a flashlight. A *flashlight*!

Her breath shuddered. She couldn't. She couldn't let it out. If she started crying, she might never stop. Swallowing the lump in her throat, Clare fought to slow her breathing. After a few moments, she flicked the storage light back on and her flare off. She reached for the door but stopped, her hand hovering above the knob.

Perhaps she should just stay in here with her flare and hope for the best. Live out the rest of her life in the storage closet. Maybe she could bribe David to bring her some rations. A paranoid giggle escaped her lips.

No!

She was not going to lose it. She was not going to sit here in a closet and wait for that *thing* to come and find her. Maybe the sun flare didn't do anything, but her gun hadn't either. She at least had some chance with the light, and she had the *Handbook* and... the article.

Clare hurried back to her desk and began to write. She no longer cared about the tone or the audience; she only cared about people knowing. They would think she was crazy, and it didn't matter. The only thing that mattered was the hope that someone—anyone—would believe. Meg had said that vampires didn't like attention and that was the whole point to *The Survivors' Handbook*: to bring attention.

Well, she'd give them attention.

They'd already found her. She was probably guaranteed to end up as somebody's liquid lunch, but if she was going down, she was taking some of those bastards with her.

It was 4:39, and Clare's stomach interrupted her petering thought flow. She'd been too upset to eat at lunch, but revenge writing had awoken the slumbering beast. She stretched as she got up and headed toward the vending machine. Maybe walking around would help get the writing flowing again. The conclusion was still eluding her.

"You going to get something?"

Clare jumped. Hayden from fashion was standing behind her, manicured hands on hips. Clare had no idea how long she had been standing at the vending machine.

"Yeah, sorry," she mumbled. Pressing her card against the sensor, Clare selected the first thing that looked inviting, and returned to her desk without another glance at Hayden.

She gnawed at the granola bar while proofing her article for the ninth time. A crumb fell in between the keyboard keys. She was trying to scoop it out with a paper clip when David walked past her desk on his way home.

"You wouldn't have that problem if you switched over to a virtual board."

"But I can't feel the buttons on a virtual board."

"It doesn't make that tapping sound either."

"I like the tapping. It's a satisfying sound." She smiled.

"You're hopeless." He shook his head but smiled back.

"Are you actually in a good mood?" She raised her eyebrows in mock surprise.

"The prospect of zombie decimation may have had a positive effect on my overall well being," he called back as he headed for the door.

Clare laughed and felt warm for the first time all day. She called after him, "Have a good night with your monsters then."

The smile died on her lips.

She turned back to her article. There wasn't much left to do there. She could go ahead and send it on to Janice, but what she needed now were fail-safes. If the article was somehow intercepted or if something happened to her, she had to have a backup plan. She could write a blog, but that would probably be deleted. David could write a program that would keep posting it, but that meant she'd have to let him know about it. He knew her, knew she wasn't insane, and even if they broke in here and searched her desk, they'd never know to search his. And since she didn't communicate with him outside of work, he shouldn't be in any danger.

Hopefully.

She grabbed a pad of paper and a pen from her drawer. She could almost hear David scorn her for using something so archaic, but the creeps couldn't find something that had no trail.

Clare's hand cramped terribly when she finally put down her pen. She folded up the paper but wasn't sure what to do with it. A sudden, terrible thought came to her. She looked around the office. There were cameras. There would be cameras everywhere! What if they looked at the footage? What if they could hack into the system?

Clare's breath shuddered again. She'd toyed with the idea of staying the night here—how could she ever go home again? But suddenly here wasn't secure anymore either.

Secure! She looked at the clock. It was 7:09. Two hours wasn't long to wait. It would give her time to wrap everything up.

And it would be worth what it cost her in dignity.

Clare was waiting in the lobby when Alex came in for his shift. A grin broke over his face when he saw her. She smiled back and was pretty sure she was the scum of the earth.

"Hey! I can't believe you're still here. You look better though." He flushed. "Not that you looked bad! It was just that—"

"Yeah, it was really early," she said, trying to save him some self respect since *she* certainly wouldn't have any when the night was over.

"Yeah." He ogled at her with those big brown eyes.

"So, I've been thinking about that offer for Chinese."

He blinked. "Really?"

Maybe there actually was a brain behind that brawny facade.

"Where would we eat though? Out here?" She wrinkled her nose as she gestured around the lobby. "It's really open."

"We could eat back in the control room. It's a little more private."

Clare smiled, hating herself more with every moment.

"Sounds perfect."

Once she started eating, Clare realized that she was ravenous. Probably looked like a half-starved animal the way she was going at dinner, but at least shoveling food in her face saved her from making brainless small talk. She perched on the extra chair Alex had crammed in the control room. While glancing at the images from her office, she nodded occasionally to whatever he was saying, some tech talk about the cameras.

She swallowed another half-chewed chunk of General Tso's and asked, "Can you move the cameras or is that the angle they're always at?"

"Nah, they're stationary. The bosses cheaped out. They figured we didn't need the 360 recorders. Not like we're a high target building, just offices." He gestured with his chopsticks while he spoke. "You can see that the five cameras cover most of your office area and the elevator. See, here's your desk right there." His eyes widened and his face turned red as he realized the implications of what he'd just said.

101

Clare pretended not to notice. His blunder was just what she needed. She set aside her chicken and stood up to scrutinize the monitor cluster.

"And here's Janice's office door. I can even see the website department's cubicles." She couldn't see between their cubicle wall and the outside wall though. Perfect.

She glanced back. He was studying his Kung Pao Chicken closely.

"Well, it's late, and I should really be going. I just need to run upstairs and get my bag. Here's a ten for dinner."

He sighed, as if the offer of money confirmed how badly things had gone.

"No, that's okay," he said to the takeout box in his hands.

Clare was sure there was a special place in hell for people who were cruel to puppies.

15

Lifeblood

Rule #8 Attempt to conceal your scent

A drian looked at the fingers on his right hand. It was a day later, and the burn still throbbed. Of course, so did the spot further up his arm where he'd tested another drop. Since the blood itself didn't glow, he'd had to be sure it still carried the property once it was thoroughly removed from the body.

It did. A lot.

Normally, all he had to do was direct his energies to heal. The process used lifeblood faster, but everything had a price. His bullet wound had healed before he'd even left the light-bearer's house, but this—

He looked at the burn again. The angry welt stung as he rubbed his thumb over it, and the energy he directed at it simply turned back. He could always cut off the index and middle finger tips. They would probably regenerate. Probably.

He took a bag of blood from the mini-fridge and poured it in a pot to warm on the stove. The smell wafted, making his gums tingle, and he thought of the sun. The feeling diminished. He thought of the way dust danced in shafts of sunlight and took a deep breath of the iron tang. The tingle returned, but his canines did not lengthen. Adrian poured the blood like a libation into a thermos and sat down to drink. He'd fail now, at the taste. No matter how many times he tried, he always failed. Adrian assumed Lachlan could manage the feat because of his age, but probably it was the bastard's sheer will power alone.

He put the drink to his lips. Taking his mind away from the exposed brick wall of his penthouse, he thought of the sun reigning hot and relentless over the calm sea. The warm blandness of cloned blood filled his mouth, and a shudder of change went through his body, causing him to grip the cup tighter. A pulse of pain rippled through him. It crashed into the tide of vampiric changes and turned them back.

Eyes wide, but vision human, Adrian moved the cup to his uninjured hand. The burn returned to a low throb. He'd wounded himself before trying to stave off the change, but it had never worked.

Probably should rule out other possibilities before getting too excited. First, he needed to make sure he could still change. Adrian brought the cup up and let the taste of blood fill his mouth.

The effects on his body were instant. Teeth, senses, muscles—all grew and changed and swelled as the vampire rose from his depths. The welt on his finger seemed a deeper red to his enhanced pupils. He swallowed then used his strongest engram. A sunrise, slow and beautiful, crested over the ocean setting rippling waves on fire. Its warmth bathed over him until, with a shiver, the change retreated.

He took another drink. The change didn't flash upon him as it had the first time. His body began to tremble (the waves were dancing with light), then shake (the sun was so bright it hurt his eyes), and with a final shudder, he lost the battle. He sighed. Still not strong enough. So, it wasn't his ability that turned back the change.

Adrian let the taste subside before going back to the sunrise again to reset his senses. He rubbed his thumb over the burn, making the pain purr, and took another drink. The tingling began, as always, in his gums, and his sight shimmered. He closed his eyes and forced the golden image to obliterate all other thought. The trembling came next. The monster wanting to be free. He pressed harder on the burn. The beast quelled back down.

With pressure on the burn and the sun in his mind, Adrian took another drink. He could feel the creature within him growl in its cage, but it didn't come out. He smiled and took a long, slow drink. The flavor wasn't nearly as good without the change, but he could live with that. It would be satisfying enough to sit at the council table and drink in front of Lachlan, in front of them all, unaffected.

Unless Lachlan noticed the burn.

He looked down at his fingers. It wouldn't work. Adrian let go, and the vampire rose from its cage. The points of his teeth brushed his bottom gums, the whir of the refrigerator grew loud, and he looked, in the newly harsh light, at the burn. It was an angry red on his pale skin. Lachlan would notice it before he ever sat down at the table.

Adrian drained his cup. Even with the change, it wasn't great. He needed to get a hold of some oxytocin to add next time. Or adrenaline. But that would require a trip to Nidhi Complex, and he'd rather drink sewage than go there when he didn't have to. Stupid bullet wound. He could've been good for another week or two, especially after the strength in that officer's blood.

He tossed his dishes in the sink and pulled on his duster. It wasn't too late. The ride to the mountains would only take a couple of hours. If he pushed it, he could probably make it back for work tomorrow, barring any complications. It was dangerous to go out again so soon, but he had the blood, and if they could tease out its secrets, he'd never have to come back here again.

He could be free.

Adrian kept his speed at a meager nine miles above the speed limit. Not that he couldn't use a fresh meal, but he didn't have the time to waste. There were all manner of devices that could detect nearby officers, but even he wasn't sure how deep the Solifugae in the Tech department had reached. They could hijack anything that connected wirelessly without difficulty, but his vintage Harley was sleek, sexy, and totally devoid of traceable tech. Perry even custom-built the radio to be compatible with an old school music player. Nothing pinged, beeped, or updated. Silent freedom, and Adrian wasn't about to desecrate his baby with anything that might compromise that.

He pulled off the main road and navigated to his favorite thick grove of pines. He grabbed the cooler, covered his bike, and set off at a jog. Adrian usually took round-about routes to avoid making a footpath to the caves, but tonight he headed straight there. He was so focused on the blood and the burn that he didn't notice the smell until he'd squeezed past the cave entrance.

Adrian unleashed his senses and allowed the human parts to submerge. His small pen light seemed to blaze, and the scent came in sharp relief.

Miriam.

That dumbass dog. She was probably wearing a trail straight to him, and no doubt she brought electronics with her during her field work. Perry had always joked that Adrian would be the death of him. Watch it be a human woman. Ridiculous.

Adrian navigated through the cave, clicking off his light as he rounded the corner to the living area. Perry was in his cargo shorts. Miriam was wearing Perry's oversized flannel and little else. Neither saw him. A vampire had entered his sanctum sanctorum, and the oversized mutt was too love-struck to notice.

Miriam's pupils were dilated as she ran her finger along Perry's bare chest. He had his arm around her and a strange, soft smile on his lips. Completely asinine. They both thrummed and glowed with the beating of their blood. Adrian shivered off his changes and cleared his throat.

Miriam jolted, and Perry's eyes flashed to yellow.

Right, because now the fucking idiot was on his guard.

Adrian came into the room slowly, hands loose at his sides. Perry's nostrils flared, and Adrian stopped. He was interrupting instincts of a different kind tonight, and he did have some sense of self preservation. A wolf was never truly domesticated.

"I see you had the courtesy to actually look normal when you barged into somebody's house this time." Miriam gave him a pointed look. Perry's flannel fell loose over her curves, just touching her mid-thighs. Damn. She was beautifully crafted.

"Hello to you too, Miriam."

"Adrian." Perry stood, shifting his body slightly in front of Miriam. The stance was protective, but his eyes had already returned to green. "You're back soon. It's a weekday."

"I know, and yet, I find myself being the one that's surprised. I'd have hoped your lady love would've given the arrangement more thought." Miriam glowered at him, but Adrian scowled right back. She was the one playing with fire. "However, since this is apparently still a thing, you might want to rig a bell system at the cave entrance. To, you know, prevent future... interruptions."

Perry cocked a sideways grin, but Miriam was not amused.

"Don't you have set visiting hours or something, Ugly?"

Adrian gave her a mock bow and let the sarcasm drip from his voice as he said, "I am sorry to trespass on your evening, dear lady, but alas, some urgent matter has brought me outside of my 'set visiting hours.'"

She didn't take the bait but instead said, "What's in the cooler?"

Adrian glanced at Perry, who gave his head a slight shake. At least he had enough sense to keep some of his research from her.

"Just some specimen I found on my way up that I thought might interest Perry."

Perry covered his face with his hand. Wrong answer then.

"Hm. That so? Could be helpful for the survey I've been doing up here. Mind if I take a look?"

He glanced at Perry again, but Perry wasn't looking at either of them, just staring off, shaking his head slowly.

She got up and approached Adrian. This seemed to wake Perry.

"You might not want—"

"You said he was safe," she said to Perry.

"He is."

"You said that you work to protect people."

"We do, but—"

She held up a finger to stop him.

"No more lies. I understand you aren't going to tell me everything right away, but you sure as hell better stop lying to me." Miriam turned a look on Adrian, and for a fragile human, it carried a surprising amount of force. She motioned to the cooler.

He unzipped it and brought it where she could see.

"Whose is it?"

Okay. Outright lies clearly weren't working, but perhaps a little misdirection... "I'm sure Perry told you that vampires have mastered cloned blood."

"He did, and that you have bags and bags of it stored up. So, that's not what this is. Whose blood's in the vials, Ugly?"

"Just some random woman's." The image of the light-bearer, her body cloaked in glow, flashed in his mind.

Miriam's eyes narrowed. "Just some random woman's blood. And you felt the need to come up on a weekday and risk your cover? Try again."

Well, Perry had certainly been filling her in on some details since they'd last met.

"She has an unusual trait that might help protect people from vampires, like a vaccine."

"And she just signed up to be a part of this research project, did she?"

Perry interjected, "Adrian is very good. He would have kept her from waking while he drew the blood."

Something must have shown in Adrian's eyes because Perry continued, "Or used a Z.I.P. when he was done."

"I don't think Ugly did either of those things. I think he just assaulted this 'random' woman and left her."

Adrian wanted to argue, but the lie died in his throat. That was exactly what he'd been doing for the past several years.

A person here, a person there. Well-placed, steady people who would be more likely to be believed if they claimed there was such a thing as vampires. He could see the face of the light-bearer in his mind, her eyes wide and mouth slack as he pulled the bullet from his stomach. At least Miriam wasn't fooled by Perry's optimism. She saw Adrian for the monster he was, inside and out.

"I have not followed Nietzche's advice," Adrian said.

"What, that women were God's second mistake?"

Adrian answered quietly, "'Whoever fights monsters should see to it that in the process he does not become a monster. And if you gaze long enough into an abyss, the abyss will gaze back into you.'"

Miriam held his look, and he wondered what she saw staring back from his abyss. She shook her head ever so slightly.

"Right." She turned to Perry. "I'm going to bed."

"Miriam..."

But she ignored Perry's pleading look as she walked back to the bedroom and shut the door.

"You sure do know how to charm the women."

Adrian shrugged. "If it's any consolation, I think that I actually like her."

Perry rolled his eyes, but a smile twitched at the corner of his mouth.

Adrian followed Perry out of the living space and down a corridor to his lab area. It was still near the edge of the mountain, for ventilation, but was far enough removed that chemical smells didn't waft into the common area. The place looked how it usually did, papers randomly stacked, microchips and gears scattered about, machines with timers whirring, and the odd beaker here and there half filled with mysterious liquid. The plate-sized black mark near the sink seemed different though.

"Didn't that scorch mark used to be smaller?"

Perry brushed some papers over it. "Just trying to up the output of the sun flare without it damaging the mortals."

Adrian snorted. "Looks like that worked."

Perry smiled. "You're an ass. Now, tell me what happened."

Adrian relayed the story while Perry stashed the blood.

"And you can't heal the burn?" He took Adrian's hand and looked over it with a clinical eye.

Adrian shook his head.

"Feeding didn't help?"

"No, but the burn combined with an engram kept the change from happening."

Still studying the mark, Perry brushed the statement away. "You would have reached that point eventually. This just helped." He pressed on the burn.

Adrian jumped slightly and wrenched his hand away.

"Still hurts," Perry said, his brow furrowed.

"Yeah. It still hurts. That tends to be the way with things that don't heal." Adrian shook his fingers and glared at his friend. "I thought about severing the fingertips. They should regenerate. Obviously, Lachlan can't see this."

Perry grimaced at the name. "Shit, no. You'd never leave R&D."

"You might never see daylight again, either," Adrian smirked. "Not if Granny dearest thinks you let her spy get killed."

"Not funny. If word gets out and Deval sees this, he might just figure out you're the one letting people go." Perry's expression was unusually grim. "No amount of usefulness or pleading from Siri would keep him from turning you over to that bastard."

His jaw clenched, and he swallowed hard. "My parents' death was utilitarian. Lachlan wanted the power in their blood, and he took it. If he gets ahold of you, he's not going to be practical. You'll be repaid for every day you've existed." Perry closed his eyes, rubbing his hands over his face. "Let's try something."

Perry led the way, lantern in hand, out of the living quarters and into a maze of twisting and tight corridors that Adrian had never been in before. When they came to a dead end, Perry pushed his light through a small opening in the rock's bottom. Then, he squeezed through after it. This was ridiculous.

"Perry?"

"Come on, wuss."

Adrian knelt down, the grit from the cave scratching at his burn, and pushed through the hole.

The cave ballooned. Perry's light didn't even reach the back wall. His light footsteps echoed off of... a lake. Perry set his lantern down a few feet from the water's edge and crouched next to it. He motioned for Adrian to do the same.

Adrian sat next to the dark water. His hands prickled where they touched the rock.

"What is this place?" Adrian's whisper came back to him in a susurrus.

"I call it the amphitheater." The room replied the name from a dozen angles.

"Original," Adrian smirked.

"It fits."

Perry grabbed a loose pebble and cast it into the water. The sound of light rain echoed back.

"You feel that?" Perry pointed to where Adrian's hands rested on the cave floor.

"Yeah, what is it?"

"It's you. You amplified. At least, I think it is."

Adrian lifted his hands. The prickling stopped. He turned them over in front of his eyes. They didn't look any different. He set them back down. The effect was immediate.

"So that's a little creepy."

"That's nothing. Think of blood."

The word sent a jolt through Adrian. This was a dangerous game.

"Why?"

Perry rolled his eyes. "Just do it. Think of the warmth, the smell, the taste."

Adrian winced. With each word an army of echoes came back and assaulted him, ripping the sensations from his memory, the heat in the back of his throat, the sharp smell, and the salty, sweet taste. The prickling beneath his palms exploded and shot through his body.

The cave was transformed. White currents flowed in an eddy, concentrated by rock formations over the lake and bounced by the water. He sat in the central current. Adrian stood and reached out. Red, translucent energy flowed in curls from him. He looked to Perry. Blue ribbons streamed from his friend into the current. Adrian brought his hand up to his face and rubbed his eyes against the irritation, but it was hard to quell the odd sense of disgust he felt at the blue aura.

"I don't think this is a good idea." Adrian could feel his instincts stirring.

"That's why I haven't brought you here before. This place seems to amplify everything." Adrian opened his mouth, but Perry cut him off. "It's worth the risk if this works. Look at the burn? Is it different here?"

Adrian studied at his hand. Despite its angry scarlet color, no red current came off of it.

Lowering his voice against the echo, Adrian said "All of me looks different. There's a sort of red current surrounding me, but the burn still looks the same. It's not giving off any kind of light or whatever this stuff is." He swiped his hand at the flow, making it swirl away.

"What happens when you direct your energy at it to heal?" Perry said, leaning to look over his shoulder.

Adrian pushed the life in his blood toward the wound and watched as the red around him intensified to maroon, concentrating and washing down his arm. His hand was enveloped in writhing light, and though the spot was lit by the glowing chaos, none of it reached the burn.

Adrian shook his head. "It doesn't touch it."

Perry stood and paced, his lips drawn in a line. Now and then, he'd gesture a hand to shoo away some rejected idea. When he pivoted, his cloud of blue rolled back over him like a billow of smoke.

"What if it's purely physical? What if it's settled into the physical state?"

"I don't follow."

Perry opened his mouth, closed it with a shake of his head, and began pacing again. "At the quantum level, matter can occupy two states at once until you observe it."

Great. Here we go. "Right. So… in either of those states is it likely to heal on its own?"

"Schrodinger said that quantum particles were like a cat in a box. Since you don't know if the cat is dead or alive until observed, the cat occupies both states: dead and alive."

"I read Nietzche, not Hawking." The mutt's science orgasm was going to give him a headache.

Perry ignored him. "You and I live our lives in that box. We straddle dead and alive. We can be in the dimension of the living or, should we choose, that of the Watchers. Maybe the light in her blood acted like an observer, causing part of you to get locked into the physical state."

Definitely a headache. "Uh huh. So that's a maybe on the healing then?"

"No idea. Your life is borrowed. It's not your own physical life. Your cells live because you will them to live, and if you can't will them to heal, maybe they can't heal." Perry raked his hands through his beard. "We don't have time to wait and see either. So that leaves us with two options: We can sever the fingertips and hope the effect is limited to its locale, but we'll have a worse problem if it isn't. Or, we can try my blood."

It was like a hit to the gut. Adrian's mouth drifted open, but no sound came out. He shook his head. He'd never laid his teeth on Perry. And he *would* never. If the draw of the blood was too strong, if he became anything like Lachlan, or if Perry died because of him...

The change left him and the cave snapped back into a stifling black.

"I don't see how that would help." Adrian's voice sounded flat, human.

"You can drink my blood since it's living, and because it's also in that dual state, it might rectify the issue."

"No."

Perry stopped pacing. The refusal of seemingly good logic appeared to have jousted him from science mode.

"It's not like I'd let you feed on me. I'd put it in a bag."

"No." Adrian's voice echoed off the waters.

"I'm not worried."

"Maybe you should be. Maybe I've been around you so long that you forget what I am. The properties of living Therian blood are fabled for a reason. Oh, wait, I know; it'll be fun science to feed that to a vampire in a place that makes everything he is ten times worse!" Worse. Worse. Worse. Worse. Worse. Worse.

"You need to stop being afraid of yourself." Afraid of yourself. Afraid yourself Afraid yourself. Yourself.

Adrian cocked his head. "Right, like that isn't the whole reason you're still

113

alive."

Perry drew closer and whispered. "I'm alive because you were a coward. Still are, I see."

The smell of Therian filled his nostrils and, before Adrian could even think, a snarl escaped him.

Adrian had seen Perry phase, but this time it was far quicker. Too quick. The elongating snout with ears and body contorting into a new shape was almost instant. Where a man had been, stood a wolf amid the remnants of break away shorts. And the vampire in him rose to welcome it.

The wolf turned toward him, and Adrian could see blue energy flow off of its body. The currents distorted and shimmered. Its heart began to race. Perry snarled, and it was like nothing that Adrian had heard before. There was murder in it. The cave brought the sound back again and again, and Adrian could feel himself slipping, his vision colored by the crimson currents streaming from his own body.

Vampires had another instinctual drive aside from bloodlust. They had a lethal hatred of Therians, and Adrian could no longer feel Perry. There was only the provocation before him, and he thirsted for it, to rip its throat out, and watch the blood fly and dance to the gurgling sounds of death. He would paint himself in it and go make war.

He readied himself for the Therian's lunge, but instead, it closed its eyes, and the snarl softened to a low-throated rumble. The drumming in its chest slowed. Adrian's fingers twitched. It would be so easy.

Except.

He knew him. Adrian hissed in frustration, and Perry's eyes snapped open, the rumble in his throat intensifying as did the rivers of blue flowing from him. The rivers deepened into purple and finally into a palpable black. The black tide engulfed him in electric animosity.

Adrian tried to lower his energy, to think of the sun, to throw off the change, but he couldn't draw himself out. He stared at his friend, hackles raised and shaking body lit by a black sun, and he searched for Perry.

The currents shifted. He could feel them welling, coursing through him and out. He *stretched,* directing his energy against the black tide, pushing it back, back until he could feel Perry. Then Adrian pulled. It felt like rising through layers of a dream until you wake. A violent shudder tore through Adrian. He blinked. The cave was no longer lit with wild currents. The change had left him.

And he had drawn them out.

A man crouched, blinking around the room and looking blank. His gaze fell on Adrian and slow recognition dawned.

"How did you...? You drew me out."

"What if I hadn't? You fucking idiot."

Perry stood. "You would never hurt me."

"Really? That's not how it looked a moment ago." Adrian felt his hands clench. The stupid, *stupid* mutt. "Our whole friendship has been one big experiment to you, hasn't it? How safe is the vampire? Well, I'm done. I'm not playing your game anymore."

Adrian pushed past a mute Perry and stalked toward the entrance at the far side of the chamber. He let the change rip through him again, and their previous scents guided his way into the darkness.

An echoing call followed him.

"You won't make it to Richmond before sunrise!"

He didn't turn back.

16

Terms

Rule #7 Never make yourself an easy target

Clare's face felt taut. She hadn't cried herself to sleep since… well, since after the accident. She licked her salty lips and pushed herself up from the hotel bed. It was 9:34 on Wednesday morning, and she didn't care. She'd made her deadline, and there was no way they would fire her when David was still on the payroll. A giggle escaped her.

Work. Ha. Right. She couldn't go back to work. Ever.

Both her lives were ruined. That thing knew where she worked and who her family was. No one, nowhere was safe. A sob turned into a hiccup as she tried to stifle it. She had severed ties before. It was just time to do it again, and this time family was included.

She pulled a spare set of clothes from her gym bag, then headed for the shower. The scalding water scoured away the nightmares as she ran through her options.

It was daylight. She could return home and grab some clothes. Then, she'd put everything in order, leave a few notes, and take a plane to somewhere far away. Maybe somewhere tropical. Or not. It didn't really matter where so long as there was plenty of sun.

Clare pulled on her clothes and did her makeup automatically, her mind ticking off places she might get a fake passport. Grabbing her bag, she headed for the door. 10:17. That left around eight hours of sunlight. It would have to be enough.

She'd been standing outside her front door for at least four minutes.

Clare had dropped her keys twice but finally succeeded in getting the key in the lock, despite the shakiness in her hand, and slid the lock open. Her mouth was dry. She put her hand to the knob, again, and took a slow breath. Nope.

Wiping her hands on her jeans, she turned and leaned her back against the door. She had to get in there. It was the first part of her plan, and she was wasting daylight. It's not like the vampire was in there. Surely there were too many windows for that. So why couldn't she open the door? She turned around and hit the door with a cry of frustration. It swung inward.

Well, that was one way to get it done.

Everything was where she'd left it. Leaning her head in, she called out, "Hello?" Because the vampire would come prancing out and say "hi" in reply if it was in there. Get a grip!

A hurried check of the kitchenette, bedroom, and bathroom assured her that the rest of the house was empty. The filled syringe that it had dropped was still on her nightstand. So it hadn't been back. It didn't mean to leave that. What was in it? Her inner journalist began to struggle. It wanted answers, had questions that no one knew to ask. Running away would not answer those questions.

Clare sat down on the bed and put her head in her hands. She couldn't stay.

Why not? Once the article got published, it would be foolish for them to kill her.

What if they did what Meg said and made her forget?

Clare snorted. That actually wouldn't be too bad an idea. People would chalk it up to a psychotic break. Even *she* would chalk it up to a psychotic break! There would be no more monsters, no more fear.

She picked up the syringe. Is that what was in there? Liquid freedom? The clear-ish, yellow fluid rolled back and forth as she examined it. How did it work? Could she just inject herself with it?

A small thought fought its way to the surface: That would still be running away.

With a yell, she flung the syringe across the room.

"I can't do this. I don't know how to deal with this. I don't know what I'm supposed to do!"

Memory of her mom came, unbidden. Her mom had been brave. She'd told Clare's dad to get Clare out of the car first.

No. Not Clare, but Elly.

No one knew that car model was faulty yet, that the batteries would catch fire in a side-front impact, but it was almost as if her mom knew. Those gentle brown eyes had been calm as she pulled a hysterical Elly forward. Something was dinging in the car, and the white light of the clock read 7:01. They were late for Elly's recital, and there was blood. She was bleeding on her recital outfit. Mom handed her through the broken window, over the median they'd hit.

"It's okay honey. Be brave for Mommy. It's okay."

She had never been brave. It was like all the brave had gone with her mother. A loving father and doting brother had never brought back what the wreck took. Years of counseling hadn't reconciled her to it being gone. She'd changed her name and separated herself from her friends and family; tried to pretend that she never had it in the first place, but she had.

And it was gone.

Gone because of a stupid recital they were late to and a patch of ice on the road. Gone, not just for her, but for her father and brother too. Her father had lost the use of his legs in the explosion that followed. Her brother had been wrecked by guilt that he hadn't been there to help. She'd watched them grieve and struggle because of something that would never have happened if not for her.

And she had not been brave.

"Oh, God." It was a moan, a prayer.

Years of being in control, of pushing it down, crumbled. The desperate cry of a little girl who just wanted her mommy to kiss it and make it better would be denied no longer. She lay on her bed and gave way to a pain that words failed.

The pain came in great waves that crashed and convulsed her before it finally ebbed to streams and then squeezed out from secret places. She had run from it for so long, and now it overtook her completely, baptizing her.

When she rose up from it, born again, she was Eliana's daughter, and she was done running. Her body shook as she stood up from the bed, but her soul was firm, broken free from its chains and alive in a way that no monster could kill. Her mother had died but lived on, and Clare had been dead while living.

No longer.

She splashed water over her face at the kitchen sink and made a cup of coffee. There was no plan that could be made, only preparations, and she would make those. When the darkness came, she would face it.

Her phone was full of messages when she finally checked it: her boss, Janice, wanting to know if she was feeling well, Janice again asking her to call (there was concern in her voice), and David. She'd been hoping for that one. He'd gotten her note, and was she alright? He'd be there, but this seemed like something bigger than her second favor.

It was almost four. She'd have to leave soon to meet him. Clare stuffed a few things into her gym bag, put on the ring her father had given her for her birthday, and headed for the door. A thought stopped her.

She went back to her room. The syringe lay at the base of the wall she'd flung it. She picked it up and placed it carefully in her briefcase. Now she was ready.

Clare was sitting on a bench outside the courthouse eating a hotdog when David found her. He sat down next to her and looked around. Her note must have sparked paranoia in even him.

"What's going on, Clare?" he said in a low voice. "Janice is worried about you. You didn't show up, and you leave me this note—"

119

"Did you mention it to anybody?"

He jerked his head back a little, offended perhaps. "No. It said not to."

"Good. I don't want them to know we're friends."

He raised his brows at her. "Them? What are you into?"

Clare inhaled and let it out in a long stream. This was harder to say than she had imagined.

"I don't expect you to believe me, but you know me well enough to know I'm solid. I'm always there on time, I always do my work, and I've never gone off the deep end on anything, especially a story."

David crossed his arms and leaned back on the bench, but he gave her a small nod.

"I was attacked two nights ago."

He jolted, his eyes sweeping over her body and face before settling on her eyes. He nodded again. "That morning you came in looking like walking death."

"Thanks."

"Did you go to the police?"

"I'm sitting here talking to you. What do you think?" She put her fingers to her temple and rubbed. "No. I didn't go to the police because—"

She sighed. Because it was a vampire. Because we live in a world with monsters. Because the Heliophiles were right. There was no way to convince what was probably her only friend that she wasn't insane, so she just went for it.

"A vampire attacked me."

David didn't move. His lips parted slightly, but that was all.

"Look, I know it sounds crazy. I didn't believe any of the Heliophiles— you know that—, but one of them warned me that they would come after me for poking into this story, and she was right. So, I can only assume all the rest of it is true too, like they can tap into our surveillance, monitor our net usage." She looked at him meaningfully.

He glanced away. "Clare, you look like hell, but you don't have a scratch on you. Maybe the pressure or the stress…"

"I have one mark." She pulled up her sleeve to show the fading needle mark.

The tight lines on his face loosened into relief. "Drugs."

"What? No! Do I look high? That's not me, and you know it."

"Drug-induced hallucinations can seem very real, Clare. It's all right."

"David, no! I'd submit to a drug test right now. I have never used drugs in my life. It, the vampire, it took my blood."

He leaned back on the bench and folded his arms again. It wasn't working. "Okay. Why? Why not just suck your blood or kill you?"

"I don't know. It took a couple of vials, but it dropped this before leaving." Clare drew the syringe out of her bag. His eyes widened, and he swiveled to look around.

"Are you crazy?! Put that thing away before you get us arrested!"

She extended it to him, but David waved his hands in front of him to ward it off.

"No! I am not getting my fingerprints on that thing."

"I know you don't believe me," Clare said as she reached over and slipped the needle into his coat pocket. He paled. "But do me one last favor and go get it tested. If I'm right, it should have some chemical compound that will induce forgetfulness. I think the vampire meant to use it on me but got distracted." She thought of his hiss, and shivered.

David ran his fingers through his mussed hair and shook his head. "On one condition."

"You name it."

"If this is anything narcotic, you go to rehab."

She felt her body relax as a smile spread over her face. "You have my word."

"*Zombie Eater 3* was not worth this."

"David, you're the best."

"I am, and I'm a saint too," he said.

She stood up, and he added, "I'll call you when I know something."

Clare nodded. "There's a hard copy of my article under your desk, in case something happens to the one I sent Janice. I'm not sure when I'll make it into work."

An unspoken "if" hung in the air.

David's face tightened again.

"Take care of yourself, all right?"

* * *

Leroy sat with his back against his headboard, Argiope's empty tank next to his bed, and searched the internet. There was information if you knew how to get it. People would tell you how to do things, poison a water supply or build a bomb, if you asked the right way.

He must have asked wrong, somehow, because he was invited to a private chat. He almost didn't go, but the person's username caught his eye. Could be another spider enthusiast.

Sanguisug:

I couldn't help but notice you in the last chat room. You were asking about something different in there.

LEroysarachnids:

I haven't narrowed down what I'm going to do my paper on yet.

Sanguisug:

Based on your screen name, why not do it on the impact of spiders on the insect population and how that affects us as a whole?

LEroysarachnids:

Do you like arachnids as well?

Sanguisug:

I think they are magnificent creatures, unparalleled in beauty and usefulness.

LEroysarachnids:

Yes! They are graceful, fast, nearly cryptesthesic in their perception of their surroundings, and the world would be overrun without them! Think of all the ants!

Sanguisug:

Haha. I couldn't have said it better myself. Ants are pests, aren't they?

LEroysarachnids:

They are the worst! As far as I'm concerned, their only purpose is to feed my spiders! Not all of my spiders are up to the task though.

Sanguisug:

That's a shame. You keep spiders too?

LEroysarachnids:

Yes! I have over 100, all local. What do you keep?

Sanguisug:

I have some exotic species, like the Goliath, but I was wanting to get into local. Where is local for you?

LEroysarachnids:

WV

Sanguisug:

That's extraordinary! Me too! We should meet. You could tell me your tricks.

LEroysarachnids:

I don't know, I'm kind of busy right now.

Sanguisug:

Ant problem?

LEroysarachnids:
   ??

Sanguisug:
   Come now, we are both spider people. I know how you feel. If you help
me get some local specimens, I could help you get some of the chemicals
you were asking about.

A frisson went through Leroy. He shouldn't. It was risky. But was it really?
They could meet, and he could feign misunderstanding if the guy didn't turn
out to be what he seemed to be.

Sanguisug:
   Are you still there?

LEroysarachnids:
   I'm here.

LEroysarachnids:
   That sounds good. When do you want to meet?

Sanguisug:
   Are you free tomorrow night?

17

Tracks

Rule #11 Do not donate blood

I t was almost nightfall when Adrian felt the summons tugging in his middle. A council had been called. He swore and rolled over.

Sleeping all day hadn't been enough after this morning. The sky was lighter than he'd seen it since his making, streaked with pinks and golds by the time he made it back to Nidhi Towers. It was so beautiful. And so painful. His skin had taken a reddish hue, and boils rose up where clothing and helmet didn't cover.

Adrian vaguely remembered staggering into the elevator and entering the code to take him to his suite. He may have been screaming. He didn't remember exiting the elevator, only being at the fridge, ripping a blood bag open with his teeth, and drinking with the cool fridge air on his face. A couple of bags later, he was on his bed, trying to heal, but it was day. He could feel the reign of the sun and its dampening on all his powers, like reverse photosynthesis.

The next thing he was aware of was the summons.

As the sun outside ebbed, his power began to flow again. Adrian groaned. Moving took so much effort. He looked down at his body. His skin was the right color again, but something was off. He turned his hands over and his blood burn glared angry at him.

The change. He must have slipped into it with the setting sun because he didn't have enough energy to maintain human form. He swore again. Adrian downed two more pints of blood from his fridge. Nothing so bland had ever tasted so good. A tingle of life filled him. He radiated it out, feeling for and righting things under the surface that had not yet healed.

That felt better.

There was only one thing left to do. Blowing out a breath of air, Adrian went to the fireplace and took down his sixteenth century scimitar from its display. It was honed and perfect, engraved down the hilt and blade. Shame to use something so lovely for something so bloody, but then, it'd probably drank plenty of blood in its time.

He braced his hand on the kitchen counter and curled down his ring finger and pinky. Damn. He hoped he had the energy to heal if this ridiculous stunt worked. Setting his teeth, he swung down hard.

Bloody fucking hell! His finger tips skittered across the counter as blood gushed from where his top knuckles used to be. The blade clattered to the counter. Adrian grabbed his hand and began pushing life to the wound. The gushing ebbed. Drawing from all his being, he pushed harder. He could feel the knitting, and relief flooded him. He'd grown bone before, but fingernails were new, and the sensation was almost slimy as the nail bed repaired and pushed forth the new nail. There was still the spot near the crook of his elbow where he'd tested the blood, but that could wait to be excised.

He would not be found out tonight.

Adrian turned his hand over with a smile of satisfaction. It had taken more life than he would have liked, but he was whole. No Therian blood needed.

The council began at midnight. Adrian was almost last in the room, and the only seat available on the far side was next to Jonathan. Of course. Adrian sat down without looking at him.

Siri, across the table and next to her father, smiled and blinked slowly at him. Suddenly, he felt her essence caress his soul. She was doing this here, where he couldn't get away from her, so she could watch him squirm. He couldn't deny the fury that rose up in him, but tonight, he would deny her the satisfaction of seeing his anger. Adrian folded his arms, squeezing down on the remaining burn to push back the change, and turned a calm eye to the ceiling.

Her bottom lip jutted a little, and she reached further. It felt like she was inside his body with him, in his soul. He wanted to kill the bitch so badly. He closed his eyes and pressed harder on the burn.

Adrian, look at me.

He couldn't fight her command, not with his energy still low, but he had enough left to fight the change. He opened his eyes—his very *human* eyes—to her and savored the confusion that swept through her, seeping out like a spreading pool of blood. Leaning back in his chair, he smiled just enough to reveal his perfect human teeth. Siri frowned at him, and for just a moment, her own pupils dilated.

Victory felt delicious. And she was far enough inside him that she could feel his triumph too. Almost two centuries under her thumb, and now she might finally get it through her pretty little head.

He was going to break free.

Deval stood, and Siri's presence in him diminished. Everything stilled. Deval motioned to Jonathan, who swallowed hard and looked down at a stack of papers before him.

"Uh, yes, well. We had some hits in Media on the *Handbook* issue. Someone writing an article about the Heliophiles. It seems she's very likely to have been in contact with us and them. I have some copies of her article here." He motioned to the papers. "Should I— Should I pass them around?"

"That would be fine," Deval replied in his usual hushed tone.

Adrian didn't have to look at the paper handed to him. It was the light-bearer. He tried to clear his mind, focus on anything but the woman with sun in her blood. Siri must not be allowed to feel his alarm. Ah, look, a grammatical error on Jonathan's report. Maybe there were more.

Once everyone had a copy, Jonathan continued. "The article has already been read and is in the editing phase. We may be able to erase it. However, if we can't, we may be able to, um, obtain useful information from the author as well as discredit her, thus preventing its release in the October issue."

Adrian quit scanning the page and let his eyes move from word to word without reading them. They were mere squiggling curiosities without greater meaning.

"Thank you, Jonathan," Deval said.

Adrian let a calm boredom fill his mind as he let the paper drop to the table.

Jonathan looked at his com, blinked a few times, and said, "One last thing, sir?"

Deval gestured for him to continue.

"My team just alerted me that a chemical analysis triggered our system. It looks like— like someone is analyzing one of our Z.I.P.s."

Figlio di troia! No. Calm and serene, like walking by the ocean.

Though not given to expression, Deval's face contorted with underlying rage. When he spoke, his soft voice trembled.

"Tyrone, you're with Jonathan. I want whoever ordered that analysis along with the woman who wrote this article. I want them tonight. And if you discover who dropped that Z.I.P., give them to Lachlan."

Like walking by an ocean of shit.

"Crystal, prepare your team for damage control on the social sites. This *will* be contained. Lachlan, tell your technicians not to mark those two when they come in. They may have to be released after processing." He closed his eyes. "This is unacceptable. I can see that I will have to clean house." He opened his eyes and looked at each of them in turn. Adrian met Deval's gaze with as much boredom as he could muster considering the shit tsunami that was about to hit. "It would be best for you that the problem is not found in your department. You are dismissed."

Deval sat and watched as they got up, some talking to others, others hurrying out. Tyrone was already at Jonathan's side asking for addresses and possible locations. Adrian rose slowly, trying to catch as much of the conversation as he could without incurring suspicion. Jonathan had a map on his com with the location of the light-bearer's house and what must be the location of her workplace marked with red flags.

Lachlan walked by, trailing a finger over Adrian's back as he turned to go.

For once, Adrian relished an excuse to bring on the change. Lach smirked at him, but Adrian let it go. Now, he could hear everything Jonathan and Tyrone were saying.

"I'll send a team to both locations. We'll want her coms as well as the woman. What about the analysis?"

It was harder to hear in the hall with all the competing noise, but he could still pick out their voices.

"It was run by Labscorp in that building there, sometime around 7 pm. The offices are closed, so you should have no problem getting the sample back. I can, um, can send you with someone from Media to help you recover and destroy any data pertaining to it."

Adrian shivered off the preparation. He could beat the team to her house, but he doubted she was there. They hadn't connected the journalist persona and her past. Yet. He'd underestimated Jonathan. It wouldn't be long before—

A whiff of jasmine hit him as Siri grabbed his arm. The change jolted through him again before he'd even recognized her touch. He whirled around, fangs bared.

"I have things to do, tonight. We all do. *What do you want?*"

He expected her usual, seductive look, but the vulnerable face that stared back at him was almost unrecognizable. He'd never seen this woman with sincere eyes, and... and need, before.

"We could leave."

"What?"

"I know you hate it here."

It took a moment for Adrian to understand what she was offering.

"I don't hate it here." Adrian said it slowly. "I hate *you*."

She flinched.

Adrian jerked his arm free and walked out.

"Kin eeye uze youur phone?" Adrian slurred, with a cup in one hand and the other draped around the oversized bartender. "Eeye seeem to have loost mine." He waved his hand around hopelessly, sloshing his drink.

The barkeeper wrinkled his nose and pulled a phone out from under the bar.

"Thhaanks, buhd-dy!"

Adrian stumbled over toward an empty corner and dialed. After several rings, a female voice answered.

"Hello?"

"It's Adrian."

A pause. "Are they moving?"

"Not as a whole, but they are mobilizing against one of your contacts. I'm going there to stand guard now, but you'll want to come and move her in the morning."

"Which one?"

"Clarity Zeitler."

A snort. "Must've written that article. I'm glad she did, but I warned her of the consequences. Let this one alone, Adrian. I vetted her after some promising hits, and she's a possible asset, but this isn't worth your exposure to Deval. I'll send someone in the morning."

Perry must have been good to his word and kept their research off the record. Dammit.

"We can't leave this one alone, Meg."

"*Why?*"

Adrian ran a hand over his jaw. The shit storm was about to continue, and there was no way to keep Perry out of it.

"She's a light-bearer. Perry is trying to isolate the compound in her blood that makes it painful to... my people."

The silence on the other line was not reassuring.

"He is, is he?"

"I asked him to keep it off the books until we could find out if it was worth pursuing."

"I see."

Perry was going to kill him. Bro-code broken.

When she said nothing else, Adrian continued, "Whether or not they manage to take her, they will kill her. They kill all light-bearers."

She sighed and then, "What's the address?"

18

Alliances

Rule #28 Keep your home alarmed

The ride back to the Shultz's opulent neighborhood seemed to take forever. Every single light seemed to turn red before he reached it, and now wasn't the time to attract attention. Once in the subdivision, Adrian struck out on foot, keeping to the tree line. Pine needles cushioned his footfalls, but there was no need. The lights were out in most of the houses.

He gained their roof with no difficulties. She had to be here. Adrian treaded to her dormer window with his breath held. If he was wrong, and she wasn't here, she was probably already dead.

He peered in.

A deep golden glow seeped out of the tangle of covers. Disheveled hair framed a face that looked drawn, even in sleep. Her hand thrashed for a moment, then stilled. Probably bad dreams. Adrian slumped against the dormer. She was safe, likely traumatized from the other night, but safe nonetheless.

He slipped to the ground and headed back to the trees to wait for Meg. She wasn't long in coming. The old woman was dressed in black leathers and as spry as ever. Adrian suspected she continued to field work for the sheer love of being in the middle of the action, that and not trusting anyone else to do a job as well as she could. Perry definitely got that gene. Stalking up to him, her eyes narrowed, then yellowed.

"What's wrong with you?" She circled him, pulling in long draughts of air. Finally, she poked his side. "You need to eat."

Adrian's throat constricted. Surely, his weakness wasn't that evident. Meg picked up on his concern.

"Don't worry. I doubt any but Deval has senses developed enough to see that." She looked at him again, up and down. "But what have you been into?"

He held up his hands. "Nothing. I just left the caves a smidge too late yesterday. Caught a little sun. That's all."

"You bloody idiot!"

She might lead the Virginia Therian resistance, but she was definitely Perry's Gran. Adrian suppressed a smile and put on his best penitent face while she lectured him on his poor choices, his egotistical lack of concern, endangering his life and all their lives, and his spectacular absence of intellect.

"I think I've heard you use this speech on Perry. Do I get to start calling you Gran now?"

"Don't get cheeky with me, pup! Our operations are stronger than they've ever been, and I will not have you jeopardizing them simply because you—"

"I know," he said. "It was stupid, and I'm an idiot for being out when I haven't recovered from it. But this," he gestured with his head toward the house, "this is more important. This might turn the tide of the war."

She snorted.

"I'll be having a word with Perry about that too! Always thinks he can handle things like this on his own. Gets into research over his head and over his experience." She marched down the lawn shaking her head, and then glanced back. "What are you just standing there for? Our people will watch the house. Go and eat before you get yourself into any more asinine situations!"

He'd been at the mansion more times in a week than he cared to in a month—or a year, really. But he needed to eat, and his regular supply of blood was low. With a sigh, he headed back toward the hell hole.

When Adrian arrived at the Solifugae mansion, there was a palpable tension in the air. No one was lounging, talking, or playing at love. Everyone seemed absorbed in a purpose or on their way to one. Adrian was given a wide berth and no eye contact. This was a chaos he could get used to.

He was threading his way to the restaurant kitchen when he heard quick steps behind him. He whipped around.

Jonathan threw his hands up in a conciliatory gesture.

Adrian cocked his head. "What do you want, Glitch?"

Jonathan glanced around and lowered his voice, "Please don't call me that. The last thing I need is a reason for the others to toy with me. I'm trying to stay alive here."

"I wasn't aware that I cared."

Jonathan jerked his head to the side, and his lip twitched up, exposing his teeth. It was the first vampiric gesture Adrian had ever seen him make. The stress must be getting to him.

"You're showing your age, Glitch."

Jonathan's face turned malevolent as it contorted with the change. He shoved Adrian against the corridor wall and snarled. "You're a prick. You know that?!"

Adrian's hand shot out and wrapped around the younger vampire's throat. He gave a hard twist. A snapped neck wouldn't disable the thrip for more than a few moments, but Adrian couldn't bring himself to do more. Jonathan was too human. Besides, someone else would probably do much worse to him before long.

Jonathan dangled limp in his grip, eyes wide, a sick gurgle in his throat. Adrian could feel the swell of energy under his hand as the boy struggled to heal himself.

"I don't play well with others. Remember, Glitch? I usually just kill disrespectful thrips like you." He dropped Jonathan to the floor.

"And yes," he said as he stepped over Jonathan's prone body. "I know I'm a prick."

Jonathan coughed, and as Adrian walked away, he could hear the thrip begin to move on the flag stones.

"Tracker." The voice was quiet and strained.

Adrian stopped and turned. "What?"

"Siri…" He coughed. "Put a tracker on your bike."

Every borrowed drop of blood in Adrian's body froze. He'd been careless somewhere and now Lach's little toy knew something. Bloody, fucking hell!

Adrian stalked over to Jonathan. The thrip had enough sense to flinch as Adrian hauled him to his feet.

"Come with me."

Jonathan hesitated for a moment but followed.

The kitchen was deserted at this time of morning. They wound their way past gleaming stainless steel counters to the walk-in cooler. Once in, Adrian moved racks of food at the back exposing another door. He motioned Jonathan to follow.

"The blood bank," Jonathan said, gaping at the floor to ceiling stacks of blood bags that extended in rows throughout the cavernous cooler.

The room wasn't a secret, but most of the clan got their blood from the kitchen stash on the Solifugae side of the mansion, not the human operations side. Adrian waited until Jonathan stepped through, then shut the door behind him. There was nowhere to go, should the boy try anything stupid.

"Before I tell you anything, can you keep my wife and son safe?"

Adrian was speechless for a moment. Was Lachlan really that foolhardy? People were often seduced by power, wealth, life, or lust, but to keep a human family alive as ransom had so many ways it could go wrong. This was a mess.

Adrian hit his fist into the door behind him. Jonathan jumped, his darting eyes seeming to take in how trapped he was.

"First," Adrian said. "Tell me about the tracker."

Jonathan took a step backward as if more space would help him in here. "She just did it the other night and, um, asked me to let her know if you went anywhere interesting." Adrian's eyes became slits. "I didn't. Well, uh, you didn't, at least it didn't seem like it. You went to the national park twice and drove around a couple of neighborhoods. That's typical of hunting behavior. It wasn't until the author of that article got flagged that it seemed interesting."

This insignificant pile of frass was far smarter than Adrian had given him credit for. "You remembered the address."

Jonathan jerked a nod. "Eidetic memory. You went to her house *before* the article was written, and I figured you're too old to make a rookie mistake with a Z.I.P.. I had to turn in the article she wrote to Deval, for my own life, but once everyone was gone, I pulled up your bike again. I was surprised when you didn't go back to her house, but then I saw you go to that neighborhood in the east heights again. I researched the owner and—"

Adrian felt his whole body tense, and Jonathan must have seen the danger. He held his hands up in front of him. "I haven't told anybody where you went! I can alter it even. Media, remember? But that's how I knew when you came back, and I went straight to find you. I figured that if you weren't wiping the author, it was because you were working to bring down all of this." He motioned at the shelves and the mansion beyond them. "I can help you, just get my family safe."

Adrian should really just kill him. Then Lachlan would have no reason to threaten his family, and Adrian's problem would be solved as well. He let out a growl of frustration.

"I can't help them if they are in Research and Development."

Hope brightened Jonathan's stupid face. "They aren't. He has them monitored. I—I can watch them anytime I want..." Shaking his head, he continued, "Lach stationed a patrol, bugged the house, has a track on the vehicles. All I can do is watch. They think I abandoned them."

There were tears in Jonathan's eyes. Adrian hadn't realized that vampires could still cry. This was a mess, and Meg was going to murder him several times over.

Adrian ran his hands through his hair. "I'm not sure who's the bigger fool: Lachlan or me."

"You'll help me, then?"

"*If* I can."

136

Jonathan nodded vigorously. "I can override his monitoring system, but I don't think I can get past the patrol." He put both his hands to his head and pulled them down over his face. "Okay. Okay. First—"

Adrian held up a hand. "No. I call the shots. If you can't deal with that, I can rip out your heart and solve both our problems." He bared his teeth. "Understand?"

Jonathan bobbed his head.

"Can you alter my bike's record from anywhere?" Another nod. "Fine. Then first, we need to get back to Nidhi Tower before sunrise. If you beat me there, go up to my office level and wait for me. I have an errand to run after I remove this tracker from my bike."

Jonathan grimaced.

"*What?*"

"It's just," Jonathan looked away, "it's better if you don't."

Siri had sullied his baby enough by sitting on, but the tracker was an invasion on a whole different level. And now this little thrip was trying to tell him he had to leave it on his bike?!

"You said you could alter the record." There was a threat in Adrian's voice.

"The record. Yes." Jonathan spoke softly, like one would to an angry dog. "But if you remove the tracker here, the program will show this as your ongoing location. It'd be a problem if Siri checks in on you. She'd know you weren't here because... well, you kinda make a scene when you are." He spread his hands in a helpless manner.

"*Cazzo di merda!*"

Jonathan gave him a quizzical look but, to his credit, said nothing.

Grabbing several piles of blood, Adrian dumped them into one of the coolers stacked on a trolly by the door. He turned to leave but stopped, "And Glitch? I need you to understand something." He lowered his voice and took a step closer to the boy. "I haven't stayed alive this long by being careless or by liking vampires. I can assure you that I am something much, *much* worse than a prick, and if I think for one moment you've betrayed me, your life will have no value."

Jonathan swallowed hard. "I know."

Adrian took the cooler and left without another word.

Adrian stared at the cursor on the borrowed phone. Meg would be livid over this, but... He rubbed his hand over his chin, then typed:

More developments. Must meet. Usual place and time.

He paused, thumb hovering over the send button. What the hell? She was gonna kill him anyway, might as well go for broke with a little snark.

Going to eat now, per your instructions.

He chuckled and hit send before deleting the thread. Adrian tossed the phone on the ground next to its cowering owner and let his eyes go black.
  The man began to scream.

19

Running

Rule #18 Do not carry an internet capable or GPS-enabled phone

Clare was running.

The creature with the glowing cat eyes had found her. Fear pumped through her as she sprinted into the dark woods behind their house, searching desperately for safety, for somewhere to hide. Her breath came out in sobs. The thing was gaining on her without even trying. It was playing with her. Branches scratched her face and hands making her bleed.

Blood. So much blood. She was slick with it. Drenched in it.

"More!" Its hiss landed on the back of her neck.

A tree root snagged her foot, and she fell. The beast was on top of her, the smell of iron was thick and viscous in her throat. She thrashed, flinging punches with all her strength, but none of them seemed to land. She might as well be fighting air.

"Aren't you late for something?" it whispered. And then burst into flames.

Clare woke up, panting, to sunlight streaming through her window. It was 3:49, Thursday. Crap. She'd napped far later than she'd planned. She struggled upright, fighting her way out of the tangle of covers, and buried her feet in the plush, white carpet. She drew in deep steadying breaths, trying to let the comfort of being back in her old room wrap around her.

Safe. She was safe.

"Elle," her father's voice came up the stairs. "You have a visitor."

Her breathing stuttered.

No one knew she was here. She wasn't in contact with any of her friends from her school days, and nobody from work knew her old name.

No one should have been able to find her.

"Be down in a second!" The words almost caught in her suddenly dry throat. She forced her hands to straighten her rumpled clothes and headed for the stairs.

Get it together. Whoever this was, it wasn't that *thing*. The sun was out. For the next three hours, she had no reason to be afraid.

She was wrong.

Meg E., her best source for her article, was sitting calmly in the living room, sipping tea across from her father. Clare swallowed. If Meg could uncover who she was and where to find her, so could others. The elderly woman smiled at her and waved her into the room.

"As I was saying," Meg continued to Eugene, who had parked his chair in his usual spot near the window. "She's been such a help while I've been moving to the community home. And no matter what she says, I know it was a bother. She keeps so busy with work. So when she told me she was going to take a little break, I thought I might surprise her with a stay at my family cabin."

Clare had no idea how this woman knew something had happened to her, but she didn't need the subtle glance to understand the message. Meg was trying to get her away for a good reason. A bolt of fear shot through her, and she fumbled with a way to say what she wanted without giving her father any suspicion.

"That sounds lovely, Meg. But what about my father and brother? Maybe they'd find a getaway peaceful too?"

"Nonsense, Elle!" Her father turned to Meg. "I know she goes by Clare, now. She told me she didn't want the family name to earn her any favors in the world, and I was proud of her for that, but I'll never adjust to it. In any case," he moved his attention back to Clare, "if you need a little time away, bringing us with you would be counterproductive."

"He's right, sweetie. It would be counterproductive," Meg said. "I'm sure your father has work to do, and staying here, he can get it done uninterrupted."

Okay. Dad and Zeke were safe. Breathe. But if they were safe, why did she have to leave?

"I really don't want to impose. Couldn't I just—"

"I insist," Meg said with the attitude of a grandparent sneaking money into the hand of their grandchild.

"Right. Sounds lovely." Lovely going who knows where with a complete stranger. "Let me just go and get my stuff packed." Her voice cracked, just a little, and her father gave her an odd look. She smiled at him, trying to cover it. "I'm sorry to cut our visit short, Dad. I know I haven't been around much lately."

He shooed her words away with his hand, "Maybe I can schedule some vacation time for us all this Christmas. We'll go somewhere nice, maybe tropical."

A small laugh escaped her, and tears welled in Clare's eyes. "Yeah, that would be great."

Eugene's brow wrinkled, and he opened his arms to her. She sank down next to his chair and was in his embrace, the familiar spicy smell of him washing over her. The tears she was holding in began to trickle over the edge.

"I'm sorry, Daddy."

He stroked her hair, but the surprise in his tone was evident. "What are you sorry for?"

She was sorry for running away, sorry for pretending that Mom didn't exist, and that his sacrifice for Clare was a mistake. She was sorry that she hadn't been brave, and now that she was finally ready to come back, she had to leave again. She was sorry for putting them in danger. Sorry she couldn't tell them the truth. And sorry she couldn't say goodbye properly.

"I'm just—I've just been so busy living my own life. I haven't made time for you, and I miss you."

With a soft chuckle, he leaned down and kissed her head. "It's alright sweetheart. You come by it honest. I've always been an over-worker myself... It took losing your mother to make me realize that I needed to stop and enjoy my family. At least you came to it in an easier way."

Easier. If he only knew...

Clare looked at him, and there was moisture in his eyes too. Allowing herself one last embrace, she tried to crystallize the moment in her memory: The warmth of him, the feel of his still sturdy shoulders, his steady breathing, the piney smell of his after-shave.

"All right," He said with a sniff. "Christmas it is then, and we'll have no excuses from you this time. I'll let Ezekiel know when he calls from the office. The matter's settled."

Clare managed a small smile. "Christmas. Somewhere tropical."

Clare left Meg and Eugene to enjoy their tea and small talk while she gathered her things back into her gym bag. She hadn't known exactly what she was going to do, but driving to an unknown destination with a woman she hardly knew was not how she'd envisioned things. Clearly, Meg was in deeper with the survivors than she let on. That should be reassuring because all the Helios had serious trust issues. Clare permitted herself a few deep breaths before she heaved the bag to her shoulder, grabbed her briefcase, and headed down the stairs.

Meg was waiting in the hall on the arm of her father's aide, the very image of a sane and respectable woman.

Eugene had wheeled his chair into the hall beside them. Clare gave him one last hug and nodded to Meg before marching out the door and down the ramp to the waiting car.

To grandma's house we go.

Meg settled in beside her, and the white Lincoln pulled away.

"You've caused quite a bit of trouble." The older woman tugged at a crease in her Caricota pantsuit.

"What's going on? How did you know where to find me?"

Meg's left cheek twitched up. "You have an unlikely ally."

"Ally? Did they tell you about the attack? Is that why you're here, to take me to stay with the other survivors?"

"One thing at a time. And, no, I'm not taking you to the survivors. You'd be a danger to them. Speaking of, give me your electronics. All of them."

Of course. What did she expect from these paranoid freaks? Track her down, give her no information, and then expect her to cut off communication with the outside world. Clare pursed her lips.

"Just let me update my voicemail real quick."

Her phone began to ding as soon as she took it off Do Not Disturb. She glanced at Meg, who rolled her eyes and motioned for her to give the phone one last look.

There was an email from Janice saying that, of course, she could take a couple of weeks off for a family emergency and to please let her know if Clare needed anything. There was also a missed call and voicemail from David. Clare pressed the button and put it up to her ear. David's voice whispered from it.

"I have a friend I traded *Zombie Eater 3* with to run your stuff at his lab. He was doing it off the books, but the computer still generates the results digitally. He called me this morning to say it's gone. The sample is gone. The digital record is gone, and he says his stack of lab orders has been rifled through. He can't tell anyone because he'd lose his job for running it without an order, but no one else seems to be missing anything." He let out a grumbling sigh. "Clare, I'm not saying I believe you, but whatever you've gotten into, watch yourself."

Oh, God. She hadn't thought of them finding the lab work. The kind of computer and manpower needed to monitor that much data was a scope she'd assumed only governments could manage. She closed her eyes and prayed they wouldn't be able to trace the labs back to David.

An impatient noise from Meg shook her out of it. Right. Suddenly, the woman's paranoia over electronics seemed well founded. Clare navigated to her voicemail settings.

"Hey, this is Clarity Zetler at *You Know It*! I'm going to be out of the office for a few weeks in a no-reception area. I'm sorry for the inconvenience, but leave me a message, and as soon as I'm able, I'll get back with you. Thanks!"

She shut off her phone and handed it to Meg along with her briefcase. It had her com and a few other work devices in it.

"Your watch too."

Clare looked down at her watch. Despite the analog appearance of its face, it was connected with her com. She chewed on her bottom lip.

"Ms. Zetler?"

"Right," Clare said as she opened the clasp and slid it off her wrist.

Meg unfolded what looked like a large bag made of foil. She stuffed Clare's phone and briefcase inside and held it out for the watch. Clare felt her stomach drop as the watch disappeared into its depths. Seemingly satisfied, Meg turned her gaze to Clare. It was the same considering look she'd given her the last time they'd met.

"*Now* will you tell me what's going on?" Clare said.

Meg tapped at her mouth with her knuckle for a moment.

"Do you remember what I said humans were to the immortals?"

Clare frowned. "You said they thought of us like cattle or dogs, but that we were useful to the Therians."

Meg smiled without warmth. "I was in favor of letting you be. Few humans are so useful as to be worth the trouble of intervening, but it seems there is something interesting about your blood."

Clare's heart began to thump against her chest like it was trying to break free, but her mind ground to a halt. She tried to swallow, but there was only sand in her throat. She could feel her mouth open. There was an implication in Meg's words that her mind refused to acknowledge.

She tried to swallow again before saying, "You said to stay away from Therians."

"I said that was best."

"You said they were unpredictable."

"Was I wrong?"

Clare's brain caught up with what her heart knew, and she pressed herself back against the door, and felt for the handle. The car wasn't going *that* fast.

She wrenched on the handle, but the door didn't open. God, no! Panic rose up in her throat. She was stuck. She was stuck in a car, and her father was not here to pull her out. And this time, she was going to die.

She slammed her palm on the opaque glass that separated them from the driver. "Let me out. I want out!" She spun toward Meg. "I want out of this car now!"

"I will sedate you if you cannot compose yourself."

Sedate her? *Sedate her?!* Clare began drawing in long, slow breaths. No no no no no. She might be trapped in this car, but that hag would not sedate her! Clare fisted her hands in her lap and settled back in her seat.

Meg studied her for a minute. "Now, if you are calm enough to be rational..."

Clare narrowed her eyes but said nothing.

"I could let you out of this car, but where would you go? How would you stay safe? You endanger the life of everyone you come in contact with."

Clare thought of David and frowned. Where would she go? If Meg's story was correct, even years ago, vampires had infiltrated society to a high degree. Meg's story...

"That story you told me for the article?"

Meg shrugged, "I borrowed it from a survivor."

Of course she did.

They're the ones who brought the survivors together. It's their new strategy against the vampires.

She was such an idiot. She'd *known* that Meg knew too much about immortals, about how they thought. And she'd dismissed it because... because she was a rational human being who didn't believe in monsters.

And now she was trapped in a car with one.

"So you aren't taking me to stay with them?"

"If my source is to be believed, you'd draw far too much attention."

Clare had a million different questions circling her mind, and even though she knew the answer to this one, it demanded to be voiced.

"So, you're a—," the word stuck on her dry tongue for a moment. "You're a Therian?"

145

"A Lycan, yes."

Oh yes, yes of course she was. Why wouldn't she be? Perfectly natural to be a werewolf. Apparently they were everywhere, those and vampires, just out running the streets. Day and night. And here Clare thought she was going to the safety of granny's house, but no. Granny was actually the big, bad wolf the whole time.

Clare dropped her head in her hands.

"So, what is your plan with me?"

"First, we need to isolate you and see if the vampires make the connection between your pseudonym and your family. You covered that track remarkably well, so we don't think they will—"

Clare jerked upright. "You did."

"No," Meg shook her head. "That was a bit of happenstance."

"Happenstance?!" Then, the meaning of Meg's words sank in. "You plan on making sure they can't track me to my family?"

"If your family decides to up and move some time in the near future, it would be better if that was not deemed suspicious."

Hope loosened the knot in her insides. "So, I might get to see them again?"

"If it is possible."

All thoughts of trying to flee a moving vehicle vanished. She might get through this, and she might get through it with her family. Forget, for now, that her father and brother were the high profile owners of Com-Soft Electronics, and their absence could hardly go unnoticed. There was a chance, and all things considered, today felt like a good day to grasp at straws. She looked at the moonstone ring on her hand, the ring they'd given her for her birthday, and let out a breath she didn't know she'd been holding.

"Okay. Then what?"

Somehow, Meg noticed the shift in Clare. The considering look left her eyes, replaced by something that bordered on approval.

"The thing that makes you dangerous to the survivors could be advantageous to our cause. I'd like to run some tests on you and on your blood—nothing invasive mind you. We would just need to draw a few vials."

Clare was back in her bedroom, staring at the glinting cat eyes. Those eyes that had wanted "only a little" of her blood. Her blood—blood that seemed to hurt them.

"They're already ahead of you. I was attacked a few nights ago. The vampire took some of my blood, but it did seem to hurt him."

Meg inclined her head, "I know."

"You know? How can you know?"

"The bit of happenstance I mentioned earlier, your unlikely ally, is a vampire defector."

They were working together. Yep. That sounded about her luck. A giggle was trying to work its way out of Clare's stomach. Or was it a sob? There was no telling really, and Meg was still talking.

"He's worked with us for years, letting us know their movements, strategies, and tech. Adrian found you because your father frequents the front he runs for antiques. He was the one who let us know about the possibilities of your blood, and the one who let us know you were a target." Meg squinted at her then, but after a moment, shook her head. "Therians can't sense it, but the vampires call your kind light-bearers. Adrian tells me that there aren't many because vampires tend to kill them on sight."

Clare held up her hands for silence. This was too much at once. The ring on her finger glinted, and its beauty seemed sinister.

"So, you're telling me… that my father buys from a vampire front, but apparently, he's not in any danger!"

"They have to keep up human appearances to avoid detection."

"And I was attacked to further *your* cause!"

"I, in no way, authorized that." Meg sniffed. "It was completely tactless."

"*And* that, somehow, I put off something a little extra special that makes vampires want to kill me. Is that about right? Anything else I should know while you're busy destroying my reality?"

"I know this must be hard for you, but you may be the most important thing we have to winning this war."

Thing? So now Clare was the thing?! No, even better, she was some sort of tool in the middle of a magical war. Her jaw tensed, but Meg didn't seem to notice.

"My grandson, Perry, is trying to isolate what it is about your blood that makes it toxic to our enemy. If he can replicate it, we may be able to spread it to other humans or, possibly, even weaponize it. We'll get him tonight and see if he's made any progress. We'd go now, but Adrian has requested to meet, and we can't manage that safely until he can leave his headquarters after dusk."

The vampire. Adrian.

Ice filled Clare's stomach. The last thing she wanted was to be in the same room as that creature again. The fact that he didn't want to eat her and was trying to bring down his own people should help. But it didn't. She could hear his growling voice in her ears and smell the death in the air around him.

No. Nope. *She* was only human, and there was no way.

She didn't realize she was rocking her body until Meg looked sideways at her.

"I don't... think I can see him."

There was a sudden depth and understanding in Meg's face. It was like the roles and detachment fell away. She reached over and squeezed Clare's hand. She was an old woman who'd seen bad things happen, and she understood.

"It took me a while too," she said quietly. "You may stay in the car."

20

Subterfuge

Rule #25 Do not attempt to make a deal with a vampire

"Have you ever seen a Therian?" Adrian asked as he and Jonathan fell into step on the trail.

The day of working in the Tower had passed by at a crawl. It was not helped by having Jonathan in his office the entire time. But night had come crisp and lit with a baleful harvest moon. It cast an auspicious feeling on the evening. And even the prospect of springing Jonathan on Meg couldn't quite dampen it.

"No. Why?"

"Just do me a favor and try not to show your age. That won't go over well."

This was met with silence. Adrian glanced over his shoulder. This part of the park was fairly open. Jonathan had stopped walking a couple of steps back, his stupid face a billboard of complete disbelief.

"You're working with Therians?" His voice was barely audible. "You must be crazy."

"They'll say the same thing when they see you." A smile crept onto the edge of Adrian's lips, only to die just as quickly. "But no matter what, you must control yourself."

"Adrian, if anything happens to me he'll kill my family!" He glanced around like beasts were ready to spring from the trees and began to back up. "I can't risk this."

Oh, *now* the little thrip wanted out. Too bad.

"*This* is the only chance your family has. Did you think we were going to move them during the night?"

Jonathan still didn't move. Ridiculous.

"You came to me for help, Glitch, and I took a risk on you," Adrian said. "You're in too deep to back out now. Either you see this through, or I walk away and let the Therians deal with you."

Adrian turned and started down the path. A heartbeat later, footsteps were hurrying after him.

Another minute of walking brought them to a sharp bend. As they neared, Jonathan slowed and drew in a deep breath. Adrian watched his pupils begin to enlarge. The Therian smell was like a battle cry, calling up instincts that no one could prepare him for. Jonathan stopped, rooted to the spot and breathing heavily, tremors shaking his body as he fought the change. Adrian did not envy him.

"Do you remember the sun?" he asked quietly.

Jonathan inclined his head, a low growl fighting to come out with each thick breath.

"Picture it."

Jonathan closed his eyes as Adrian continued. "Feel its heat. Let it make you squint. Walk through it with your wife. Go through every memory you have of it until you find one strong enough."

After a moment, the tremors slowed, then stopped. Jonathan looked at Adrian with surprise in his grey, human eyes.

"Don't get cocky yet. It's a nice trick, but it's harder the greater the provocation."

"I'm... not sure I could handle any more 'provocation.'"

The boy wasn't ready, but they didn't have a choice. Adrian hadn't been ready that first time either. "Just keep that memory. If the change happens, whatever you do, don't move or make a sound until you're back in control."

Jonathan took a breath, and they started walking again. He shook his head slowly as they neared toward the bend. Trees hung low there, making the

150

space feel closed in. At the elbow of the curve was a wooden bench. A solar light, styled to look like an old lamppost illuminated the spot in a soft amber light. Jonathan stopped again. Adrian paused with him, fighting his own impatience. This moment was dangerous. And though the thrip's human memories would tell him this was just a harmless little old lady sitting on the bench, Jonathan's instincts would be screaming a different story.

"Ready?"

Jonathan had begun intensely studying the ground and didn't answer. Ready or not, then... And when Adrian started walking, he followed.

Meg's lips were a flat line, and she stood without offering any greeting. Over the years, Adrian had tested her limited patience constantly, but bringing in a rogue vampire without telling her earned any lashing she might dole out.

"Why?" She pointed at Jonathan.

It was good the boy wasn't looking at her. The anger in the Therian's eyes might have killed him where he stood. Still, she hadn't attacked Jonathan or yelled at Adrian. All in all, not a bad start, but the tension in the air was palpable. Should Jonathan snap, he was dead. Well, honestly, if either of them snapped, Jonathan was dead. Entering a fray with Meg would be like expecting to survive a fight with a tree shredder. And Adrian wouldn't touch that mess. Best just to hope the tree shredder felt like talking.

"Deval made him the head of Media. He found me out—" Meg's body tensed like a coiled spring, and Adrian found himself shifting his body between the two of them like a fucking idiot. "But he came to me for help instead of turning me in. He's got an engram, and Lachlan is holding his family in exchange for services."

At Lachlan's name, a soft growl escaped Meg.

Shit.

Now Jonathan was trembling, fists clenched. Meg froze, watching him, waiting. He drew in a deep, shuddering breath and let it out in a slow stream. His body stilled and fingers uncurled.

Bloody hell, that was close.

Still watching him, Meg spoke. "That makes no sense. That bastard is too

151

old to do something so foolhardy. More like he sent a little pet to find us all out."

Jonathan's jaw tensed. It felt ridiculous defending the thrip to Meg, but…

"Despite my reckless reputation, none of the Solifugae would imagine me suicidal enough to work with Therians." Meg didn't look convinced or amused. "When he found me out—"

"And how the hell did that happen?" Meg was several inches shorter than he was, and many times more intimidating. *Madonna santa.* This was a terrible idea.

"Siri placed a tracker on my bike. He was tasked with watching it."

Meg's lip twitched, but she swallowed her growl. "I told you to watch for that! Gave you tech to sweep your vehicles!"

How did this turn back around to him?

"It happened while I was away from home." Hopefully, he could steer her away from the topic. "Anyway, I believe Lachlan took the risk with Jonathan so he could kill me without serious repercussions. This one," Adrian motioned his head toward the boy, "could do my job, and Deval can be forgiving so long as company operations are maintained."

Meg brought a knuckle up to her pursed lips.

"He seems quite young."

And he suffered from a chronic lack of proper vampire etiquette. Adrian sighed. "It may be difficult, but he has near unlimited access to information right now, and they have no reason to lock him out. Yet. He only wants his family's safety in exchange. They're under guard and surveillance at their home."

She tapped her mouth.

"Look at me, boy."

Jonathan looked up. His eyes were already black, and when Meg cocked her head at him, he began to tremble again.

"You were much older, Adrian, and even then, there was some trouble." She shook her head.

"Please," Jonathan spoke softly, his trembling less, eyes still dark. "You can kill me after I help you if I can't… can't control myself. I don't care. I just need to know my family is safe."

She raised her brows. "Do you really mean that? Because this is likely a death sentence for you."

The look of intensity on his face made even Meg stiffen.

"I died nine months ago. If you told me you'd help my family, I'd walk back into the Nidhi Complex tonight and rip everyone apart until they took me down."

Meg snorted. "I doubt you'd get past the door."

Adrian chuckled. "Frankly, I'm surprised he's survived this long, but since you aren't going to kill him outright, let me make introductions: Meghan Erwyn this is Jonathan..."

"Jonathan Howards." The thrip thrust his hand forward. His voice had held no rasp, and his eyes... his eyes were gray.

Damn, that was quick. And irritating as hell that Adrian was perpetually underestimating him. But he had to admit, the kid was starting to grow on him.

"He learns fast. Maybe he'll last a while."

Jonathan chanced a small smile.

"Don't get your hopes up." The smile froze, but Meg continued, "He does have a sort of... lost puppy quality to him."

"It's annoying, but he grows on you. Blame it on the engram."

"You have one of those, and you still aren't that likable."

Jonathan choked on something that might have been a laugh. Useless thrip.

Meg began to walk down the path, and they fell in step with her like members of a pack. Adrian caught the smile on her lips and felt a twinge of relief. This might actually work.

While they walked, Meg grilled Jonathan on his family's situation and made a plan. The family could go with the survivors in Colorado until more suitable arrangements were made. Jonathan would work for Meg until the vampires locked him out. That wouldn't be more than a few days, but in the chaos over the article, they might get more time. Adrian would have to get Perry from the mountains. With all the commotion, Meg wanted him—and his research—close at hand. Perry could go back to his troglodytic life in a week or two.

As they neared a sidewalk that fed onto the greenway, Meg pulled a disposable phone from her bag and handed it to Adrian.

"Use it only—"

"For a week, and then incinerate it. I know."

She jabbed his chest. "That's right young man! I swear, you get less respectful every year."

"Comes from hanging out with your grandson, I imagine."

"I'm sure it does, and if you keep acting like him, I'll start treating you like him. You both need a good thrashing."

Jonathan laughed, and Meg turned on him, "Shut it!"

The laugh died abruptly, and Adrian burst out with his own until tears pricked at the corners of his eyes. A sense of warmth and contentment eased in to replace the laughter. He smiled at Jonathan. "That's your welcome to the family."

As they neared Meg's vehicle, Adrian could see a golden glow through her tinted windows.

"She's with you now?" He glanced toward Jonathan. The kid was getting a lot of exposure for one day.

"Well, I was hardly going to leave her alone at the base. Clare's skittish enough as it is, thanks to your little stunt. The last thing she needs is to see someone in half phase walking down the hall." She looked at Jonathan. "That will pose a bit of a hazard with you as well."

"Once he has things set up at the base, he can sneak back into my flat and work from there," Adrian said.

"Absolutely not! There will be no travel between the two locations! That kind of recklessness will get us all killed." She sighed. "I was thinking that when he was done here, he might be able to infiltrate an operation in another region."

"It may be time for us all to move, Meg. Lachlan will have noticed where Jonathan spent his day today, especially once his family is gone. And Deval has already decided to clean house. We use the momentum to try and pull down as much of the infrastructure as we can and then leave."

"It's worth considering. But I'm only leaving once Lachlan's bleeding out at my feet," Meg said the name with a growl. "You get my grandson back here, and we'll talk it over."

21

Meetings

Rule #28 Do not go to secondary locations

C lare could hear voices from inside the car. There were two people with Meg on the walkway. As they approached the car, the driver got out and opened the back door for Meg. Against her better judgement, Clare leaned forward to look at the group, now stopped under a lamp post.

There was a man with a baby-face, light brown hair, and light eyes dressed in a simple polo with slacks. He shifted on his feet as he watched Meg. Next to him, and slightly shorter, was the handsome man from the restaurant. This could only be Adrian. He looked different in the light and without the glowing eyes, but this was the monster. She thought of wrenching the ring off, but it wasn't her father's fault that filth had touched it.

That's how he knew her real name! He met her in the restaurant, followed her home, and attacked her.

All the fear and anger she'd experienced over the past few days welled up in her. Perhaps it was knowing that Meg was there, perhaps it was righteous indignation—or just a complete mental breakdown. God knows, she'd earned it—but maybe she was done running. Clare pushed herself across the seat and out of the car.

All three froze as she strode up to Adrian. She took a deep breath, planted her feet, and punched him in the jaw on the exhale. There was a gratifying pop and a trace of blood where her ring had made contact. Oh, she was definitely keeping it.

She shook out her stinging fist, then thrust a finger at him, "You!... You..." but words, her life-long friends, finally failed her.

Adrian raised his brow, but he pushed his jaw back into a normal angle.

"He is a prick, isn't he?" The baby-faced man grinned.

"Skittish?" Adrian looked to Meg who wore a sideways grin.

"You deserved it," Meg said back to him.

They seemed to be making light of this, and Clare was not done. "That didn't hurt near enough after what you put me through. Do you have any idea the kind of hell...?" She groaned through her teeth. "Your image has been haunting me every time I close my eyes! That smell, it's not really there right now, but that tang."

"I'd just healed," Adrian said.

"I don't care, and I don't want to think about what nasty things you might have just been doing! I wake up with that smell in my nose! I've been afraid for my life every minute I've been awake since then, and it's because of *you*!" Clare was on her toes now with her finger in his face. It was like taking her life back from the person who'd held it hostage.

He stood there, quiet for a moment before saying, "I'm sorry."

"Yes. You are." Clare said and huffed back to the car leaving the three of them standing there. She slammed the door behind herself for good measure.

Meg was chuckling when she got in a moment later.

"Well tonight has been full of pleasant surprises."

The driver and other man got in the front seat. The glass rolled down between them. Baby-face was smiling as well.

"That was incredible! I'm Jonathan, by the way." He thrust his hand back toward her as the car began to move.

She suppressed a smile. It had felt pretty incredible.

"Clare," she said, taking his hand. As soon as she closed her hand on his, he jerked and wrenched it away looking from the hand, to her, and then back.

Meg tilted her head a little to the side. "Did it hurt?"

"Not hurt really, it was more unpleasantly warm. I just wasn't expecting it."

"You can see it without the change, then? Tell me what it looks like," Meg said.

"What?" But they ignored her.

Jonathan took his eyes from his hand and studied Clare. Her sudden liking for anyone who would call Adrian a prick was fading. Standing with the other two, Jonathan could have been anything, even human. Here, looking at her like that... No. *No.* Her heart began to race. She tried to swallow around the lump in her throat. Meg needed her. She wasn't going to put Clare's life in danger. Right?

"It surrounds her, moves with her, like a cloud of light. It's like—um, it's like she's walking in her own patch of sunshine."

Clare glanced down at herself in the dim car, half expecting to see something different, but she looked the same as she always did.

"It's really beautiful, a little..." His voice trailed off as he tried to describe her special, vampire attractant halo. "It calls to my instincts a little."

Meg's head snapped from Clare to Jonathan.

"How so?" she said.

"It feels dangerous, like when the sky is getting light."

Right. Great. Clare edged back in her seat, but Jonathan noticed.

"No! Please, don't. I'm not—I wouldn't hurt you. I'm just trying to help." Clare didn't move, and Jonathan slumped a bit. "I'll put the window back up if that will make you feel better."

Even at night, it was hard to be afraid of something that looked so defeated. "You can leave it down."

"Do we really smell bad?" he asked in that same, dejected tone.

Meg snorted.

"Well," Clare sniffed tentatively. "Not at the moment, but when Adrian broke into my house, he smelled terrible."

"Like old blood," Meg said.

"Yes, like that!"

"After they feed, they sweat out the waste in their pores. It happens when they use energy to heal too."

"I had just shot him."

All dejection disappeared and a full grin lit Jonathan's face. Adrian must really be a universal bastard.

"Makes me want to shake your hand again. I won't though," he added quickly.

"Jonathan is a new vampire," Meg said to Clare. "I know more about his kind than he does right now."

Clare's inner journalist sat up.

"Like what?"

"They don't teach them how their bodies work, and most of them don't care for a long time anyway. Jonathan is different because he has his memories intact."

"He remembers being human?"

The vampire and Meg both nodded. Then, she continued. "It's uncommon, but an error can occur in the restructuring of the brain before the conversion from human to vampire is complete. A fragment of memory, an engram, is all it takes to derail the process, but it must be a strong one. Adrian has an engram as well."

The flow of information gave her a sense of control, like an anchor in the midst of all this insanity. She grabbed onto it.

"So, he has a vampire's instincts but human memories on top of them?"

"Yes, but it does dull the instincts a little. That is to our advantage, yours and mine. But it's a distinct disadvantage for him. In dealing with us, he can put his vampiric inclinations aside, but in dealing with his own kind, any lingering human quirks make him seem more like something to kill." Meg turned to Jonathan. "Ironically, that's probably why Adrian let you live. He's never been bothered by killing vampires, considers it a bit of a calling, I think. But he still holds some regard for human life." She shook her head. "It'll probably get him killed one of these days."

"So what else might a new vampire not know?"

"Don't think I don't know what you're doing, young lady."

"What could it hurt? The worst I could do is write another article that no one would believe."

Meg's mouth twitched, and something in her posture relaxed. "Do you know how to *stretch* or *beckon* yet, Mr. Howards?"

His brow creased. "I've heard of it. I've never done it, but I felt Lachlan do it to me." At this, an intense look flitted across Meg's face.

"You haven't encountered Watchers yet either then." The look of confusion on Jonathan's face must have mirrored her own. He shook his head slowly.

"Kenyon, you're a better storyteller. Why don't you explain?"

Clare had forgotten about the driver. He hadn't spoken all day, and she was surprised, now, to hear a quiet Irish accent answer back.

"In Ireland, they talk of thin places. A liminal place where the barrier between the physical and spiritual worlds is tenuous, and humans can get a glimpse of the other side. We immortals can walk in that place anywhere. We can use our body as an anchor and let our soul stretch out into the other side. In that realm, we can reach into the souls of others, of people or even animals. If we can captivate a soul, the body will follow."

He focused on the road as he spoke.

"It's not without risks though. The higher realm is not empty or filled only by souls passing through. It's full of things that watch. They take many forms, some beautiful, some terrible. Whatever else they may do, they are intensely interested in humans, not their affairs, but their souls. They only interact through the veil, touching souls not bodies, but sometimes the soul begins to take the form of the Watchers surrounding it, growing stately or twisted in turn."

His words painted pictures in Clare's mind.

"When an immortal steps fully past the veil and walks in the dimension of the Watchers, we have no defenses, and all Watchers can be dangerous. They are fierce about the ones they guard. They can sever the webbing that anchors a wandering soul to the body, and we do not know what happens then, but some say that the twisted ones feed on the dark souls of the vampire."

His mesmerizing cadence left an emptiness in its wake.

160

"What does an immortal do, then, if it encounters a Watcher?" she said.

Kenyon's melodic voice filled the car again. "If it takes no notice, then one may simply pass by, but if it fixates, we must hurry back through the veil."

Fascinating. Not exactly clear, but fascinating.

"How does it work? How do I do it?" Jonathan said. He must be fascinated too.

Kenyon sniffed. "You may not do it here. Not here with us, but it would be an important skill to learn."

In the passing street lights, Clare could see the dejected look settle back on Jonathan's face, but he didn't pursue the matter any further.

"Why not?" Clare's inner journalist was affronted for him.

Jonathan cast her a look that said it was fine; he didn't need an explanation. But she did! When the driver said no more, she looked to Meg.

Meg sighed. "Reaching into a soul is a delicate business. Done well, it is like a caress. Done badly or forcefully... Jonathan, can you explain how it felt when Lachlan *stretched* to you?"

In a slow motion dance, Clare saw him shudder and close his eyes. When he opened them, the pupils had nearly swallowed his whole eye and reflected the headlights of passing cars with a cat-like gleam. At her sharp intake of breath, his focus snapped to her, and Clare felt her heart begin to pound. He turned his head to stare at the passing houses.

"No," he said in a foreign, gritty voice that did nothing to slow her racing heart.

Meg continued, seeming to ignore his transformation from baby-faced man into threatening beast. "That response was elicited by one of his own kind. We are his natural enemies, and I can assure you that Mr. Howards is exercising considerable willpower just to appear human in our presence. A poorly done *stretch* in our company could turn fatal for him. It would be best if Adrian teaches him."

"And in a place far from humans," Kenyon added.

The rest of the ride was taken in silence. Clare's inner journalist had been quelled by those eyes.

22

Maintaining

Rule #23 Do not try to fight an immortal

T hey turned off at a low warehouse just off I-95 with a gate blocking the entrance. Kenyon leaned out and pressed his palm to the biometric pad outside the guardhouse. The gate rolled away, and he maneuvered the car around to the back of the building.

Semi-trucks were backed up to some of the loading docks along the length of the building. One loading dock and ramp stood empty. The bay door was open by the time they reached the top, and they drove into the bare-walled bay. As the door lowered, closing them in, Clare felt a stab of fear. She would finally get out of the car, but she was still trapped.

"Kenyon, would you please let everyone know about our unique guests? Have them vacate the halls until we situate everything, and get someone to make sure spare quarters are ready.

The driver left the car with a curt nod, disappearing through a door on the far side of the room, and Meg turned her attention to Jonathan.

"Are you maintaining?"

He continued to stare out the window, but shook his head.

"The smell is overwhelming." His voice sounded raw and threatening again.

"Will you need restraints?"

"Will they attack me?"

The misery in his growling voice filled Clare with a wash of sympathy she was unprepared for. He sounded like he was having a worse week than she was. And that was hard to do.

"My people are accustomed to Adrian. They won't attack you, unprovoked."

"Well, I think—I think that might be a—be a good idea." His words began to come in pants.

Meg nodded and pressed on a biometric square by her handle that Clare hadn't noticed before. The door unlocked, and she went out and rummaged in some sort of storage cabinet. Clare sighed. What kind of things do you deal with to have to have hidden locks on your doors?

"I'm sorry," Jonathan said over his shoulder.

"Sorry?"

"For frightening you."

"Oh." Clare wanted to say something comforting, like it wasn't his fault or that it was okay really, but she knew, without saying them, that they would be hollow. She'd be lying if she said she was happy to be stuck in a car with a vampire who was having difficulties. Or to be stuck in a car at all. Her therapist had locked her in a car to help her overcome that fear. Repeatedly. And it really did help some. Perhaps exposure would help here too.

"Could you turn around? If I see you in the light, maybe it won't be as bad. Your eyes wouldn't have that glow at least."

He took a deep breath, and his whole body slumped a little. It was like watching someone resign themselves to something terrible, but he turned. There was no back-lit look to his eyes in the light of the garage bay, but their complete blackness made Clare blink. With whites showing only in the corners, they looked distinctly evil.

Well, that was no help. Clare glanced at her bare wrist. No watch either. She had one last place to turn for comfort. She unlocked the pit and let out the screaming journalist.

"Why do they do that? Your eyes I mean?"

"I'm not sure about all of it, but our pupils grow and dilate. It lets us see more. I can see the heat of blood under your skin," He swallowed hard. "And my ears change so I can hear its pumping. The hearing, that's not a visible change though."

"And you grow...?" Clare trailed off but brought two fingers to mime at her lips.

Jonathan parted his lips in a soundless snarl that showed off glistening, sharp points.

There was a muffled shout from outside the vehicle. His door was ripped open. Meg wrenched him out by his shirt and threw him against the wall. He landed in a crouch, despite the dent his body left in the cinder blocks. He rose with a growl into the cloud of falling dust. Meg began to advance on him with a snarl of her own.

"NO! He was just showing me!"

Meg paused, and Clare seized the moment. "I asked to see his teeth. He wasn't trying to hurt me." She clambered over the passenger seat—stupid locks—and reached for the open door.

"Stay." Meg barked the command in a voice that was neither old nor human, and Clare froze with her hands on the door frame.

Jonathan stood tense and ready to spring. Each quick breath was covered over by the harsh rumbling that poured from between his sharp, bared teeth.

Without turning her face from Jonathan, Meg knelt and picked up something by her feet. She tossed it to him. The speed and precision as he snatched it from the air were beyond Clare's eyes. He glanced down at the object, back at Meg, and began to shake.

"Close your eyes and think of the sun." Her voice still held a threatening edge.

"Can you turn away from me?" he ground through his teeth.

"Not until you put those on."

He closed his eyes. The growl subsided, replaced by a moan that quickly ratcheted up to a cry of frustration. He lowered himself in jerky, forced movements to the ground, and, keeping his eyes down, put the white, metal bands around his wrists. Metal wire, a pencil's width thick, connected the bands and attached to another pair for the ankles. The shackles closed with a snap, and he lowered his head to his knees, heaving in air.

Meg turned towards Clare. For a moment her face was... different. But the expression was so fleeting Clare wasn't sure what was wrong other than the yellow, canine eyes.

Clare finally peeled her hands from the door frame and stepped fully out of the car. Meg strode toward her. The shuffling walk she'd affected before vanished, and a sense of power seemed to exude from her. This truly was not a human. Clare swore under her breath.

"I don't know what you intended to do, but you just put yourself in *serious* danger. It doesn't matter how nice he seems, he is too young to control himself!" Meg jabbed a finger at the still heaving vampire. As if Clare needed more of a reminder.

"I'm sorry. I just reacted. I didn't want you to hurt him."

"He will heal. You would not." She turned to go. "Come on."

Clare looked back to Jonathan. He hadn't moved from the floor. "What about him?"

"He needs a minute," Meg snapped and continued toward the door.

Clare tried to take in her surroundings as they entered the building and headed down an empty corridor. Doors lined both sides, and she could hear voices coming from behind a few of them. Six doors down, Meg stopped and pressed her thumb to a small pad next to the door. It clicked, and she pushed the door inward. The room inside was like a hotel room. It was lit with soft yellow lights, and a bathroom door stood open to her right. Clare's bag already lay on the bed. It looked like it had been riffled through.

"The door will lock when I leave. I think after the spectacle in the bay you can see why that's a good idea. You don't know how to act safely, and it won't do to have you wandering the halls."

"I'm not going to ask anyone else to show me their teeth." The thought of being locked in was disconcerting.

"You put his life in danger. And your own. You are not leaving this room without an escort!"

Clare gritted her teeth against the heat pricking at her eyes. She was not going to lose it in front of this woman.

Meg sighed. When she continued, her voice was softer. "It won't be for long, and there's a speaker system built into the door jamb if you need anything. For now, just try and get some rest."

The door shut behind Meg with a strong click, but Clare tried the handle anyway. Nothing. She turned back to her room. No clock. Not that she had anywhere to go. She checked the dresser—empty except for a change of sheets. The nightstand drawer held a notepad and pen. Very quaint. Clare resisted the urge to check under the cushion of the chair because... because that's something crazy people do. Why would there be anything there?

She began to pace the room, the room she was locked in with no way to tell how long she had been there. She'd left her father's house because it was implied that she needed protection, but she wasn't sure this was the sort of protection she wanted. Clare could leave and risk attracting vampires to whoever she was with or she could stay and be safe. Safe had always been the right answer, but making herself disappear no longer felt quite so safe.

After what was probably five minutes of pacing, she heard steps in the hall outside her door and talking. She pressed her ear against the seam of the door.

"—family. You can coordinate with my team, and we'll move in the morning. I want you working on bringing down your people's networks from inside Nidhi as soon as they are secured."

"Where will you take them once you have them?"

"Back here at first. What? Is there a problem Mr. Howards?"

"I—Well, I..."

"You don't want them to see you like this?"

"I'd... I would rather they thought I was dead. It's not like I can be a part of their lives anymore. Can you tell them I was killed, and they're being moved as a—as a witness protection thing? Can you do that?"

"It wouldn't be difficult, but—"

Clare strained but couldn't make out any more of the conversation. She suddenly felt very small and very tired. It would be easier to think in the morning. Taking solace in routine, she flossed and brushed her teeth, then

166

combed out her hair and dressed for bed. Before turning off the light, she glanced around. Still no clock. She huffed and plopped onto the bed. She rolled on her side and reached for the lamp on the nightstand. Her fingers lingered over the switch. It was bad enough to be trapped in the room, but to be trapped in the dark, in a building full of monsters… Clare took a slow breath, closed her eyes, and twisted the switch.

When she opened them, the soft red glow of a nightlight near the bathroom greeted her. She let out a sigh of relief and stared at it while she counted. Somewhere around the 530's she started to lose track and skip numbers. She never made it to 600.

23

Restraint

Rule #9 Keep all main arteries covered

Once Adrian made it back to the Towers, he swept his bike. The magnetic tracker was stuck to the frame behind his exhaust. He placed the little fucker in the wheel well of the company BMW. Nothing conspicuous about it showing him at home.

Bike cleansed, he headed off to the woods for his third time in a week. It was a new record. He shortened the couple hour ride considerably with a reckless pace that would have infuriated Meg. Then again, most things he did infuriated Meg. All in all, it was quite enjoyable.

Until he got to the cave.

Miriam's smell was still strong at the entrance, and his last parting with Perry hadn't exactly been a shining example of civility. Not wanting to interrupt anything, Adrian called out as he neared the entrance to the living quarters. A minute later, Perry was standing there, bare chested and scowling. This was going to be great fun.

"I see you're still alive. Manage to heal those fingers?"

Adrian held up his hand and wiggled the digits in question.

"Scimitar."

"Idiot. At least you didn't get burned to a cinder."

"I did develop boils, if it makes you feel better."

The scowl cracked. "It does, actually." Perry chuckled, despite himself, and shook his head. "Come on in. Mary's asleep. She's here until Sunday." He slapped Adrian on the back hard enough it almost knocked him off his feet.

Adrian followed his friend into the living room and sank into a chair.

"So," Perry asked, dropping onto the sofa and kicking his feet up on the coffee table, "if you don't need help with the burn, what's happened?"

"It's a long story, but the short of it is," Adrian took a breath, "your grandmother asked me to come and get you because we had to move the light-bearer, I found another engram defector, and we might have to move operations to another state."

Perry blinked. "Wait. You told Gran about this?"

Of all the statements, of course, that was the one Perry latched onto.

"There was another summons. They were going to take the light-bearer in, and I had to tell Meg about what we were doing with her blood to convince her to step in."

"What happened to off the books?" Perry glanced back toward the bedrooms and lowered his voice. "She's going to flay me!"

Adrian snorted. "Not too badly. She wants you to bring everything you've got on it so far." He grinned. "If you've got something spectacular, she might even forgive us for going behind her back."

Perry sighed and sank further into the couch. "No luck there, but it's only been a few days. Tell me about this defector."

"He's the head of Media."

Perry let out a low whistle. "Nicely done."

"I didn't do it," Adrian said. "He cornered me. Siri put a tracker on my bike, and he'd been monitoring my movements. Told me he'd change the data, but he wanted help getting his family free of Lachlan."

Perry sat up, all traces of humor gone. "What does Lachlan have to do with this?"

"Lach glitched him on purpose and has been using his family as a bargaining chip to keep him in line. Your Gran is preparing a tactical team. When everything's ready, they'll extract his family from their house. In return, we'll get some orchestrated chaos on the part of our new guy at Nidhi Complex."

"So, what? We just have to trust this guy? For fuck's sake, he's under Lachlan's blood! I can't believe Gran agreed to this. Dammit, Adrian! What happens if Lachlan decides to *stretch* this guy, and he can't stay calm? What if he exposes us all?!"

"Since when did you start playing it safe? Is your Gran wearing off on you because this is exactly like what she said when she met me."

"She had a point."

"She had a point? Who are you today? Look, Meg thinks the intel he could get us is worth the risk."

Perry raked his fingers through his beard causing his face to take on a bushy look. "Is Gran thinking about making our move now?"

"Maybe. Jonathan, the engram, was with me all day, and when his family is gone—"

Understanding and fury lit in Perry's eyes. "Lachlan will come after you both."

"Exactly. Leaving was my suggestion, and I think she's favorable to the idea. She just wants Lach first."

"About time." Perry's face had a look of deadly calm. He was in.

"About time for what?" Miriam came blinking into the room wrapped in one of Perry's ubiquitous flannel shirts. Her hair hidden beneath a deep purple headscarf.

"I didn't mean to wake you sweetheart." Perry stood to wrap his arms around her.

"You'd have had to anyway. We need to go tonight," Adrian said.

"Hello to you too, Adrian," she said, using his name for once. She gave Perry a questioning look. "What's he talking about?"

"It's nothing. I just have to help my gran with a few things."

"*Things.* Like… she needs groceries or like you're going to do something stupid?"

Perry grinned, still holding her. "Probably just needs eggs and bread."

"And your boy here can't handle eggs and bread."

He lowered his voice to a mock whisper, "With those scrawny arms, I doubt he could hold a gallon of milk by himself."

Miriam pushed out of his embrace. "So this has nothing to do with you going after that guy who killed your parents?"

"You've got remarkable hearing for a human," Adrian murmured. They both glowered at him.

"Okay, yes," Perry hedged, "that is part of an operation that may happen, but I'm not being called in for that."

Miriam raised her brows at him.

"Adrian told my Gran about the vaccine I've been working on, and she needs what I've got so far."

"Good. Then there's no reason I can't go with you."

Adrian smothered a grin. This was going to be glorious.

Perry choked. "What? No."

"If all you're doing is working on that vaccine, and I'm off until Sunday, I don't see why not. You were doing that while I was here anyway. Besides, you need to introduce me to your grandmother."

Perry reached for her again. "Look, baby—"

"Don't you 'baby' me." She shoved his hands away. "I'm not stupid. And I'm not staying here while *you* go off and do something absurd. I know you. You're not going to sit back while something big is going down."

Adrian smirked. As ridiculous as it was for Perry to have taken a mate, he had certainly found his match.

"I told you what he did." Perry rubbed a hand over his face. "I can't just—"

"No. Stop. I know you loved your parents, but… can't you live for me now?" Her voice rose, accentuating the question, and then lowered as she added, "Besides, how would I know if anything happened to you? Adrian doesn't know where I live, and your people don't know me."

Perry pulled her in close, "I will always come back for you."

After a moment, she leaned up and kissed him. "We'll take my car."

Damn. She was spectacular. Maybe Adrian should take negotiation lessons from her. And Perry—Ha!—that dumbass mutt was so screwed.

Perry stood there with mouth agape as Miriam headed back to the bedroom. Adrian walked over and patted his friend on the back in commiseration. As he passed by where she'd stood, he caught a whiff of something. Relaxing, he let the change wash over his body and took a deeper breath.

Shit. No wonder the mutt was acting strange. Adrian looked at Perry who just nodded in answer.

"Does she know yet?"

Perry shook his head. "This early, it might not take, so I haven't said anything."

Adrian opened his mouth, to say what, he wasn't sure, but Perry cut him off.

"You may as well get a head start. Let Gran know to be expecting an extra visitor."

Adrian left with Perry still looking toward the bedroom.

The roads were empty as Adrian passed under the strobing streetlights. Usually, the sound of the pavement under his bike was calming, but his mind was too full.

Everything was about to change. By next week, Adrian would either be dead or his life would be new. With any luck, Siri would be killed, and Paul's death would finally be avenged. The Therians might move and do it all over again to a different coven, and Meg would certainly continue her work with the survivors. As for Perry, hell, that was going to be interesting. And for himself…

Well, one way or another two centuries of subversion were coming to a close. Adrian might finally be free.

* * *

Leroy had set up the meeting in a park outside the city. It wasn't anywhere near his apartment, in case the guy turned out to be some sort of police informant, and Leroy had caught an excellent Dolomedes over the stream here once. Win-Win. Once the meeting was over, he could go hunt for some more. Of course, that sort would be hard to find at night, but strap on a headlamp, and the biggest hunters were easy to find. Their eyeshine made them coruscate in the leaf litter, like diamonds glinting in the dark. The brighter the shine, the bigger the diamond.

Leroy shifted the gear strapped on his back as he waited under the light at the trail entrance. The park was closed after dark, but that wasn't enforced. It was ideal actually. No one would interrupt them, and there would be no cries of disgust at his beauties. He fidgeted his headlamp into place and swept it over the ground. Tiny glitter. Not what he was after. He wanted something much bigger.

A snap sounded in the underbrush. He spun around. Coming up the trail was not what he'd been expecting. A man with long, white-blond hair, lab worker looking white clothes, and intelligent blue eyes strode up to him. This could not be his guy.

The man extended his hand. "Leroy?" The stranger had an odd foreign accent Leroy couldn't quite place.

"Yes?"

"Walk with me." The man turned back into the forest gloam. He didn't introduce himself or even wait to see if Leroy followed. Whatever he thought a police informant would look or act like, this wasn't it. There didn't seem to be any harm in listening to him at least. Leroy's headlamp cast long shadows as he hurried after the man.

When Leroy caught up with him, the man said, "I saw your exhibit on Monday. It was a shame what they did to your spider."

"I don't remember seeing you there." Surely, he'd remember someone like this.

"How could I miss an expo on arachnids," he said. "It's a shame that I couldn't stop those two boys."

"Filthy—"

"Ants!"

Leroy looked at him. That wasn't what he'd been going to say...but yes.

Yes they were.

"They should be fed to your spiders for what they did."

Leroy could feel his eyes crinkle. Yes, yes they should.

"It would be fun to watch, wouldn't it?" the man asked.

"It would be perfect."

"I've done it."

"What?" Was he actually saying what Leroy thought he was saying? Had he found someone... someone like him?

"Fed the filthy ants to the spiders. We could do it with your ants too. That is, if you thought you were able."

Leroy was silent. The man's strange, near glowing, blue eyes stared intently. He appeared serious. Kill Leroy's ants? Kill his ants. He would love that.

"How would we do it?"

"Certainly not quick and painlessly."

Leroy felt the grin spread across his face before he could hide it.

"And that's just the reaction I was hoping for."

His grin faltered.

"Oh, don't worry. I've been looking for someone like you, someone who sees things the way they are and isn't shy about what needs to be done. I've been searching for a famulus, if you will."

Leroy didn't know what that was—he'd have to look it up when he got home—but it was about time someone recognized his skills.

"So, what do you think? Do you want my help with your ant problem?"

Leroy hesitated. He had to be careful. This could still be some sort of set-up. But if it wasn't...

"Yes."

The last thing he remembered was black spider eyes, gleaming in the darkness. The biggest diamonds he had ever seen.

24

Expecting

Rule #6 Avoid places that operate primarily at night

Meg was waiting for Adrian in the loading dock when he pulled his bike in.

"Where's my grandson? Why didn't he ride with you?"

She'd made a fuss when Perry moved up on the mountain, but Adrian suspected that she was secretly glad. Even if she couldn't keep as close an eye on him up there, he was further from trouble.

"He'll probably be an hour behind me. He had to pack up his equipment and research, and... he's coming with someone."

Meg went still, but Adrian could see the hurricane forming inside her. He just hoped it'd wait to make landfall until Perry arrived.

"He's coming with someone? Like you did this evening when you started this whole mess?" She looked at him, apparently wanting an answer.

Shit. That air of practiced nonchalance was terrifying. "Yes, ma'am."

"And did *you* know about this 'someone'?"

"Only since last weekend."

Meg walked up to him. That he had to look down to meet her eyes never made her seem less intimidating. The strength of her age oozed from unseen places into an almost visible quality.

"Only since the weekend. I see." She planted her hands on her hips and painted her face with mock confusion. "But didn't we meet on Wednesday? Yes. I'm quite sure that we did." Her eyes narrowed, all traces of sarcasm gone. "You didn't think it was important to tell me that there was someone with my grandson?"

That damned hurricane was getting closer. He was so fucked. "I met her by accident. He didn't want me to know yet either."

Open shock swept over Meg's face. Oh hell…

"Met *her*?" There was considerably less nonchalance in her voice. Which was somehow more terrifying.

"Yes, ma'am."

"Therian?"

Shit. Shit. Shit. "Human."

For a moment, calm descended, and the car bay was silent. Then, the hurricane hit. "Perry is with a human woman, and he's bringing her here—tonight of all nights?!"

"That's correct."

Her eyes lit yellow and snarl curled over her words. "Is there anything else you would like to tell me before he gets here?"

Adrian opened his mouth, then shut it. He might be fucked, but he didn't need to be *that* fucked. He shook his head. Not for a world of nights.

Meg growled and then, blessedly, began reigning the hurricane back in, storing it up for her stupid ass grandson. Poor bastard. He didn't stand a chance.

"Come on," she snapped. "Your vampire could use help."

She gestured at a dent in the cinderblock wall and the small pile of debris beneath it. Adrian grimaced. Holy hell. The kid hadn't even made it in the door. Meg shook her head.

"He's alive. He's just young. Doesn't know how to behave." She snorted. "Neither does the girl, come to that." She spun toward the door. "Inside. Now."

Her growls trailed behind her as she stalked through the building. "Brings me a new vampire, and now Perry's bringing a woman, and with all this going on. No sense. Brainless, thick-headed pups. I'll kill them both when this is over. Both of them."

Adrian considered saying that she could just sic the light-bearer on him again, but after what he'd just seen of the cinderblock, sass was probably not his best option.

Adrian followed Meg to the last room in the hall, the control room. At the sound of the door opening, Jonathan jerked his head around from his console to see who'd entered. His body relaxed when he saw Adrian, but his eyes stayed black. Kitsune, a Kumiho from Japan, was the only other person in the room. He rose to greet Adrian.

Adrian grinned. Sune had always been one of his favorites.

Despite Perry's repeated assertions to the contrary, Adrian still wondered if there wasn't something extra in the perception of the fox people. Sune was reserved but had accepted Adrian after only one long look. The other Therians had needed much more convincing. It made sense that Meg had called on him to work with Jonathan.

"What have you got in place?" Adrian asked as Sune approached.

"Control already had the program to infect and erase their network, including online memory. Jonathan's been setting up channels with each of their hubs. After we secure his family on Monday morning, he'll execute the codes. We've gone over the schematics of his house and figured the safest way was to send Clare to the woman's work place around 10 am."

Adrian blinked in surprise. Why send her? Sune raised a brow and then went on to answer Adrian's unasked question.

"Jonathan says that Lach keeps tabs on all sorts of video feeds during the day. We're certain he has some hired thugs for a dayshift. They wouldn't recognize a Therian, but if our plans go awry and Lachlan's watching…"

"Then he knows at least Jonathan's been working with you." At the mention of his name, Jonathan shifted at his station. "And how's the thrip been doing?"

"He's still reactive, but twice I have seen the grey of his eyes. He can't maintain it yet, but he's doing very well. I believe we can remove his restraints unless he'll be in a group of us."

Adrian hadn't noticed the restraints—Jonathan had kept his back toward them—but now he saw the white bands around his wrists. His stomach tightened.

"Is that still necessary?" he asked Meg.

"Yes." Jonathan said, never turning from his computer. "If it's all the same, I'd like to keep them on for now. I'd rather not die tonight."

"You were much older, Adrian," Meg said gently.

Resigning himself to a chair, Adrian said, "So that's the whole plan?

Sune went back to a console two down from Jonathan, and Meg sat as well.

"No. We're going to try and enter the manor," she said.

Adrian rubbed a finger over his eyebrow.

"How?"

"Jonathan's confident he can jam the doors that lead from the front of house operations. Since the front house is mostly human, we can bring them down with tasers. If we can make it through without raising an alarm, we'll catch the vampires unprepared and weakened by the sun." Meg cracked her knuckles. "Our hope is to take out the computer backups. Jonathan said he can take out the online memory. Without being able to reboot, Deval's whole enterprise will be crippled for years. Jonathan is willing to sneak in and disable them. But since they're in the basement, through R&D..." Meg shot a glimpse at the boy.

"If Lachlan *stretches* him, it would give everything away."

"Precisely."

"Not that it isn't also very convenient for you," Adrian said to Meg.

She gave him a dark smile. "All the way from Ireland I have followed that bastard. He ripped my heart apart, and I plan to return the favor." A flash of yellow returned to her eyes and was gone. "The only thing I want Jonathan to do is make sure the codes are in and the doors are open. Keep him in the tower with you for as long as you can without suspicion. It'll be better for all of us if he doesn't run into Lachlan."

"I may be able to come up with an excuse for tomorrow." Adrian sighed. "But there is no way I can keep him there over the weekend. What about me?"

"You may want to pack and bring your valuables here before Monday morning. Just be there during the attack." A grin spread across Meg's face. "I'm sure you'll find useful things to do. You need to make sure Jonathan is in a secure location first. Battle is no place for him."

Kitsune turned from his monitor, "Can you secure him in the east side tunnels? I'll be making incendiaries all weekend to bring to "celebrate" with, so he'll need to be somewhere out of the way."

Those tunnels spilled out by the river about a mile away. Usually no one was there during the day, but...

"The blood bank is safer. No one will be trying to get through there. It's through the restaurant cooler in the front house. Just have your people steer clear of it, and he should be good until night."

Sune inclined his head and then returned to his screen.

"How much longer, Glitch?" Adrian asked. "We'll have to leave in no more than an hour to beat the sun."

"I'm done. I was just writing a quick bit of code for a data dump from Media to here Monday morning. I'm going to ask the other departments to send their data to help with the 'search for the leak'. If I can get anything helpful, I'll save it on my media mainframe and that will transfer it before the virus hits."

Damn. The kid was getting more likable by the minute.

"Meg," Sune glanced up from his screen. "We have a visitor."

Adrian felt his grin returning.

A Jeep was sitting at the guard station, Miriam behind the wheel. Perry pushed his face forward to wave at the camera. Even with the green night vision video, Adrian could make out the sideways look she gave Perry. Adrian glanced at Meg. She was staring at the feed intently, the first hint of the returning hurricane leaching into her eyes.

Perry must have become impatient with the delay. He leaned over Miriam and pressed his hand on the panel.

Meg rose with deadly calm and strode out the door. Adrian followed. There wasn't a chance in hell he was missing this.

She marched down the hall, Adrian on her heels. The door to Bay 5 bounced against the wall as she slammed it open. Stopping just inside, she stabbed the control pad to the outer door, and then crossed her arms, waiting.

The Jeep came up the ramp and into the bay at a creep. Miriam cut the engine. For a long moment, nothing happened, but Adrian could hear the faint murmur of a heated conversation. Finally, Perry emerged, arms wide.

"Gran!"

And the hurricane made landfall. "Peregrine Ó Luain!"

A flush rose to Perry's neck and cheeks. He glanced back at the Jeep. "Gran..." he ground through his teeth.

"I don't care if you are embarrassed! Imagine how I feel!"

Meg marched toward her grandson, the full fury of a wronged matriarch bearing down with her. Adrian snorted. Poor bastard. This was gonna hurt.

"First, I find out from Adrian that you're conducting experiments on resources we don't even know about." She rammed a finger into Perry's chest. Adrian felt his friend wince from across the room. "Then, he tells me that you're not only involved with a human woman, but you're bringing her here! Here!!" Meg shoved harder, and Perry staggered back out of reach, rubbing his chest.

"The reception is bad, Gran." He ducked his head. Ha. Like that scolded puppy routine was gonna work this time.

"Don't you give me that cock and bull line! You could have come down off your mountain anytime. You could have sent word with Adrian. But no. I find out like this!" Meg thrust her arm toward the vehicle. "You have outdone yourself this time. Didn't I raise you better?"

"Gran, listen—"

Oh, good luck with that, buddy.

Meg rolled right on as if Perry hadn't spoken. "It was one thing when you brought us Adrian. You had a *passable* excuse for your blatant disregard for our rules. Rules, may I remind you, that were put into place after what happened to your parents. But this time! How do you explain your disrespect for your people, your cause, and your grandmother?"

180

Perry swallowed and glanced at Adrian. Oh, hell no. He wasn't touching this. He'd already had his share of Hurricane Meg. Adrian was just a spectator this time. He grinned wider, folded his arms, and leaned against the wall.

"Like you never break the rules to do field work."

Going on the offensive was definitely the wrong move.

"*I* have more acute senses than anyone in this tribe! My insight is necessary to assess some people or situations. What you are doing is in no way comparable."

Miriam chose that moment to emerge from the driver's side. Damn. That woman had balls walking into a storm like that.

Meg turned her steely look from Perry to Miriam.

"I apologize, ma'am, for coming unannounced. I've been trying to get Perry to introduce us for some time, and as he's been reluctant to," Miriam shot Perry a look. "I decided to impose." She stepped between him and Meg and extended a hand. "I'm Miriam Elizabeth Walker. Your grandson and I have been together for about six months now."

Meg's nostrils flared, but after a long glare, she shook Miriam's hand. "Meghan Erwyn. I wish I could say I was pleased to meet you Miss Walker.... Miriam Elizabeth? Where do I know that name?"

"Miriam Elizabeth Benjamin was my dad's hero. She was an inventor in the 1900s."

"I see. And what do you do, Miriam?"

"I'm pursuing my master's in forestry science. I was doing a wildlife survey this spring when I met Perry."

Meg harrumphed. "I would ask if he's been a gentleman, but I can smell that he hasn't."

Perry gestured wildly behind Miriam's back, frantically mouthing the word 'No'. Adrian nearly choked. *Madonna Santa.* You couldn't get theater this good.

Miriam, oblivious, narrowed her eyes at Meg, hands planted on her hips. "And just what is that supposed to mean?"

And now for the kill. Adrian almost felt bad. Almost, but not quite. Perry brought all this on himself.

"Ah," A vindictive smile spread across Meg's face. "I can see he likes keeping both of us in the dark." The look in Perry's eyes reached a truly impressive pitch of terror. "It seems he may have neglected to tell you that you are with child."

Miriam's lips parted slowly. She turned her head to Perry. He looked from his grandmother's triumphant face to Miriam's darkening one.

"I just noticed a couple of days ago. This early, it doesn't always take so I..."

"You didn't think I'd want to know anyway? I mean after all that talk about being careful, taking measures. You said the trait could pass!" She slammed her palm against his chest, sending him back another step. "After all that, you didn't think I'd want to know?"

"We were both careful. It shouldn't have—"

Miriam put her hand up to stop him. "Don't! Just don't talk to me right now." She turned back to Meg. "Do you have a room that I can stay in, Ms. Erwyn? I don't even want to look at his face."

Meg offered the taller woman the crook of her arm and led her out of the loading bay while apologizing for her inconsiderate grandson.

Adrian turned to his friend, who stood staring at the door, mouth open and hands limp.

"Relax," Adrian chuckled. "It could have gone worse. At least now they're united against the same dumbass enemy."

Perry apathetically raised his middle finger.

Adrian laughed and slapped him on the chest, drawing another wince. "Come on, idiot. I'll help you unload and tell you the plan."

The lab was on the far side of the warehouse. Safer to have it away from main operations in case the mutt decided to tinker and blew something up. As they were coming back from their third and final trip, Kitsune was bringing Jonathan down the hall. His gait was awkward against the restraints, and he kept his face turned down. Adrian sighed. The kid was actually doing good, all things considered.

Perry cocked his head at Adrian.

"Your grandmother," Adrian said, "thought it was necessary. He's very young."

"We've got it from here. Thanks, Sune," Perry said.

Jonathan looked up at the new voice, but Sune simply inclined his head to them and turned back down the hall.

"Glitch, this is my friend, Perry."

Perry gave him the signature lopsided grin and extended his hand. Jonathan held out his own, dragging its companion up with it by the long metal tether.

"Ah, hell. I can't. This is absurd." Perry reached for the coded release panel. "You've probably never even made a *human* kill."

"I have." Jonathan's face was drawn tight as he pulled his arms away from Perry.

Adrian felt a stab in his gut. Fucking Lachlan. There was no telling what he'd inflicted on the boy before turning him loose at the manor.

"I'd rather you leave them on." Jonathan continued, "Adrian can take them off when we're alone."

"Are you with us?"

Jonathan looked around confused.

"We don't have time to break him in, genius," Adrian muttered to Perry. What they really didn't have time for was this shit to go badly.

"I just want to know if he's with us."

"I don't understand what you're asking," Jonathan said.

Perry motioned him into Bay 5. Jonathan's eyes kept darting to Perry as he hesitantly plodded in. Adrian didn't feel much more enthused than he looked. After they were all in, Perry pressed a few buttons next to the biometric pad. The lock slid into place with a loud click, and Jonathan's body went rigid.

"I want to know if you're on our side."

"Of course I am. I wouldn't be here if I—Please stay back. Why did you lock the door?" Perry had been approaching him. That dumbass dog was too cocky.

"I'm going to take off the restraints, and I didn't want to worry about anyone coming in while we were doing that."

"Can, um, can Adrian take them off?" A desperate growl was in his voice as he turned his eyes back to the ground.

"He could, but then you wouldn't learn control. I know our smell is overwhelming here, but if you're going to work with us, you need to be able to trust yourself." More like if Jonathan was going to work with them, *they* needed to trust *him*. The stupid thrip might be able to hide his intentions if he really meant them harm, but he was too young to squash his instincts.

Jonathan started to say something, but Perry interrupted, "Adrain can restrain you if things get out of hand, but they won't."

Heaving a sigh, Jonathan held out his wrists. Adrian tensed. Jonathan seemed innocuous, but so had Siri. This was insane. Then again, fighting was what had convinced Perry that Adrian was trustworthy.

With a few taps on the release panel, all the cuffs snapped open and fell to the ground. Jonathan stepped out of them, rubbing his wrists. Then, Perry released a growl. Jonathan's head snapped up. His humanity evaporated as he slid back and snarled. The vampire was awake, and Perry intended to fuck with it. Idiot. His eyes were yellow and his voice deepened, but there were no other physical signs of the beast. At least he was holding back some.

"Now, either you're going to attack me, or you aren't. Which is it?" Perry rumbled as he continued to approach. Jonathan began to shudder. "No! Don't try to come out of it. You can't become more than what you are until you accept what you are, and you *are* a vampire."

With a burst of speed, Perry closed the space between them. Jonathan's back hit the wall, and a growl tore from his throat. All shuddering was gone. His eyes were black, and he pulled his lips back in a toothy snarl.

"There we are!" Perry roared. Adrian let the change wash over him in case the dumbass mutt pushed too far.

Jonathan drew his body down like a snake preparing to strike, and Adrian felt his own body tense. With the slightest of movements, Perry jerked at him. Jonathan threw his body into him with an animalistic cry. Adrian drew in a breath. Perry could easily flip but instead fell with Jonathan landing on top.

Jonathan reared back to strike… with his fist. Damn dog had been right. Adrian let out his breath. Jonathan's fist hovered for a moment and then dropped. A shiver ripped through him as the change left. He awkwardly got off of Perry and stood. Adrian snorted. The kid did good.

"It's gone," Jonathan said with a human voice. "I don't understand why it's gone."

Dusting himself off, Perry got up. "At your age, the change comes with the desire to kill. I was trusting your engram to help you realize you didn't really want to kill me."

Jonathan turned wide, grey eyes on Adrian. "Why didn't you stop me when I lunged?"

"No teeth. I would have broken you the moment you used your fangs."

Perry snorted. "You'd never have gotten the chance. I could take him and you!"

Jonathan just blinked at them, looking as stupidly human as ever. Damn kid was definitely growing on him.

"Don't worry," Adrian said. "Next time he'll make it harder on you."

"You're both out of your minds!"

Probably true.

"But it worked, didn't it?" Perry smiled at him. "Not that the effect will translate to all Therians, but just knowing you can stop yourself will help. Next time," his grin broadened, "we can try it with me in full phase."

Jonathan shook his head.

"All right," Adrian said. "Enough playtime, Glitch. We have to get home before daybreak."

Jonathan sighed. "Are you really going to keep calling me that?"

"Yep."

Perry slapped him on the back. "It's a good name for a techie."

Adrian gave Jonathan a lift back to the greenway where he was parked. "You have any Z.I.P.s on you?" Adrian asked as the younger vampire slipped off the back of his bike.

Jonathan frowned. "Of course."

"Good. Pick an alley and get a quick meal. That's the excuse you used yesterday for coming to this side of town. Use it again. Say the hunting's good."

Panic flooded Jonathan's face. "Can't I just get a blood bag from you?"

Shit. The thrip hadn't even hunted before, but there wasn't time for coddling.

"No. Fresh smells different from cloned if you know what you're looking for, and Lachlan does. He's going to want to talk to you when you get back from spending time with me, so your alibi needs to be solid. Just use the Z.I.P. What they don't remember doesn't haunt them. Also, you reek of dog. Buy a change of clothes while you're out. You can shower and change at a truck stop." Adrian began to pull away, but a thought stopped him. "And I'm sorry… about your kill."

Jonathan looked out into the night, jaw clenched. "He made me."

"I know. This isn't the same."

It wasn't. There would be no death tonight. But if he hadn't already, Jonathan was about to realize that vampires enjoyed hunting and hurting. It was gonna fuck with the kid too. Adrian turned away. He just needed to get home, get a shower, and get some sleep. Day would come far too soon.

25

Curiosity

Rule #20 Do not talk openly about vampires

Clare woke to the same red glow she'd fallen asleep to. So, it wasn't a dream. She was still here and had no idea how long she'd slept or, more importantly, what time it was. She'd had enough. Flinging back the covers, she stormed over to the speaker by the door and mashed the button.

"Hello? Anybody out there?"

A light melodic accent issued from the speaker. Kenyon. "Good morning, miss. Can I get you anything?"

So it was morning. Clare leaned her head on the door jamb.

"Breakfast, answers, and out of this room. Oh, and a clock would be nice too."

"I'll see what I can do."

Sure. Great. You do that.

Clare ran her fingers through her tangled hair, then turned on the light. She squinted against its brightness. This was all ludicrous. She snatched her bag from the dresser and stomped to the bathroom.

Her reflection caught her as she passed the mirror. She stopped. The face staring back at her had dark rings under the eyes and that look—the look that all the Helios had. The look of frightened prey.

Clare sank down on the cool tile and put her head in her hands. No tears came. No thoughts came. There was nothing but the warmth of her breath on her face. Her breath was real. It said she was alive, and that would have to be enough. As she pushed herself up from the floor, there was a knock.

"Just a moment!" In a flurry, she changed, pulling clothes at random from the bag, and yanking her hair back into a ponytail. A little breathless, she called out, "Okay, you can come in now."

There was a metal snap, and the door opened. Clare had been expecting to see Meg or even Kenyon. Hell, she'd even welcome Jonathan after being trapped in this windowless box with only her own useless feelings.

Instead, a tall, broad stranger filled in the doorway, a breakfast tray in his massive hands. With his full beard and red flannel, he looked like something right out of *Hunting Today*. If Hayden ever saw him, she'd immortalize his fashion sins in her column, but Clare thought he had a bit of that old style lumbersexual vibe going for him.

"May I come in?" he asked.

Clare blinked. "Oh, of course. Sorry. I was expecting Meg."

"Gran's had a long night." He gave a crooked smile. "I'm Perry."

"Clare," she said mildly. "So... she's your grandmother?"

He smiled. Clare had seen that same half smile on Meg's face, but that was where the resemblance ended.

"Yeah, she's something, huh?"

That was one word for her. Perry crossed over to her bed and set the tray down. The smell of eggs and coffee made her stomach rumble. She plopped down on the bed and dug into the food, only realizing several bites in that she hadn't thanked Perry... and that he was still standing there, watching.

She covered her mouth while trying to speak around a bite of toast. "Thank you. For the food." She swallowed. "I don't mean to sound ungrateful, but how long will I be stuck in here?"

Perry wrinkled his nose. "It might be a few days. There's a lot going on, but there're some things you could help us with. If you're willing."

Clare poured a little creamer in her coffee and stirred. She didn't know if she was willing. "Things like what?"

"I'd like to run some tests with you."

With her, not on her? Well, that was refreshing. "And what do I get out of all this?"

"Out of this room, for one." Oh, she was in already. "And Gran warned me you'd use any excuse to ask questions. So, how about, while we work, you can ask whatever you want?"

Clare's fork was paused halfway between her plate and her mouth. A blob of egg fell off it, splatting onto the tray. She barely noticed. This man had no idea what he was getting himself into.

"Deal!"

Clare followed Perry down the corridor, haranguing him with every possible question. When they reached a stairwell, however, she stopped. There was a whiff of bleach and cleaner that reminded her of hospitals. The smell still made her stomach churn after all these years. At her silence, Perry turned. He didn't ask any questions, just waited. She shook her head, trying to scatter the feeling, and followed him down.

The door at the bottom opened to reveal a large laboratory with half a dozen workers and two clocks. It was 8:54. A little of the tension flowed from her body, and she took in the room of white and stainless steel instruments. The outside of the warehouse looked rundown, but everything inside was cutting edge.

"You have your own lab?"

"When you live as long as we do, you start to tinker. Mostly, we were trying to unravel our own mystery." He wove through work spaces filled with gleaming equipment.

"*Were*? Did you find your answers?"

"Not as many as we'd like, but for now, we've changed our focus."

Clare shot him a look, and the look was not lost on him. He turned his eyes to the ceiling, then sighed.

"Gran said there was a sun flare in your bag."

Clare stopped walking. "So they did look through my bag."

His voice was gentle. "Did you expect we wouldn't? Anyway, that's our tech. The survivors wouldn't come forward without some sort of protection, and we can't sit around and babysit them all day. So, we've been focused on researching ways to keep humans safe." He started walking again.

"Which is where I come in?"

He nodded and motioned her toward a padded chair with an L-shaped armrest. A desk stood next to it, and a white cabinet and mini fridge perched upon that. Clare sat down, trying not to watch as he pulled vials and needles from the cabinet. She was glad she'd stopped eating when she did. The sights and smells brought acid up her throat.

He pushed back her sleeve, explaining as he prepped her arm.

"We have some vampire blood from Adrian."

She looked away with a huff, and he chose that moment to stick her. She twitched in surprise, but the pinch was almost painless. He filled several vials as he continued his explanation.

"We'll use his blood to see how it reacts to various components of your own. I want to try and isolate what makes your blood so potent. There." Perry pulled the needle free and placed a bandaid over the spot. "Now, if it's alright with you, I'd like to take a very small amount of his blood and see if your skin has any physical reaction to it."

Clare pulled her arm back to her chest. "Mine burned him."

"Correct."

"What if his burns me?"

"It probably won't. I've been working with samples in the lab, and the results were promising. Besides, I plan on using a very small amount, just enough to be able to tell."

Probably? She twisted the ring on her finger. The ring her father had given her by way of a vampire. What the hell. What did it matter? There was no coming back from this trip to wonderland.

"I'm crazy. This is crazy, for the record."

"Is that a 'yes', for the record?"

Clare begrudgingly extended her arm back to him.

A full grin broke across his face, like Santa had just brought him presents. He didn't have to look so pleased about it.

Perry took the rack with her blood, placed it in the mini fridge, and pulled out another, darker vial. He drew up some into a syringe and turned it on her. Her internal cringing must have been partly external because he stopped, put out his own hand, and added a single drop to the back of it. It didn't spontaneously combust or turn into a mini cobra.

"Just that much," he said.

Chewing on her bottom lip, she held out the back of her hand. As he neared her with the syringe, she found herself with her eyes squeezed shut and her neck knotting up.

"Did you do it yet?" she asked. Then she jumped a little and opened her eyes. "How cold do you keep that fridge?"

"Does it hurt?"

"No. It's just really cold, like a miniature snowball."

"No. It's not." His eyes were alight. "You're sure it doesn't hurt?"

She looked down at the drop of red. Eerily, it wasn't warming to her skin, but it didn't hurt.

"It's just uncomfortably cold. How long does it have to stay on there?"

In response, Perry wiped it off with the alcohol wipe he'd used to prep her arm. They both looked down at the patch of skin. There was no indication that anything had been there.

He let out a little whoop that made Clare jerk.

"Okay. So, I guess that's good then."

"This is great!" Perry was becoming more animated as he spoke. "We're working on cloning some of your cells, and if your attribute is present in the cloned blood, we could win the war with squirt guns." White teeth showed through the huge smile on his face. Then, his grin drooped a little. "Adrian's pretty sure the attribute isn't physical. He may be right, but we'll exhaust all of the tests anyway."

Clare bit at her thumb. "If it's not physical, what is it?"

"Adrian said he tried to *stretch* and soothe you." Clare's stomach twisted, and Perry added quickly, "To keep you asleep while he drew your blood, but even that was painful. So, he thinks the attribute is something in the other realm, something ethereal if you will."

191

He had tried not to wake her that night, tried not to be the thing that haunted her days and dreams since. Whatever his intention, just thinking about him brought up flashes of the attack. Then Clare remembered the dream she'd had that night, the burning cold that brought her awake. No, that wasn't quite right. There was the ice, and then a voice. It wasn't the rasping voice of a vampire. It was quiet but strong, calling her awake, like her mother used to when she was a girl.

"What is it?" Perry asked, turning his head, doglike, to the side.

She shook away the memory. "I was just remembering a dream I had the night he took my blood."

Perry considered her for a moment. "Did you feel his *stretch*?"

"I think. Maybe. I felt something cold. Much colder than this." She gestured to the spot that was no longer on her hand. "But then I heard a voice telling me to wake up, and when I did, he was there."

"I don't think that was a dream. Adrian said there was a Watcher with you."

A Watcher? The things that scared the immortals? Right. Of course there was. What was it Kenyon had said about them?

"What do they look like?"

Perry scratched his head. "Seeing in that place isn't like seeing here. You see from yourself, not from your eyes. So, they might not look how we 'see' them. Their forms can be fire, light, shadow, or darkness. But they all have eyes, and the eyes are watching."

She looked around her. "Is it here with me now?"

"Distance is different there too. There's space," Perry motioned around his body with his hands, "but that's flexible. It's about connection. Your Watcher could be anywhere. However, when Adrian touched you, it felt his touch through its connection to you, and distance didn't matter. It was right there."

"But why would it wake me?"

He shrugged. "They can't interact with matter in our dimension, so perhaps that was its way of protecting you."

Clare went back to chewing on her thumbnail. There was so much she didn't know. She glanced at the clock. It was 9:35. Friday, how could it only be Friday? Last Friday seemed decades ago.

David had to be at work by now doing normal productive things and probably preparing to waste the whole weekend gaming. She wondered what he thought as he passed by her empty desk. Did he believe her or think she was off on a heroin holiday? The odds were he was worried, but what could she do? She doubted she could contact him, and what would she tell him if she did? *Hey, don't worry, some werewolves are keeping me safe, and I'm about to become their new secret weapon.* He might be better off thinking she was on drugs.

Perry was saying something.

"What? Sorry. I wasn't listening."

"I was saying, if you're willing to try, I'd like to see if I can sense anything different about you by *stretching*."

Clare frowned. "Isn't that… uncomfortable?"

"If it's done wrong, but I'm as skilled at that as I am at drawing blood."

She looked at the bandaid on her arm. It hadn't even hurt. She didn't want to be willing, but if she was honest with herself, she was intrigued.

"Do I have to do anything?"

"Not a thing."

"Will I feel anything?"

Perry shrugged. "You might."

Clare shook her head. "We've already established that this is crazy, so why not?"

Drawing in a slow breath, he closed his eyes. Clare found herself mirroring him. She sat in the dark for a moment before opening hers. His were still closed. Was it silly to be disappointed?

Then, she felt it. It was soft but distinct. She could feel him there with her. He'd been there with her all morning, but this was different. It was like the difference in seeing a picture of a person and meeting the person. She found herself reaching out after it. And then it was gone, like a rustling breeze had whispered through her—not her body, but her being.

Perry drew in a sharp breath, and her eyes flew open. Clare had no idea when she'd shut them.

"Are you all right? Was it the Watcher?"

He focused on her, eyes searching and piercing, and she felt herself leaning away.

"You grabbed me."

Her mouth dropped, and she shook her head. "I—no. No. I didn't. I mean I did feel you, for a moment, and then you were gone…" Clare trailed off. She had felt herself… reach. Was that what it was?

He went on like she hadn't spoken. "You shouldn't have been able to. I've never had a human do that and never heard of any…" Suddenly, he was up past his desk and in her space. "Are you human?"

She squeezed herself back in the chair as he leaned in and sniffed at her. "What else would I be?" She only half joked.

"I'm going to partially phase. Don't be alarmed."

Before she could object, his eyes had turned a golden wolfish color. They scanned over her body as his mouth and nose elongated. What had been a beard was now fine golden brown fur covering his face. Clare clamped her hands on the armrest of her chair and willed herself not to, as he had said, be alarmed.

The new wolfman took in deep draughts of the air around her and reached out a hand toward her, fingers slightly stunted and covered in the same tan fur. The movement caused her to flinch, but he continued to hold his hand—paw?—there in the air. Swallowing at nothing in particular, she looked into his face. His animal eyes held human understanding while he waited.

He was waiting for her.

Clare held out her hand. His touch was soft and strangely pleasant as he turned her hand over looking for something she couldn't even fathom. Then, suddenly, there was the ephemeral feeling of his *stretch*. It was quicker and lighter this time, like the flap of a butterfly's wings. Had she not already known the feeling, she would have missed it altogether.

With something between a snort and a sigh, he released her and turned back toward his desk. By the time he'd rounded it, all that remained of the

194

experience were his yellow eyes, and in a blink, those were gone too. For the second time in twenty-four hours, words failed her. Hopefully it wasn't going to become a habit.

Perry didn't seem to notice. He was busy writing on his com, but she prodded her inner journalist back to the forefront. She could process later.

"Does it hurt?"

"Hmm?" he said, not looking up.

"Changing like that, does it hurt?"

Stopping, he thought for a moment before saying, "It feels like I'm stuffed into this form and set free in the other." He went back to his typing.

"You didn't speak when you wanted my hand. Can you speak in that form?"

Still typing, "Yes, but it sounds menacing, like a dog growling, and I didn't want to frighten you any further."

"Like the vampires."

He looked up this time, his face trying to express annoyance but failing. "Similar." Then, he was writing again.

"So, what's the diagnosis?"

"You're definitely human."

"I'm so relieved," she said, with what she hoped was passable sarcasm. Then her thoughts drifted. "Was the Watcher there when you *stretched*?"

Perry nodded. "It's fire, and it's fierce. The moment I touched you, its eyes were on me." He gave the com one last tap and set it down. "Come on. You can ask questions on the way, but we need to get you back to your room for now. Gran's gonna want to hear about this."

That sounded about as alluring as eating tree bark. At least here she had answers. And the time.

"Do you have any books I can read? Or a clock? Something other than just pacing the floor in there? I feel like a prisoner."

Perry frowned. "I'll see what I can come up with."

26

Behavior

Rule #15 Practice yoga, meditation, or other heart slowing exercises

Adrian could have slept most of the day, but three hours after going to bed, he headed down to work. Vanessa rose when he entered, biting her lip. She informed him the man from corporate was back, and he was waiting in Adrian's office. His show the other day must have convinced her that Jonathan was unwanted. Hopefully, it was good enough to convince more perceptive eyes that might have been watching.

Jonathan didn't seem to hear Adrian as he entered. Wearing new smelling clothes, he sat in a side chair with his head in his hands. There was a healthy flush to his skin.

"Back again, Glitch?"

Jonathan raised his head and looked at Adrian for a few blinks before saying, "I'm sorry. I got, um, distracted last night and figured there was no reason to try and race the sun home."

Good. The kid remembered to play along.

"Just stay out of my way. I don't have time for your ineptitude," Adrian said, sitting down at his desk and looking at his com. "Come to think of it, I'm surprised you have time for it. I don't see any updates on the author of the article or the person who ran the Z.I.P.. If things don't start happening, Deval might feel the need to call another council. I doubt that would go well

196

for the new head of Media."

"We've tracked down the person who requested the analysis on the Z.I.P. and have an extraction plan in place for tonight." Jonathan said, but his voice was a blank monotone. Adrian looked up.

The younger vamp's eyes were bright with misery. Shit. The kid was probably orchestrating the death of whatever poor bastard was unlucky enough to find that Z.I.P. A fact that clearly wasn't lost on him.

That sort of feeling would get them all killed.

"Well, congratulations. You may live another night."

Adrian took out a piece of paper and a pen. If the thrip couldn't school his expressions, he probably didn't know how to keep his emotions from Lachlan either. Jonathan needed help if any of them were going to survive the weekend.

Lachlan likes a challenge. Don't give him one. If you can sense what he wants, try to bring up a thought or feeling that looks like it. If not, you need to wall yourself off, create a pocket in your mind where you can go. It can be a walk in the sun or perusing an art gallery. Anything calm that can't be used against you. If that doesn't work, go to something that infuriates you, but you have to pick something they won't find interesting. The more Lachlan provokes you or stretches you, the deeper you go into your pocket. I find revulsion to be particularly effective with Siri. She doesn't want to feel that from me, and the more she digs, the more of that she gets. Any anger or fear that might slip through, she then attributes to how I feel toward her and not what I am trying to hide. Find something like that to use with Lachlan.

Adrian folded the paper and tucked it in his pocket. He'd find a time to slip it to Jonathan before they left. He didn't know whether or not the office was under video surveillance, but every keystroke was damn sure recorded. So, it had to be business as usual. He contacted his vendors, looked at wares, scheduled shipping, and for kicks, searched *"The Survivors' Handbook"*. That should be considered work related.

The book reviewed well. Though there was a trend among the comments suggesting it was supposed to be a work of fiction and not a serious exposition on the existence of vampires. That would be Media trying to put out fires. It could actually be Jonathan's idea. It wasn't bad either.

Deval had seen Jonathan's potential to head media over his glaring youth and experience in other fields. That was Deval's gift. Beneath his quiet exterior was a keen perception and watchfulness. His knack for being able to see a person's abilities was what made Nidhi the force that it was, both financially and in the vampire world.

In human resources, Adrian saw little of the other factions, but smaller covens popped up and were cut down all the time. Nidhi was one of the big six in the U.S. It seemed immortal. And that would make gutting it that much more of a blow.

Adrian was lost in thought when Jonathan cleared his throat. Adrian glanced at the clock, just past sunset. He stood and walked around the desk, dropping the folded note onto Jonathan's lap as he passed. Jonathan palmed the paper.

"Try to get home tonight, Glitch. I can tell by your fresh glow, you were enjoying the sights, but I'm sure there are interesting whorehouses on your side of town too."

Instead of responding, Jonathan flashed Adrian just the slightest bit of teeth. Disrespectful and very vampiric. Adrian wasn't sure if he was acting or not. If it was an act, he'd gotten better very quickly. If it wasn't, he'd probably picked a surly meal last night. It was a good attribute to go into a fight with.

Adrian took the lift up to the penthouse. He often wondered if Deval had chosen him to run Human Resources as a ploy to separate him from Siri. Her obsession was laser-focused and certainly hadn't escaped the notice of her doting father. But whatever the reason, Adrian had lived here for decades before the big technology push at the turn of the millennium, and it was the one space he didn't feel watched. He glanced around. Various artifacts, most of them sharp, graced the exposed brick walls. There were books but no electronics. Soft lighting came from old styled fixtures.

With an uninvited pang of regret, he realized that he would never return to this oasis. His bike had been his freedom, but this had been his safety.

All these years, he'd used it with little thought. But humans, vampires, sunlight—nothing reached him here. He'd always assumed that he would bunk with Perry in the caves when the time came to leave, but now there was Miriam. When this place was gone, Adrian would be free but adrift. It would be nice to appreciate something before it was gone. But if the way he'd appreciated family, life, or the sun were any indication, that just wasn't his style.

Well, if he was going to be out to sea, he'd need provisions. Adrian grabbed a cooler and took all the blood from the fridge. Then he relieved the walls of a few of his favorite pieces—a cruel looking seventeenth-century karpan dagger, a small nineteenth-century khanjali with scabbard, an engraved revolver from the twentieth century—and tucked them into a leather duffle. He grabbed several changes of clothes, though he always kept a few at the caves, and a 50 count box of Z.I.P. shots. That should do.

Out of habit, he looked at his reflection in the cracked mirror at the door before leaving. He'd told himself that he kept the mirror because he needed to make sure he wasn't bringing breakfast on his shirt when going to deal with the humans. Adrian told himself that it was a valuable antique, even cracked. He'd told himself that he didn't even notice the crack anymore, just looked around it.

He lied to himself.

He loved the crack, its brokenness, the way it cut across his reflection severing his head from his body. It reminded him of what he deserved for killing his brother. It reminded him of what they all fucking deserved.

Adrian paused, then reached out and let his finger trace up the crack. It sliced into his flesh, and a trickle of blood ran down, filling the dark space in the silver with deep crimson. He closed the wound and looked at the bleeding neck of his reflection. His reflection stared back at him looking human. And sad.

What did it know, anyway? Adrian let the vampire rise and snarled at the black eyes in the mirror.

Clare was tired of lying on her bed and reading. Not that A *Tale of Two*

Cities wasn't amazing, but her eyes were sore and her brain hurt. She'd gone over the morning in her head again and again, trying to assimilate the information...which only made her think of question after question that she hadn't asked.

Closing the book, she glanced at her dresser where a tiny analog clock was now perched. It was 6:56. Her dinner tray sat next to the clock with what remained of her steak and potatoes, not that she'd been all that hungry. It was hard to work up an appetite laying around all day. Tossing herself back onto her pillows, she expelled the air from her lungs. This was impossible.

She rolled off the bed, stomped over to the speaker, and rammed the button.

"Heelloo? Is anybody out there?"

It was Meg who answered. "Yes, Ms. Zetler?"

"I'm slowly losing the will to live in here. Is there any way I can get some electronic devices? I mean, I get no internet, but how about T.V.?"

"We can't allow anything with internet capability outside of restricted areas and devices." She sounded tired.

"Can I just come out? I already saw somebody get all hairy this morning, and I won't freak out. I promise. I'll stay out of people's business. Maybe I could just run laps in the corridor or something. Anything. Please?"

There was silence on the other end, and then, "It's been a long day Ms. Zetler. I doubt you're the only one here 'losing the will to live.'"

Then in the background Clare heard a female voice say, "Perry won't be done for a little while yet, and I'd like to meet her. We could keep each other company." Please, God. *Anything.*

"Company sounds great to me." Clare wedged as much perkiness into her voice as she could, hoping to sway the outcome.

She could hear Meg's sigh through the speaker. "Fine. Just stay to the lounge and kitchen areas."

The door gave a click, and when she tried the handle, it swung inward. Sweet freedom!

Clare bounded into the hallway, but it was empty. A moment later, a door opened at the far end of the corridor. A tall, black woman emerged wearing a khaki button-down shirt, faded jeans, and hiking boots that were clearly well used. She gave Clare a little wave. Clare waved back and waited while the woman strode toward her with an enviable air of confidence

"Miriam." The woman thrust out her hand when she'd reached her.

Clare shook it eagerly. "Clare."

Miriam smiled. "Oh, I know. I've been hearing all about you. They make you sound like a magical unicorn."

"They?"

"You know, the Therians," she said.

"Oh. Sorry. I just assumed you were one of them."

Miriam shook her head. "Human, like you. Come on, the lounge is this way."

The woman led her down the hall to a door opposite of the one marked Bay 3. Inside were two couches and a coffee table scattered with playing cards and outdated magazines. Clare sat down, and Miriam took the seat closest to her on the other couch.

"Thanks for rescuing me," Clare said.

"I was bored too. You can only sleep so long, even after a long night."

"You are not kidding! Did you come in last night too?" Clare leaned in as they spoke.

"All the way from the Allegheny mountains," Miriam said, leaning in as well. "I didn't get to bed until six this morning!"

"How late did you sleep?"

"Perry woke me up around one." Her dark eyes twinkled. "He had a lot of apologizing to do."

Despite the tone in her voice, Clare knew that look. The woman was in love. How did that even happen? How did...No! This was her one advocate for freedom, and she was not going to have her rabid inner journalist offending her.

Clare's face must have betrayed her, though, because Miriam raised her eyebrows.

"What? You disapprove?"

"No! I just... um..."

"It's because I'm black isn't it?" Miriam shook her head.

There was a deep pause as Clare's mouth fell open.

The severe look in Miriam's eyes gave way as she tried to choke back a laugh. A moment later, they were both giggling.

"I'm sorry," Clare gasped as she sank back against the couch. "It just took me by surprise."

"Took *you* by surprise? You should have seen the look my daddy gave him when I brought him home for Sunday dinner. I think it half scared Perry!"

The giggles started up again, then turned into outright laughter. It shouldn't have felt familiar or comfortable but it did, and when the laughter tapered off to a contented sigh, Clare said, "So, do your parents know?"

"Oh girl! I wouldn't even know where to begin. I told them I met him while doing a wildlife survey, which is entirely true. They've always tried to set me up with quiet academic types, so it was bad enough bringing this hulking, white, mountain man home." Miriam restrained a chuckle at the memory. "The fact that he's good with scientific jargon helped a little, but they still looked at him like he was a backwoods redneck trying to woo the queen of Sheba."

They were laughing again when Perry poked his head in the lounge door.

"There you are." He looked at them stifling their giggles. "What's so funny?"

"You are. What else?" Miriam said, giving him a pointed look. It was too much for Clare, who was snorting between her fingers.

Mock offense filled Perry's face. "Woman, do I need to put you in your place?"

Miriam stood, eyebrows raised. "I know you're not even going to pretend to be in charge."

Perry strode over to her with a roguish grin and said, "No, ma'am," before giving her a kiss.

Clare felt a swell of regret at their closeness but pushed it down. Keeping everyone at arm's length had its drawbacks, but relationships brought pain and complication.

Miriam pulled back from him a little. "I'm still mad at you."

Perry's eyes were penitent. "I know. I've been very bad."

"Stop it."

He pulled her tighter to him and nodded as if in earnest to her request.

"I mean it, Perry. Behave!"

"Yes, ma'am!"

Miriam's dark cheeks were tinted with red as he released her, and they settled down on the couch. Clare watched as he reached for Miriam's hand and wove his fingers through hers. While talking after breakfast, he'd said he was three hundred years old, but he looked like a star-struck school boy. She couldn't fathom how such a relationship could end well, but the love painted all over their faces made her hope it for them.

27

Apology

Rule #21 Do not try to reason with a vampire

Adrian parked his baby in Bay 5 and ran a hand over her dark blue finish. He kept that bike looking damn fine. It was a good bike, and this was the one place he never worried about her. He gave her a pat, then grabbed his stuff and went in.

The sound of happy voices floated down the bare hall. Familiar voices. Instead of setting up in his quarters, Adrian followed the sound. Through a slightly ajar door, he could see Perry and Miriam, and across from them was the light-bearer, Clare. They were playing cards. Her eyes were crinkled up in mirth, and the glow around her seemed soft, like the first warmth of dawn.

Adrian pushed the door open more fully.

"You should know, Perry cheats."

Clare started slightly and turned around. Her eyes widened and then narrowed as she took him in.

"How dare you impugn my honor, sir!" Perry said.

If looks could kill, then Clare's would be making him ill at the very least. Hell. He might as well keep going anyway.

"He can tell by your heart rate when you're bluffing or excited about a hand."

"There's no honor among thieves this week, is there?" Perry said. "First you rat me out to Gran and now in front of the ladies. You sir, are dead to me." And then Perry got up and gave him a hug of welcome.

The couches were arranged in a "U" shape. The light-bearer sat catty-cornered from the love birds, so Adrian took the far side, setting his bag down next to him. Her eyes followed his movements. She had more sense than Perry or Miriam. At least she knew when a monster was near.

"Are you staying here too?" The pitch at the end of her question was just a little too high.

"At least for the weekend."

She twisted a ring on her finger. Not just any ring. That ring. Siri had slipped it off her own finger and gifted it to him when he was promoted to human resources. He'd left it at the mansion, but it was catalogued under his name and put in storage along with all the other useless things he'd left in his quarters. Selling it was to be the beginning of seeing all of those gone, but it had followed him. Siri always seemed to follow him.

The thought caused his vision to ripple, and the soft glow around Clare grew brighter for a moment before he pushed the change back down. But she'd seen. It must have been in his eyes, and dammit, now the air was thick with adrenaline.

Miriam might not be able to smell the adrenaline, but she'd definitely picked up on the tension. Her gaze snapped from him to Clare. "Don't you at least have the decency to apologize to the woman you assaulted, Ugly?"

Shit.

The woman he'd assaulted. Thanks for fucking mentioning it. We'll all have a real nice evening now.

But then a smile tugged at Clare's lips. "Ugly?"

"It fits, doesn't it?" Miriam smirked.

The smile broadened. Impossibly, it made her face even brighter. Adrian looked away.

Perry cleared his throat and began gathering up cards. "You want dealt in?"

Adrian was stuck on what Miriam had said. He could apologize, but what the hell would that accomplish? He wouldn't suddenly be safe in Clare's eyes and able to sit back and play with them. He couldn't take back what he'd done. He couldn't put Clare back in her home or at her job. *Porca troia.* He'd exploded her world, and somehow he didn't think an "I'm sorry" would ever cover that. And besides, it was for the cause. What did it matter as long as in the end her blood turned the tide of the war? Wasn't that what it was all about?

"What good would an apology do?" Adrian lurched to his feet. "The truth is, I'd do it again. I'm responsible for most of the stories in *The Survivors' Handbook.* And that look in her eyes," Clare flinched as he flung a hand in her direction, "is the reason all of Nidhi is scrambling right now. I've done what I'm supposed to do. I've risked my life to expose them, and if this works, it will save countless other lives. I am done apologizing."

He scooped up his bag and spun towards the door, but a hand on his shoulder stopped him. He jerked around. Clare's face was inches from his, but this time she didn't flinch. Her nose flared and jaw jutted. Adrian readied himself to be struck again, but she didn't draw back.

"You had a choice," she said. "Don't act like there wasn't a better way or any other way."

What did she know about choice? "One day with immortals, and suddenly we have an expert."

"You could have shown yourself without hurting anyone."

"Humans believe what they want to believe," Adrian said. "They're very good at convincing themselves they don't know what they know."

Clare opened her mouth as if to protest. He didn't give her the chance. "Even with your interviews," he put a finger in her face, "did you believe any of them until you saw me? Would you have believed if I hadn't touched you? Or would you have told yourself a thousand lies for the rest of your short, little life and died wondering?"

She blinked, and Adrian knew he'd hit a nerve with that last statement.

"Where you're wrong," she said slowly, "is touch doesn't have to hurt. That's what makes you ugly."

She walked out before he could give a retort, the room a little dimmer than before.

"Shit." Perry said. "And I thought I was having women troubles."

"You should give your boy some lessons on relationships." Miriam said to Perry as she got up. "I'm gonna check on her."

"Relationship with Clare?" Adrian said to her. "Do you think I even give a fuck about her? Is that what I'm risking my life day in and day out for? I'm not going to go and grovel because, the point is, it doesn't matter how she feels or how I feel. I can't take it back and I wouldn't. I'm focused on something much bigger, and everything else is just a distraction!"

Miriam looked at him for a moment longer before shaking her head and pushing past him.

Perry sat alone, an eyebrow raised. "What?" Adrian said. "Are you going to try and fix me too?"

The mutt suppressed a grin. "I would, but I'm certain you're far beyond even my exceptional skill. Just got to deal with you as you are."

"So you keep telling me." Adrian offered him a faint smile.

"That was pretty bad though."

Bad? It was a total clusterfuck. "Not my finest hour." Adrian sank back onto the couch. "But where are we wrong? We've done all this trying to expose the Solifugae."

Perry shook his head. "That's only the cherry on top. It's personal for both of us." They were silent for a few moments. When Perry spoke again, his voice was a whisper. "I've wondered how much different we are from Lachlan."

"We are nothing like him! We don't take pleasure in their pain." The idea, the comparison, was ludicrous. Whatever kind of monster Adrian was far paled next to that bastard. "We aren't torturing or killing anyone."

"No, we didn't take pleasure in their pain, but we didn't try to spare them any either. We got what we wanted regardless of what it cost them."

"What happened to 'we are what we are'? We are immortals."

Perry took a deep breath. "We've been fighting monsters long enough. I don't want to become one."

"So what are you telling me? Are you done with your Gran's operation?"

"No. I—" Perry ran a hand through his hair. "I just want to do it differently after this. My son might be human. I don't want his life to be like cattle for vampires, but I don't want it to be at the whims of my people either. We can do better. We have to be able to do better."

A rare look of pain came over Perry's face, and Adrian felt a flare of protectiveness. Perry was older by almost a century, but he'd always been so carefree, like a younger brother. Like Paul.

The conversation of the night came jumbling back. Paul was dead, and nothing Adrian had been doing was going to bring him back. There was no "I'm sorry" big enough, but Adrian had lived long enough to have a second chance, a second brother, and he'd damn well do better this time. He could do right by Perry and his new forming family.

Then something struck him.

"Your son?"

"I'm just guessing. I *stretched* to feel it. Kinda wanted to say hello." A wistful smile fleeted across his face. "It's tiny strand of life is so strong. Feels like a fighter."

Adrian was going to start doing better now.

"Don't come to the battle on Monday. Let Meg take care of Lachlan."

"Fuck that. I'm not letting Gran go in alone."

"The whole tribe will be there. *I'll* be there."

"But I —"

"You have a son, Perry." Adrian put a hand on his friend's shoulder. "It's not worth him growing up without you. I'll look after your Gran."

The conversation had continued as Clare walked down the hallway to her room, but she didn't stick around to listen. A mixture of emotions battled in her. She was angry, furious really, but underneath that, she was afraid, and sad, and as she stared into her room, lonely. She didn't want to go in and be stuck, but she didn't want to stay out with the possibility of randomly running into Adrian, either.

The numbers on the clock read 10:25. It was a nice, round number. Easily divisible or multipliable. Probably a good time to turn in for the night.

Clare eased herself into the room and held her breath as she shut the door. It latched but didn't lock. She let out the breath in a long stream. She could still get out.

A knock on the door jarred her.

"Yes?" She stared at the door but made no move to open it.

"Are you okay?"

Miriam.

Clare opened the door a crack. "Yeah. Thanks. I'm just…tired. I think I'm gonna head to bed."

Miriam gave her an understanding smile. "You want to make it a sleepover?"

Yes. Yes, she did.

"I'll be fine."

"I'm sure you will, but maybe I need some time away from all that testosterone."

Clare almost snorted. From the way Miriam looked at Perry, that was highly doubtful. It was sweet of her to offer though.

"Thanks, but—"

Miriam turned toward the sound of quick footsteps in the hall, her face tightening. Obviously, it wasn't Perry. Clare jerked the door shut. The footsteps stopped.

"I assume this is Clare's room."

"I don't think I'd tell you either way, Adrian."

Thank you, Miriam.

"Just let me by."

"You were a little extra Ugly tonight, you know that? How much would it hurt you to just apologize to her."

Adrian's voice was a little quieter when he spoke. Almost…polite. "You're not wrong about me, on any account."

The prick couldn't even say the words: "You're right".

"Anyway, I came to apologize to her."

"I really don't think she wants to talk to you right now."

"Oh for fuck's sake!" There went polite. "First you want me to apologize, and now you're not even going to let me try." A string of—was that Italian?—poured through the door. Whatever it was, it definitely sounded profane.

There was a long silence. When Adrian finally spoke again, his tone was only slightly less combative. "For what it's worth, I told Perry not to go."

There was genuine surprise in Miriam's voice. "You what?"

"I told him not to go to the battle on Monday." There was a moment of quiet. "He has too much to lose now."

There was a small catch in Miriam's voice. "Thank you."

"Can I at least knock and see if she'll talk with me?"

"Yeah, I guess." Miriam's voice started soft like she was still thinking about other things. She raised it a little as she added. "But if she lets you in, I'm going to be right out here in this hall the whole time."

Clare's heart began to beat faster.

"Fine." It sounded like he was grinding his teeth. Served him right after—

A sharp knock struck the door. Clare jerked back several feet. "Yes?"

"It's Adrian."

Really? And here she'd thought it was the white rabbit coming to invite her to a tea party. God in heaven. "I know who it is. What do you want?"

"To give you a proper apology."

"I thought you were done apologizing."

Adrian heaved a sigh that she could hear even a few feet from the door. "I'm aware I've been an ass tonight."

"Just tonight?"

"Clearly, it's a fundamental flaw of my character." The mockery practically dripped through the door. Clare rolled her eyes.

"Please."

...That sounded sincere.

Clare groaned. She was going to do it. She was actually going to let him in. After everything! What the hell was wrong with her?

She yanked the door open. He must have been leaning against it because he half fell into the room, nearly colliding with her. She stumbled back as he righted himself. Huh. That was the first awkward movement she'd ever seen him make. By the look on his face, he clearly hadn't expected it either. It was almost enough to make her smile. Almost.

"Fine, but the door stays open." She stalked across the room.

To his credit, Adrian only came a few steps inside. He didn't speak right away, but rather, looked at her. Probably not at her but at that fantastic vampire attractor halo she had. Great.

"Do you know anything about it?" She shifted her weight, looking down at herself.

He blinked. "About what?"

"The glow? They said it was a vampire thing, and they didn't know much about it."

Adrian shook his head. "I've heard of your kind, but you're the first I've ever seen. Supposedly, there are more in the old country."

She could almost laugh. Well, wasn't she special. The stuff of legend. To a vampire.

"If you want," Adrian dredged up the words slowly. "I can go in a little earlier on Sunday night before the battle and try to dig up some information."

She blinked. "That wouldn't expose you at all?"

"You were seen at Nidhi's restaurant, so it shouldn't be suspicious if I'm making inquiries."

"Then, yes. I would like that."

Adrian nodded and looked away. Was this his way of apologizing?

"You said I didn't even try, but you were wrong."

And he was botching it already.

"I did try. I tried to keep you asleep. You wouldn't have even known, but the light around you is painful and—"

"So it's my fault you had to traumatize me."

"No. That's not what I meant." He ran his hands through his hair, revealing a wounded expression. "Almost none of my memories are human. I've lived for nearly two centuries now. Over a hundred of those years were spent in direct contact with a creature that can force me to do whatever she wants. Or kill me with a thought. I am well acquainted with nightmares. I compared my actions with those I knew, and by vampire standards, mine were almost philanthropic. I knew I was a monster, but I thought if I could take down the others, I could make it right."

He looked at her then. His dark eyes glittering in the low light, and Clare felt a stab of unwanted sympathy.

"But I can't make it right. I killed the person I loved the most. And nothing I have done—none of it—can change that."

It was like a punch in the gut. Clare knew that feeling. She knew what it was to feel like death, sorrow, and everything was her fault and to be helpless to change it. And he'd been living with that for centuries. She swallowed.

His voice was quiet. "But I am sorry."

She cleared her throat, and then, "Not that I'm one to talk, considering that I literally changed my name in order to run away from my past, but... an early millennial author once said that resisting pain only made it worse. That we should lean into the pain."

He frowned. "What does that even mean?"

Clare shrugged. "It made sense when I was ready for it."

Adrian studied her for a long moment, then nodded and pushed off the wall to go.

"Wait!"

He glanced back.

"Is Jonathan going to be okay?"

"He'll be fine. He's surprisingly good at what he does. Instead of tracking you, he currently has our people bringing in some guy who ran an analysis on one of our Z.I.P.s. I'll make sure he's safe before the battle."

Clare's ears began to ring, and the floor seemed to tilt beneath her. David. She'd asked David to have that syringe analyzed. If they had him, if they killed him..."

"Are you alright?" Adrian was suddenly much closer. Clare reached up and grabbed his lapel.

"Is it David Reese? Do they have David?"

Adrian tried to pull back, but Clare tightened her grip.

"I don't know."

"You dropped a syringe at my house. I gave it to my friend to convince him I wasn't losing my mind. I need you to tell me if he's in danger because of me."

Adrian pulled himself free and stepped back. His face had gone stiff and distant.

"If it's your friend," he said, "there's nothing that can be done."

"But you work there. You can find him."

"If I go asking about someone they just picked up, it'll raise eyebrows." He sighed. "Besides, they might not kill him. There's a good chance they'll just wipe him."

Clare put her finger in his face. "But you don't know that! This is our fault, yours and mine, and for once we might be able to make something right. Maybe tonight, we save a life instead of ruining it."

"There is no 'we' here! You going would be like sending a lamb to the slaughter. Hell, I'm surprised you made it out of the restaurant alive the first time, what with that light."

"Fine," Clare said. "You go for us."

"No!" He leaned in, frustration and something like pain lining every word. "The Therians are planning a fucking *attack*. This is not the time for me to start acting strange. More than one life could be lost if I do."

"He'll die because of me. I can't let that happen. Not again!"

"If I do what you're asking, many more here could die because of *me*."

"You don't know that."

"And you don't even know that it's your friend they've picked up." Adrian ran a hand over his face.

"Please." She reached for his arm, but her hand only met air.

"I'm sorry, Clare."

And he was gone.

28

Companion

Rule #13 Always carry something that will make noise or draw attention if attacked

C lare sank to the floor.

She thought she'd separated her business and private life. She thought she'd avoided making friends while she focused on her career, but somehow between their snark and walls, David had become dear to her. And now, the monsters had him.

Adrian said they might not kill him, but really, why not? David had no family nearby, all his friends were online, and if he didn't show up for work, they'd think the slacker just quit without giving notice. What reason did they have to let him live?

Pain squeezed her heart, and she gasped against the sobs. She couldn't live through that kind of crushing guilt and sorrow again. But what could she do? Not only was she human, but she had an actual death attraction surrounding her.

Her sun flare was still in her bag though, and Perry said that her blood could win the war with squirt guns. If that actually worked, then she could have a weapon for both her and David.

Perry had pulled a couple of vials of blood from her that morning, and she doubted he'd had time to use them. It would just be a matter of getting to the lab unnoticed and getting out of the Therian compound. That would probably be a walk in the park compared to trying to find David with the vampires.

It was a ridiculous idea that would likely get her killed. Not that she'd been living much anyway, and she'd rather die trying than sitting around counting the minutes while David was tortured and killed. Clare twisted the ring on her finger.

Transportation would be tricky. They were too far out of town to walk to the Pulse transit station, and she didn't have her phone to order a ride. She might be able to hitch her way there. Clare had always thought that was dangerous, but all things considered, it was probably the sanest thing she was considering. She definitely couldn't go back to her father's and get her Mini. Enough lives were in danger tonight because of her. Hopefully, she'd just get lucky along the way.

The whole way. She'd need to get lucky the whole way.

Taking a deep breath, Clare got up. It was 11:04, and who knew how long David had. She ran her hands over her hair and clothes. This would require looking like she was absolutely confident in what she was doing.

Her door opened into an empty and quiet corridor. Head up and shoulders back, she marched to the stairwell at the end of the hall. A faint waft of disinfectant carried from the lab up the stairs and soured her stomach. This was a bad idea. Her knuckles whitened where they gripped the metal railing.

Her father had given up the use of his legs rescuing her, and she was just going to throw her life away? Her mother had died… Her mother had died for her and told her to be brave. Clare swallowed the dryness in her throat and started down the stairs.

David was not dying for her too.

The lights were still on in the lab, and there was a smattering of people. She nodded to those who looked her way but went straight to the area Perry had been working that morning. She was on an errand. Perry needed her to bring up some vials to—well, she didn't ask what, but he needed them.

At his desk, she mumbled out loud, "He said in the fridge, top shelf." She opened the fridge. There were clear bottles with who knew what in them and several vials of blood. Three vials had her name in a scrolling but hurried hand. Clare grabbed them, shut the fridge, and began walking out like she knew exactly what she was doing.

"Where are you going with those?" A small, red-haired woman with amber eyes was looking right at her.

"Perry said to bring them?" Could they smell fear, like dogs?

"That sounds about right." The woman didn't seem suspicious per se. "What's he need them for?"

Clare tried to stay calm. Perry had sent her out. She was just running an errand. "I'm sorry. I didn't ask."

The woman shook her head and tsk'd.

"Here," she pulled out a black pouch. "It's safer to transport them in this. Perry can be a bit scatterbrained about this sort of thing."

The woman unzipped the pouch. It had a reflected, insulated interior with black, elastic loops. Clare kept her breathing even as she slipped the vials in and zipped it up.

"Thanks."

"Of course. We look out for each other around here." The woman gave her a small smile. "Look, I heard about you, and pretty much all of us know what it feels like to be thrust into this life against our will. I know it seems bad now, but it gets better."

"Do I look that rough?" Clare tried to joke.

"No. But I can smell the tears on you."

Clare looked down. The tears were still close, but at least they were giving her a cover instead of giving her away. Might as well run with it. She slumped her shoulders and let the fear she was feeling surface. The woman frowned and put a hand on Clare's shoulder.

"If you need to talk..."

"Thanks," Clare said, "but I think I'm just going to get this to Perry and turn in."

She could feel the woman's stare on her back as she walked away, but Clare made it out of the lab, blood in hand. As soon as she was out of sight, she resumed her confidence act. The fewer people that stopped her the better, but at least she didn't have to worry about her emotions giving her away if they did.

She made it back to her room without incident, shoved the pouch with the blood into her work bag, and walked back out. The nearest bay to her was marked 5. She popped her head in. No people, one vehicle. A dark blue motorcycle stood next to the wall. She hadn't ridden one since her rebellious late teen years, and even then it wasn't much. It felt too exposed and unsafe.

Clare trotted over to it. The keys were in the ignition. She wasn't exactly in riding gear, but it'd probably be the easiest way to get out of the compound. She strapped her bag on the back and walked the bike out the small pedestrian door.

Once outside, she got her seat. The bike was bigger and heavier than the one she'd played around on. With a turn of the key, it seemed to roar to life, but no one came running. Leaving the light off, she pulled in the clutch and pushed down into first gear. Clare let out the clutch and began to walk the bike forward. She really, really didn't want to do this.

Clare eased on the throttle and let her feet up. The bike glided around the building to the gate. The gate was closed, but there was enough space on the walk-through next to it. She slowed it to a walk and putted through, hoping no one was watching. As soon as she was on the road, Clare gave it as much speed as she could without freaking out. Despite the bike being well-balanced and easy to ride, that turned out to be about 40 mph, but it was better than walking.

The heat of the bike on her legs caused Clare to stop at the first 24 hour supermarket she could find. The cashier working nights must have seen some crazy things come through because he didn't even look surprised when a long black coat, spiked choker and cuffs, thick dark pants, boots, perfume, two squirt guns, and a funnel came down the conveyor belt. She went into the store bathroom to change and walked out looking every bit like a Heliophile. A small part of her had to admit, she rocked the look too.

There was one more element she wanted. Clare wasn't even sure if it would help, but she set a course through downtown and stopped at the Cathedral of the Sacred Heart. Its castle-like exterior reminded her some of the Nidhi restaurant. It had beautiful stone columns and turrets. Inside it was even somewhat similar. The floors were polished marble and the walls gilded, but instead of smelling of food and—her imagination filled in—blood, the church smelled faintly of incense.

The church had changed over the years from more of a historic society to a well known, community-centered place of refuge. The doors were never locked anymore, and parishioners each signed up for a time, so someone was always there in case of a need. That person was in a back pew with their head bowed.

At the sound of Clare's boots on the hard floor, she got up, and Clare was surprised to see someone dressed similar to herself. She was young, barely a woman, and clothed head to toe in black with piercings in all kinds of places.

"Hi. Do you need help or prayer?"

Clare was pretty sure that saying she wanted to use some holy water—just in case that helped—to dilute her blood enough to fill two squirt guns would not get her anywhere. But what came out of her mouth surprised her.

"I don't know if I believe in prayer, but I'm planning to free my friend from a vampire compound. If whoever you talk to doesn't mind interfering in that sort of thing, I'll take all the help I can get."

The girl blinked once, slowly, and then nodded.

"Would you like me to pray with you now?"

"Since I'm not on speaking terms with any deities, I'll let you handle that. But do you mind if I take some holy water for the road?"

"It's better to have living water in you, but you're welcome to the water here."

And that's about how she remembered church people, minus the sharing part. That was a nice addition.

The basin of holy water was located in a square of stone. It felt odd, no matter what she believed or didn't, plunging a neon orange squirt gun into it.

With weapons stashed conveniently in her long coat, Clare headed south on 76. The restaurant had been outside of Richmond a little way, and while she didn't remember the name of the road that they'd turned on, she did remember it was off VA-711.

The air was cold and stinging as she finally got confident enough to go the speed limit. City turned to suburb turned to trees and land. And then she saw it: a black, back-lit sign, with fancy white letters proclaiming "Nidhi Manor" and nothing more.

The road seemed like a private drive, but there was no gate or cameras that she could see. Still, she came in at a crawl. No need to announce her presence with engine roaring and guns soaking. Trees made a beautiful arch overhead that let in dappled moonlight. Then, the drive opened to a large estate lawn and a huge sprawling building.

The front was old and posh, but behind that, newer sections had been added on. There was no telling how big it actually was or where in all that she would find David. This was definitely a fool's errand. There was no way this could work, but she'd rather die trying than live with not having tried at all.

Clare shook her head and looked for a place to park the motorcycle. The front parking lot was empty but well lit, so she took it off the road into the grass at the edge of the lawn. The ground squished under the tires from the recent rain, and when Clare tried to set it on the kickstand, either she did it wrong or the mud caught it. Whatever the reason, the bike stood for a moment and then toppled on its side. She cringed at the noise and, after a moment of debate, grabbed the keys and left it on its side. The clock under the speedometer read 1:18, and every second she wrestled with the motorcycle could be the one that David's life hung on.

The jog across the grounds seemed eternal despite her hurrying. Side doors would probably be more dangerous of an option, so she decided to check the front first. Each step brought her closer to the mammoth red doors and the complete futility of what she was doing.

Hopefully, the long coat blocked out most of her light, or whatever the glow was. If it didn't, she was basically her own spotlight walking up to the devil's lair. The large, vertical door handle was cold to the touch, and her heart was beating so hard it might as well be taking flight, but the door opened with silent ease. Of course it did. If dinner wanted to walk in the front door, why stop it?

Clare took a breath and stepped into the dark building.

It took her eyes a minute to adjust from the moon and floodlights on the building, but the room was lit. Dimmed lights in sconces showed a scene in grey: tables with chairs inverted on them for the evening, large double doors likely leading to a kitchen, the balcony and staircase with their own double doors.

That was probably the way she needed to go, but for a moment, despite the need to hurry, Clare couldn't move. Her throat constricted, and everything in her begged her not to do this. She didn't know where those doors would lead or what she would do when she got there. David could already be dead, and then her death would mean nothing.

A few tears slipped down her cheeks, but she took off her boots and carried them as she ran across the polished floor and up the stairs on silent feet. The movement seemed to wake something in her, and despite a tremble in her hands when she shoved her boots back on, Clare felt a surge of strength. She was here, and she was going to do this no matter how it ended.

Before opening the door, she pulled a squirt gun from her coat. It seemed less likely to draw attention than the Sun Flare. She'd poured her blood into the guns outside the cathedral. Now to see if it actually did anything.

The door opened into a black corridor. Pitch black. Clare put a hand to the wall, but as the door closed behind her and sealed off the light, the darkness felt suffocating. She was trapped and couldn't breathe and was about to die. There was a pain in her chest, and her knees felt weak. She couldn't die here. Not like this.

Move!

But her legs didn't move.

"Be brave."

The words fell from nowhere and left no echo, but Clare was sure she'd actually heard them, and they left a warmth in their wake that unfroze her. One hand on the wall and the other holding the gun, she moved a foot forward and then another. She'd thought this through. No more thinking now. Just moving.

About ten steps in, her boot kicked a door. She found the handle and cracked it open. It was another balcony. This one was lit with soft, golden light and carpeted in deep red with mahogany wood trimming everything. Seeing no one, she stepped out but stayed close to the wall.

Her trick of walking with her head up, looking like she knew what she was doing, probably wouldn't work here. Maybe if she found a computer or something, that would help. What she really needed was a map that said "You are here" and had "Dungeons for Bad Humans" clearly labeled. Clare sighed. This really was foolhardy. She might as well just walk down the stairs and announce she was looking for the new prisoner.

Voices wafted from below. She ducked down and listened. The sound carried as if they were walking.

"The sooner they find the writer the better. Deval is in a foul mood." The voice was deep and harsh.

"I would've thought having new information would ease his pressure on Security." The second voice was female.

Perhaps she was in line for a little luck. Hopefully, David was giving them whatever they asked for and this "new information" was going to buy him time.

The first voice scoffed. "He's putting the brunt of the responsibility for the leak on Security and Media. Justin's dead, and Tyrone is still alive only because he can *soothe* better than anyone. None of us are safe."

"Jonathan seems to be in good graces."

"Only because he found the guy who ran the Z.I.P. and seems confident that he can bring in the writer in a day or two."

Clare couldn't help her gasp, but she held her breath afterwards hoping the sound hadn't been heard.

Jonathan. If he was working both sides...

He'd seemed so sincere. But he must seem sincere here too for them to believe him. What if the Therian attack was a trap? She let out the breath, quiet and slow. She had to get through this and warn them.

The conversation appeared to have stopped, but she wasn't sure if they were still down there or not. And then the air was knocked from her lungs. An icy, sickening presence seemed to weigh on her body, and she sank to the floor. Suddenly, she felt a ripple of alarm go through the weight, and she understood.

It was *stretching* her. And it had met her Watcher.

For once, Clare didn't think. She reached back, like she had when Perry *stretched* her, latched on to the fetid thing that had touched her, and held. The alarm rippling through it began to radiate out in spikes of fear. Pain throbbed through her body as it struggled against her. Just as her grip began to slip, there was a surge of warmth, and the thing she'd been holding onto was cut away.

Clare found herself on her knees with her hands out in front of her. Her palms tingled with pinpoints of pain.

A cry sounded from below.

Clare grabbed the squirt gun that had fallen to the floor and began to sprint for the door she'd come through. A thud landed behind her, and she could smell the tang of vampire. Her glow must show through the coat because, as she whirled around, she registered a stunned looking, blonde woman.

And then Clare started shooting. The woman's face contorted with pain as lines of harsh red bubbled up across her nose and cheek. And then Clare was flying backwards. Light splintered her vision as her head slammed to the ground, and everything went dark.

29

Siri's Play

Rule #5 Be aware of who and what is around you

A drian was whiling away the time in the control room with Kitsune
packing explosives for transport when he felt the pull of the
summons. He swore and slammed his fist on the desk, startling
Sune who was working across from him. The other man raised a brow.

"Work is calling me in."

Who knew what the damn reason was this time. With Jonathan working
to cover things up, they couldn't have made any progress with their search.
Shit. Maybe that was the problem. The kid had better have enough sense
not to act any differently around him if he saw him at Nidhi. Hopefully, the
extra clothes in his bag didn't smell of Therian.

Sune nodded. "Be careful."

"Always."

Adrian grabbed a change of clothes and headed for Bay 5. The bay door
swung open and... he stopped.

His bike was gone.

No. Oh, *hell* no. No one in this warehouse was stupid enough to steal
his...

Shit.

He bolted back down the corridor to Clare's room and pounded on the door. No response. He grabbed the handle. The door swung open with ease. The bed was empty. No. No no no no. She couldn't be that stupid. No one could be that fucking stupid!

Adrian sprinted back to the control room and pulled up a console, ignoring Sune's pointedly curious look. He scrolled back through the footage at the front gate. Come on, come on. There! The camera didn't capture her glow, but it was definitely Clare. Dammit. That was two hours ago. She just waltzed right through without triggering the gate, and nobody even noticed. And with his baby in tow! Sune watched over his shoulder as she made a somewhat wobbly start and drove off camera.

Adrian was still staring at the spot he last saw her on the screen. "Nidhi has one of her friends. I told her it was suicide to go."

"The Teacher said that was the greatest love."

"This is not the time for proverbs." Adrian let a breath out through gritted teeth. "If I don't contact you, call off the attack."

The Kumiho nodded.

"Inform Meg, but don't tell Perry. He needs to keep out of this one." Sune narrowed his eyes. Adrian ignored him and headed back out the door. "I'm taking Larry."

Larry sat in Bay 9, a shadow of his former glory. Perry had bought the grey F150 Lariat truck new decades ago when he was doing some renovations on the cave and managed to get in, out, and up more spots than Adrian thought possible. The exterior looked like hell, but it still ran. Perry had removed the VIN number when he sent it to live with his Gran so it could be used on just such occasions. Adrian found the keys on the dash, and after turning over a few times, the antique combustion engine roared to life. He peeled it out of the bay.

Consciousness trickled back in along with a pounding headache. A silky, female voice was speaking.

"No. I am not asking you to keep this from my father. I am merely asking you to wait until morning to tell him."

A bass voice replied, "You may not value my life but I do. If anything happened to her before she was processed—"

The silk rose in volume and turned to steel. "I'll make sure she is still alive in the morning. But if you alert my father before I'm done with my business tonight, I will personally arrange a visit with Lachlan for you."

There was the sound of a door clanging.

"I know you're awake. You may as well open your eyes." The voice was flat and commanding.

Clare opened her eyes to a bare concrete room. A pair of red stilettos stood out against the grey wall, followed by high waisted black pants and a red blouse that accentuated a voluptuous hourglass figure. The woman was beautiful with caramel skin and long black hair. The vampiric black eyes were a bit of a drawback though.

Clare was unbound—because really, what was a puny human going to do?—but she'd been stripped of her coat and weapons. She pushed herself into a seated position without taking her eyes off the other woman.

"Where did you get that ring?" The question was loud in the small room.

Clare blinked. Not exactly the first question she'd been expecting. She looked down at the moonstone on her finger. In a way, the thing had gotten her into this whole mess, yet she couldn't think of a single reason how it could be important. The truth should work here.

"From my father. For my birthday."

"You are a skilled liar." Clare could feel herself bristle. So much for the truth. The woman continued. "That is the ring I gave to Adrian, and we found his bike outside."

Crap.

"I know he's still alive, so either you overpowered him, or," the woman's face crinkled as though she caught a whiff of something foul, "he is in love with you. He wouldn't part with his bike for anything less. Though falling in love with something as revolting as you would be a new low, even for him."

Adrian had referred to the creature who could kill him with a thought as a "she." From the possessive look in her eyes, this must be the witch. A tiny spark of what might have been anger lit in Clare's chest.

"I stole the bike."

225

"Where were you when you managed to wrest it from him, and why bring it here?"

And this was where the answers ran out. There was nothing Clare could say without endangering someone.

The woman's look hardened. "Why are you here? What are you doing with Adrian?"

Clare didn't answer. Faster than she could blink, the woman was across the room, landing a blow on her cheek that slammed Clare against the floor. Her teeth sliced into her tongue and a coppery taste filled her mouth.

"You've had some dealing with Adrian," the creature hissed. "On top of that, you've assaulted my friend, somehow severed a guard from his anchor, and you're a light-bearer. I'm sure you realize you're going to die. The amount of pain you feel, though, is entirely up to you."

Clare pushed herself up from the cold concrete, willing her head to stop spinning, and spat. She was aiming for the eyes but missed, badly. The glob of blood and spittle landed on those oh-so-neat trousers instead.

The woman shrieked and swiped her hand across the splatter. Only to shriek again. Small streaks of red were blossoming on the creature's skin. Good enough. Her interrogator began drawing in deep breaths of air, eyes narrowed, and Clare tensed her body for another blow.

"You," the woman snarled through clenched teeth, "have just opted for a world of pain. I would do it personally, but I know someone much more creative than I am. He'll make you hurt in ways you never imagined. I'll watch though, and whatever your dealings with Adrian, when I'm done with him, he'll watch too. And he'll enjoy it."

The cell door slammed behind her and locked.

A muffled shout came through the door. "Tell no one that she's here until morning! And don't go in there. This one is dangerous."

Dangerous. Locked alone in the small space, she felt anything but dangerous. She swallowed another coppery mouthful and wiped at her lips. Her hand came away with a small bit of red. Sure, it hurt them, but it didn't devastate, at least not in small quantities. It certainly wouldn't get her out of this room. She was going to die trapped in here, without having

226

helped David, and managing to endanger plenty of other lives in the process. That was going to be her end: trapped, alone, and worse than pointless.

"NO!" It was a scream, a declaration, a decision.

She got up and punched at the wall, splitting her knuckles. Well, that accomplished a whole lot. She paced the small room. There had to be something. Maybe when that creature came back, Clare's newly bloodied knuckles would... would what? Sting her real good so the guard had to come in and help?

The guard. Clare stopped pacing. She'd killed one vampire already, no blood required. She closed her eyes, took a breath, and tried to recapture the way it had felt when she was holding on to the vampire. Despite what she'd heard about Watchers and the danger, she was going to figure out how to *stretch* and get the hell out of this place.

Adrian stalked into the council room. He needed to get this over with and find Clare. The mansion had seemed conspicuously busy, but he was surprised to find that he was the first one there. He had the farthest to travel. He was never the first one.

A prickle started at the base of his spine. Shit. Whatever this was, it wasn't good. He turned to leave. As he did, Siri and Lachlan appeared in the doorway. Jonathan trailed behind them, his head down. Then, Siri took a key from her pocket, closed the door, and locked it.

Unease turned to dread, dread to anger, and anger slid into fury. He welcomed the blast of sensations as the change ripped through him.

"You don't look happy to see me, my love," Siri said.

Happy to see the conniving bitch who'd damned him? She was delusional. Delusional and blocking the exit.

"Unlock that door."

Siri settled on the edge of the table, her red blouse billowing over tight black pants. It should have been a non-threatening stance. Adrian had spent far too long in hell for that. Her ease was more menacing than a snarl.

"Why did you call me here?" he ground out.

"You're always all business, aren't you?"

227

You have no fucking idea, sweetheart.

Siri trailed her finger along the wood grain of the table. "I could have anyone you know. My father said your engram and your hate would keep you from me. He told me long ago to give up on you, but I never could." She turned wide, doe eyes on him. *Madonna Santa,* what he wouldn't give to gouge them out with his bare hands. "You see, even without an engram, something of ourselves carries in the crossover. And I'm rather like my father." The finger stopped moving. "Tenacious once I decide what I want."

Adrian let disgust ripple through him while the *troia* kept running her mouth. The thought of Clare briefly flashed in his mind, and he pushed it out. If Siri caught even a hint of it—no if she hadn't mentioned her, chances were Clare wasn't here.

He focused on what was in the room. Lachlan had stayed in front of the door, smiling with sincere happiness, which meant nothing good. Jonathan was behind him, never looking up. If that little thrip had—

"I want you, Adrian, and you want me."

The growl erupted from his throat without a thought. He'd sooner castrate himself than bed her again.

She pouted prettily. "Or you would, if you could let yourself. You wanted me back on that pier, and if not for the unfortunate mistake with your first meal, that desire would have carried through in the crossover."

"Don't even allude to my brother, you whore."

She laughed. The bitch actually laughed.

"And what would you call a man who sold his soul for a piece of ass? And you did. Gladly. I didn't have to beckon or soothe. Oh, no. You were only too happy to worship my body. I'd never felt anything like it." She slipped down from the table and came over to him. Adrian went still. "I turned others, had my way with them, even forced it a few times. But there was nothing like the raw passion you unleashed on me that night." She ran a finger down his chest, apparently relishing the memory.

He could feel the fury and hate rolling inside him, and he dug into it, feeding it with every image he'd ever had of her lying dead at his feet. She wanted passion? Let her feel that.

Her smile faded. She dropped her hand and stepped back.

"But *that* is all I ever get from you." She sighed dramatically. "I've heard when you stop fighting, that's when it's truly over because the other person doesn't care enough to fight. It made me hope you'd come around after a few decades, maybe a century. I didn't want to force you to my bed and lose that chance. I suppose I should have gone to Lachlan sooner, but I wanted to try the civilized way first."

Figlio di trioa! As if things weren't bad enough already, Lachlan was involved. There was no telling how deep this shit-hole was about to get.

"It turns out he's known for a long time how to get rid of an engram. The only problem is that it would reset you completely, and your knowledge has become extremely valuable to my father. He'd hate to lose his top man in Human Resources. So Lachlan found a solution for that too, of course." She favored the pair at the door with a glowing smile, and Adrian made his move.

He crouched to spring, but his feet never let the ground.

She'd been toying with him, waiting for this. The moment his muscles coiled, the will was cut from them, and he slammed onto the ground, one leg bent beneath him at an odd angle. A thousand profanities went through his mind, but not a breath got past his lips. He couldn't even blink. Siri had finally gotten tired of the fucking chase, and he hadn't even seen it coming.

She stepped into his vision and bent over him, her black hair falling in a halo around her face.

"You see, darling, after spending a few days in the tower with you, Jonathan is quite confident he can run your operations. He's got a lot riding on this too. I told him he could have your old haunt for him and his family, since you won't be needing it any more." She stroked his face. Bile rose in his throat, and he couldn't swallow it back. "I've assured him I can glitch his wife with the proper blood prompt, a cousin perhaps. We've seen how it goes when siblings are used." She paused to smile at him. "The child will have to wait a few years, but there's no reason he can't live with them until then."

One vampire he had trusted, and that'd been one too many. They'd kill his friends, and he wouldn't even know it. Oh God. He might even help slaughter them.

Pulling up all his energy, he tried to break her hold, but there wasn't anything to break. She had taken all but the barest trace of his life. And she was only stronger for it. Siri ran a finger down his jaw, and his skin tingled in its wake.

"I'll do it right this time." She leaned down and kissed his lips, her hair feathering over his cheeks. "Then, you'll be mine willingly. I'll end this torment for both of us."

Hell. This was fucking hell.

"All right, Lach. You may have him now. Leave him a little dignity when you're preparing him. And I don't want any marks on him when I come to finish it. He won't be able to heal, and don't think I won't notice."

"Wait!" It was Jonathan. "Can I have his bike? You said you had the keys."

Cazzo di merda! He was gonna kill the thrip, rip his heart out of his chest. Adrian stormed and raged, but his body did none of those things. There was the light tinkling of keys flying through the air.

Lachlan didn't say a word, but stood over his body with a look of glee. He ran his tongue over his teeth. Adrian watched the room spin as his body was hoisted from the floor and slung over Lach's shoulder.

For one upside-down moment, he caught sight of Jonathan's face, unreadable and vampiric. The little shit. Adrian would never even get the chance to kill him for this.

Siri stood close next to Lach. There were burns on her hand... *Madonna santa!* Clare.

"I was wondering how you'd feel about that." Siri's face came into his vision. "Your girlfriend did stop by. Interesting choice. Didn't seem to want to talk much though. I'm glad to know I haven't been wasting my time with her. Anyway, once we've got you all fixed up right, we can celebrate by watching Lach try to unravel her mysteries. You'll finally be able to enjoy the thrash and screams."

Adrian felt something hot and wet slip from his eye.

30

Waiting

Rule #24 Vampires can also be religious, so don't expect supernatural help

There was no time, no waiting, only the edge of her body like a wall around a house: solid and unyielding. Both times she'd gotten outside of it, she'd grabbed on to someone who was intruding from the outside. It was a lot harder trying to jump the wall from the inside. Breathing slow and even, she gathered everything that felt like her and pushed. The wall didn't budge and neither did she.

She leaned her head against the cold concrete of her cell. Maybe Perry was right. Maybe humans couldn't *stretch*.

Clare frowned.

Stretch. Not push, not get out of, but *stretch*. Clare's breathing slowed as she once again let her awareness grow until it included her body and the essence of herself. This time, she didn't try to break free from her body. She felt its firm hold. This was her anchor. Now, to find something close to latch on to.

Perry had said that distance was different, that it was about connection. So, David should be easier to find than the guard outside her door, but once she figured out how to find him, she should, in theory, be able to find the guard too.

Clare went deeper into herself, finding the place that held David in her heart, and then tried to direct it outward.

And she felt the *stretch*.

It was as though a line in her heart was connected to David and would know him anywhere, in any form. She reached out along the line. It was like spreading out her fingers just a little farther and just a little more. There he was, a mass of life more complex, substantial, and more... well, more *David* than she'd ever known.

There were spots of pain in the ever-moving fibers that made him up, but not too many. Mostly, the life was shimmering with fear, so many fears. In the writhing of them, she could catch strands that were concerned for her. He had told them things about her, he didn't even know why, and was she even still alive?

"I'm here." There was no voice, but Clare said it to him all the same, said it from herself into him. "I'm alive, and I'm going to find you."

A filament of confusion surfaced and hardened. "It's okay. It's me," and she reached out and touched. The vibration of his confusion smoothed under her contact.

"Clare. Where are you, Clare?" He wasn't speaking to her like she had to him, but the question filled his being.

"It's going to be okay. Just... Just rest, alright. I'm going to fix this." As she said it, she could feel it transmit through her touch. The mass of his life quieted. She did it again. "Rest." His edges became more indistinct, and she pulled them close. "Rest." She spoke it into him with all she was, and he accepted it. His life became still, *soothed,* and he slept.

When Clare opened her eyes, her arms were outstretched, and she could still feel him. The connection had always been there, but it felt almost like a solid thing now, and she was sure she could follow it to find him in the mansion.

As soon as she managed to get out of this room.

If she could figure out how to find the guard in that place, she could try and get him to open the door like she'd gotten David to sleep. It was a long shot, but it was a long shot that she'd still be alive in the morning too. There was nothing to lose.

With a deep breath, Clare closed her eyes and fell into herself. Last time she'd looked for a connection she knew. This time, she had to find a connection. This thing had touched her. It was guarding her. They had breathed the same air. They walked the same dimension. They both lived...

What she'd experienced before was like looking through the peephole of a door. She'd seen only that connection right in front of her. But now the door had exploded and sucked her out in the process. A web of life flowed in connection with hers and, with a painful draw, pulled at her. Too much. Too broad. She tried to pull herself in, pushing back against a rushing current. It hurt in places Clare didn't have.

Warmth, heat, life, death, giving, and consuming. Power. Fire. It saw her. She could feel its gaze on her soul. It approached. For a moment she thought of letting go, flowing away wherever the current might take her. But she was done running.

"Find your anchor," the voice sang into her.

In the maelstrom of sensations, her anchor was like a mountain she'd forgotten, and just being aware of it made everything suddenly stop. With a snap, she was inside of herself, the edges of her body a wall of safety. The Watcher was on the other side. It had helped her. She could even feel the line that connected them. It went heart to heart.

Without really meaning to, Clare pulled on the connection. The flame pulled back and pulled Clare out. The *stretch* was gentle, and instead of a massive current, she found herself in a calm place. Connections webbed out from her. Heat warmed her.

"You went too far out." The words danced into her with a pleased familiarity. *"You were searching through time, but it's connections flow to places you cannot walk with an anchor. This is space. It is harder to walk than a soul connection and less sure, but it is safer than walking time."*

Clare had a million questions.

Amusement rippled through the fire, but the words that filled her had a tinge of sadness. *"Our time is short. The fight is coming. I will give what help I can, but you must go now."* It placed both hands on the webbing, and a pulse went out.

"This way." The words and the strand seemed to be the same thing. Clare followed them, thinning out until she came to a dark thing. Boredom and irritation moved in its frozen life. She reached into the ice, and the ice shuddered and bucked. Curling tight around it, she spoke.

"Open the door."

Her words didn't even penetrate it, but it turned to grab her. As it did, the presence of her Watcher flared, and she felt visceral fear resound inside the frozen thing.

"Let me go!"

She could actually hear the words. They came from far away and right outside the door. The ice under her hold deepened and became sharp. She held tighter and cried out against the piercing cold.

"Open the door!"

The Watcher advanced. Panic and pain flowed up through her hands, but then the door latch slid open.

Clare let go, snapped back into her body, and opened her eyes in time to see shock on the guard's face. Then, with an exhale, he dropped to the floor next to her. She was out of the room before she could think, her hands tingling with remembered pain.

Three heavy doors were in the hall outside her room. It was harder to find the connection this time. That part of her was weaker, tired maybe, but finally, she could feel him. Right there, at the end of the hall. Whatever tech the vampires were supposed to have, the doors were locked with a massive, manual slide. They must not have people breeze into the den of death looking to free friends too often. As she pushed the knob, it slid on well-greased rails, and the door swung open. The room smelled of stale urine. David was still sleeping. His hair was more unkempt than normal, and the bruising on his wrists made Clare's gut twist.

As if he could feel her standing over him, David opened his eyes.

"How are you here? Alive?" His voice was hoarse, and she didn't want to know why. Clare threw her arms around him, but he flinched.

"Are you hurt? I'm so sorry," she said.

234

He waved the comment away. "I'm sorry I didn't believe you, but you can't be here. They're looking for you."

"I know. Can you walk?"

David nodded but winced as he got to his feet. It was going to be slow going. Clare darted out the door and checked the hall. Still empty.

"I don't suppose you paid enough attention to remember the way out of here?"

"I was hooded. Why don't you know the way?"

"I was unconscious."

"What?" David raked his hands over his shaking head. "We're going to die!"

"Probably." She held out her hand, and he took it.

"If we get out of this, you never get any favors ever again," he said, walking gingerly.

"Deal."

They stole down the hall and paused, listening before looking around the corner. There was another short hall and then the brighter light of an open room. They hugged the wall, and as they got closer, Clare could see low couches and an enormous fireplace. Equally enormous windows stood on either side showing the lawn.

"This is an outside wall." She whispered. "If we follow it, we'll come to a door."

"We'll be eaten first."

"Probably."

He followed after her. The next room didn't have a door, but it had a window that might open. Like moths to a flame, they both went to it and pushed. Like the bolt on David's door, it slid easily. Clare couldn't escape the thought that if even one human had ever broken free, that wouldn't be the case. She motioned for David to go first.

He pushed up, but his face contorted with pain. His hand went to his ribs. Clare guided him to sit down on the window sill. If this didn't work, she'd haul him out by the shoulders. One way or another, they were getting out that window. But David managed to lift his legs over and ease his body to the other side.

He cleared the window and smiled back at her, but then his smile froze. Clare refocused her eyes to see her reflection in the top windowpane. A large man stood behind her.

"Where're you two heading, sunshine?"

The beast's arm was tight around her in an instant. She threw her elbow back into his middle with no effect.

"Run!" she said. But David stood there, frozen.

"Come 'ere, boy."

David's face shot back and forth between panic and blank, and Clare understood. His body didn't move, but it was only a matter of time. She allowed herself to go limp as she followed the connection between her and David.

His life was going cold under the creature's blanket of ice. Clare pushed between them and felt it flinch in surprise at her touch, but only for a moment. When the thing grabbed, it's hold went deep. The tremor of pain that went through it mirrored her own as the cold penetrated through her core. Then, heat came roaring in, screaming a terrifying battle cry. The ice exploded into mist that dissipated into nothing.

A thud snapped her back to the physical world. The body sprawled out behind her, and David stared at her with his mouth open. She scrambled through the window, grabbed his hand, and pulled him as fast as he could go toward the woods at the edge of the lawn.

"What the hell just happened?" He half trotted along, still holding his side.

They made it to the woods, and Clare wasn't about to stop.

"They can get inside you."

"Yeah, I realized that, but how did you get there too?" David slowed and looked at her. "Did they do something to you?"

"No. It's not that. I…" was some kind of probably-human freak with a fiery companion. "I just felt what they did and did it back."

David narrowed his eyes at her but allowed her to pull him further in the woods. She wasn't sure of the direction they were going, but the more distance they put between them and that place the better. Weaving between trees was difficult with spotty moonlight and noisy with David's limping along. Leaves crunched and twigs snapped under their feet. When they stopped for a breath, another twig snapped, and both their heads turned toward the sound. They heard a deep huffing.

"Clare?" It was a low, growling voice, how she imagined a bear would sound if it could talk. David stiffened. "You got out! Where's Adrian?"

"I don't know. I got out by myself. Who are you?"

A hulking form stepped into the moonlight. It stood upright, but the moon illuminated fur, and claws, and yellow eyes.

"Shit!" David's voice was panicky. "Werewolves. Really? Really?!"

"Calm down!" she shot back. "They were hiding me."

It stepped closer, and David backed away.

"It's me, Perry. Adrian's not with you?"

"No. I haven't seen him."

Just then, Clare became aware of the presence of many things moving through the woods around them. Meg appeared, a black cape around her, looking small and human next to her grandson, but she assessed the situation like an army general. Her eyes flicked from Perry to Clare and David.

"He's still in R&D," Meg said to Perry. "Come on." With barely a sound, they merged into the flow of bodies pouring through the forest. After the Therians had passed, a hand touched Clare's shoulder. She spun around. Jonathan stood there, looking grim faced after the others.

"What's going on," she said.

"They're here for Adrian. And for battle." His voice was rough.

"Is this because of me? Did Adrian come after me?"

Jonathan shook his head. "This was coming. You may have sped it up a little, but it was going to happen with or without you."

"What about you, your family?"

He blinked a few times. "The Therians are in route there too."

"Why aren't you there?"

"That was never the plan," was all he said.

David hung back until Jonathan pulled a small electronic screen from his pocket. The glow drew him closer until he could look over his shoulder.

"Are you trying to break into a quantum code system? That's uncrackable."

Jonathan glanced up and then back. "I'm already in. I'm executing a program that loops the security feeds. The security system has fail safes, so it won't hold for long before the program is flagged, but they don't need long. They just needed me to buy them enough to breach the perimeter."

"So, what do we do now?" Clare asked.

Jonathan finished typing and folded the screen back into his pocket.

"We wait."

31

Bleeding

Rule #26 Never accept a vampire's blood

R esearch and Development was cool and clammy. And empty. God only knew where Lach had sent the other workers. It took some time to prep him alone, but eventually, Adrian's body was stripped almost naked—*we wouldn't want you to wake a new vampire with any reminders, just in case*—and strapped to an incline table. His head was angled down with both arms strapped above it so that his wrists hung well off the edges.

They were going to drain him.

Adrian tried to *stretch*, to reach out and warn Perry, but his life clung to its anchor. Must be how it was for the humans. Ha. Here at the end, he got to feel human again for a moment. And it really fucking sucked.

Lachlan was tightening the strap on Adrian's left arm and humming "Music of the Night" to himself, when he stopped. Adrian felt his arm being turned. His blood burned. Shit! Shit shit sh—

Pain stabbed at his elbow. *Porca miseria!* For the barest second, Adrian was glad he couldn't move. He didn't want to give that psychopath the satisfaction of seeing him grimace. The angelic face came into view, and Lach squatted to be on the same level.

"Did that hurt? I imagine it did. Get the mark from that girl?" He rammed his thumb into the spot again. Pain flared. "Been doing a little research yourself, have you? Figure how to heal it yet? That might be important to know. You think Siri would mind if we ask you before we proceed?" Lachlan grabbed Adrian's jaw, turning his face toward him. "You wouldn't mind would you? No, of course not. You'd welcome staying in your absurd existence."

The bastard gave his cheek a slap. "It's likely I'll still hate you after all this, but I'm sure your disposition will improve. That is, so long as it works." Lach leaned down, letting his breath wash over Adrian's ear as he whispered. "Honestly, I'm not entirely certain you'll live through it. You'd have to accept her blood again, and between you and me, I think you'd rather die."

Lachlan straightened, his smile widening. "Either way, it's going to be a good night."

He had a choice.

Adrian had thought that because he was already hers, she could force this, but after all this fucking time, he still had a choice. The boiling, impotent rage began to abate, and the quiet that replaced it was something he hadn't felt since he'd been human. It was like feeling the power of the tide rolling in, wiping away all that had happened since it'd been gone. This night, his choice would be different.

He'd carried Paul's stricken face as a reminder of the monster that he was, but it had been Paul's memory that kept him from being a monster. And he would not lose that. Nor would he become the thing that would hunt down Perry or enjoy Clare's death. Adrian had hated himself, but now, there was nothing he wanted more than to remain himself. And they couldn't take it. His years of hatred and revenge had been wasted, given away, but this moment was his.

And he would win it.

He and time hung suspended, and despite Lachlan's humming while he busied himself, Adrian was calm. Fuck them. They could kill him, but they couldn't change him. He would go as himself.

Perhaps once he was severed from his anchor, he could warn that dumbass mutt that Jonathan had betrayed them. No one really knew how that worked, but he would try. It would be his eulogy, and it would be for his friends.

This time, his dying would bring no more death.

Siri's light footsteps broke his reverie.

"Sorry that took so long." She was talking to Lach, but she stroked her fingers down Adrian's exposed stomach. "Father's been having fits trying to find "the leak," and I needed to make sure everyone kept quiet about what we're doing. Is he ready?" The bitch ran her hand through his chest hair. So much for his moment of calm. But he wasn't going to be in her power for much longer.

"Yes," Lach replied, "but I'd like to have a little chat with him first. The straps will hold solid. You can revive him."

"What is it?"

Lachlan's form drifted past, followed by Siri's black pants.

"I found this on him. I assume he got it from the same place you got yours. It might be good to know what he's been doing with that girl before he can't remember. Besides, you haven't healed from yours yet. There may be a trick to it."

Siri huffed. "You want to delay this? I don't care what he's been doing with that girl, and we can heal anything but brain and heart removal. We're running out of night! And father will put a stop to this the moment he hears anything." She stroked his face. "He values Adrian too much."

There was a smile in Lachlan's voice. "I can assure you, my lady, none of my people will say a word. And if you've silenced the people on your end, then we still have a couple hours."

"Fine, but you're wasting your time. He's beautifully stubborn that one." There was affection in her voice.

If Adrian didn't want to rip her arms from her body, he might pity her.

A wave of life crashed into his body, and the change left him. He didn't strain at the bindings. There would be no point. He reached out to *stretch*, but Lachlan mashed down on the blood burn, and the *stretch* was lost in its bright pain.

"Ah, I knew that hurt. I like it much better this way." Lach's sentence ended with a growl.

Siri rolled her eyes, but Lachlan looked down at him with a hungry, black gaze. *Madonna Santa.* This was gonna hurt.

"How did you get such a token?" The bastard muttered as he traced the spot on Adrian's arm. "What do you and the little light do that gets messy?" Revulsion twisted Adrian's stomach as Lach the licked burn. "Still tastes like thrip." He lowered his face to Adrian's, and his smile faltered.

"Look. He finally learned to control himself after all these years. Damn. He's no fun at all this way."

Siri frowned. "Yes. So I see."

A sharp pain sliced into Adrian's wrist. He tensed. He'd endured worse. Hell, he'd inflicted worse—chopping off his own fingertips—but if Lach had his way, he'd endure far, far more before the night was over. A moist thread of blood slid down his palm to drip from his fingers. Focusing his energy, Adrian stanched the flow.

"He can still heal, but he hasn't restored this. I may have been wrong."

A note of panic touched Siri's voice. "It can't be healed?"

Something was thrust deep into the burn, and despite himself, a groan escaped Adrian's lips. He couldn't deaden those nerves. On the edge of his vision, he saw Lachlan lift a bloodied scalpel to his nose. He frowned and handed the instrument to Siri, who sniffed it as well. She wrinkled her nose.

"Smells dead," she said.

"Aye, it does." Lachlan turned back to Adrian, eyes gleaming.

Blood was flowing freely from the new wound, running slick down his arm, and he couldn't stop it. He hadn't thought about the veins when he'd chosen his test spot. Adrian drew in a deep breath. It was only the cephalic vein. Good for a meal, bad for bleeding out. Damn. That was worse.

Siri thrust her hand at Adrian. "Is there a way to fix this?" Her frantic gaze flicked to Lachlan. "Is it possible he's not healing to spite me?"

Lachlan licked fangs. "I'm sure I could persuade him to tell us."

She bent over Adrian, clutching at his chest. "As much as I love you, this is too dangerous to let go." He wouldn't give her the satisfaction of saying a damn thing. Her fingers bit in, bruising deep into his flesh. "Tell us, Adrian, or you bring this upon yourself!" There was a slight tone of desperation in her voice. Well, maybe one damn thing.

He opened his mouth to speak, and Siri leaned in to hear. *"Vaffanculo,"* he whispered in her ear.

She jerked back and swept the instruments off a nearby table with a scream. She grabbed the edge, flipped it, and turned black eyes on Lachlan. Shit. He'd never actually seen her lose control before.

"Fine! He's yours."

Lachlan sucked in a breath of expectation.

"But do *not* kill him or, so help me, I will rip your fucking head from your body!" Adrian could hear the crashing of tables and the tinkling of glass as she stormed off. Her voice trailed back, "Come for me before he's bled out!"

Lachlan turned to him. "As much as I'd hoped, I never thought I would finally get you."

Adrian closed his eyes against what he knew was coming next. He could feel the trail of Lach's fingernails, as the bastard debated where to start. The sensation stopped at his midsection. The sear of the scalpel ripping into his abdomen was nothing to the wrenching pain as Lachlan reached in and pulled out a handful of his small intestine.

Fucking hell! Adrian strained at the straps, a guttural cry of pure rage and agony ripping from his throat. All humanity left him.

"What? Having control issues again? Is the human form not suited to a little discomfort? You really don't need intestines anyway. Why those aren't erased when we transform has long been beyond me."

Focusing his energy against the damage did almost nothing as long as that bastard's hand was still in his body. So he tried to cut the signals coming from the nerves to stop the pain.

"I do hope you hold out a long time. As soon as you tell me what you've been into, my fun is over." Lachlan pulled out another loop and laughed as Adrian's teeth clenched tight enough to snap.

"See what a good time we can have together?" Blood was seeping onto the table and dripping to the floor when he withdrew his hand. He bent down to pick up one of the instruments Siri had scattered. Panting, Adrian rushed to pull his body back together.

When Lachlan righted himself, he was holding what looked like a drill.

243

He pressed the trigger, and the bit whirred. *Figlio di puttana!* Leaning over Adrian's right side, Lach felt along his ribcage. Finding a bone, he rested the bit over the spot, and began.

Adrian jerked which only drove the bit in deeper. He tried to keep the screams in, to dull the pain, but when the drill broke free of the bone and plunged into his lung, the sounds turned to wheezing anyway. His lung began to collapse, and he fought desperately to keep it inflated. Lach pulled the bit from his chest and examined its glistening tip as Adrian scrambled to repair some damage.

"I've found the lungs to be a superb place to cause pain," Lach mused. "Let's do the left side now, shall we? I'll have to go a bit lower, must mind that heart of yours. Unless you're feeling chatty, that is. No? Excellent."

Dio santo. The pain was everywhere. Adrian tried to mend and stanch blood flow, but Lach knew his craft. He forced the drill down into Adrian's chest and swirled it until it drew out a gurgling cry. Adrian thrashed against the straps as Lachlan reversed the bit. Blood filled his mouth, and the life was soaking out of him. Shit. He wouldn't be able to heal much more.

"I do love working with tools."

Adrian spat his blood at the son of a bitch.

Lachlan tsked. "My pants were still good, and now you've ruined them. I may as well get them really stained now. Let's pull a bone, shall we?"

He set down the drill and took a step back to consider.

"Hmm, I think the tibia. What do you think?"

"I think you can burn in hell," Adrian growled through clenched teeth.

"And the silence is broken! Well, I must be doing something right." Lach pulled his palm back and slammed it down on Adrian's leg.

A groan slipped through his teeth when the bone snapped, but as Lachlan began yanking on the splintered end, Adrian's reserves finally ran out. His screams echoed through the empty laboratory. Lachlan smiled and pulled harder.

A muffled explosion shook the building. Lachlan's hands slipped from the wet bone, and his eyes darted around. Shouting and fast footfalls echoed from above. It was a fucking ocean of pain. Adrian was able to quell the bleeding while Lach was distracted, but the bone was another matter.

Siri flew into the room. Her eyes locked on the mess of Adrian's body and blackened. She was next to him in a breath of time, fingers on the exposed bone. Adrian let out a cry as she pushed it back into his body. Then, she spun back to Lachlan.

"We have to finish this now whether he talked or not. The mansion's under attack."

"By whom?" Lachlan asked, as though wanting to know who'd stopped by for dinner.

"Therians," she snarled. "Who else?"

Therians. There were Therians. Here. Oh God, he hurt. Thinking hurt, but how... Jonathan. The thrip took his bike. He told them, and they came early. *Madonna santa.* They came for him in the night.

"Shouldn't we be helping then?" Lachlan asked in the same disinterested tone.

"Adrian might bleed out before we got back!"

The bastard rolled his eyes. "Your attachment is unfathomable, but as you wish."

He grabbed a scalpel from the table. The slice barely registered in the tide of Adrian's pain. He could feel his remaining blood gushing through the cut in his neck, but he was past the point of healing.

"How will we know when it's time?" There was actual worry in Siri's voice.

"You'll feel his thread begin to break."

Another explosion was followed by the clanking of things falling in the lab. Siri began to pace, but he gave up following her with his eyes. He was tired, and damn, it was cold. Why was he cold?

A roar filled the lab, but he couldn't come and spar. So tired. It must be day. His eyes drifted closed.

Lachlan laughed, and Siri let out a bloodthirsty cry. What had their panties in a twist? The bed he was lying on was knocked on its side, but it didn't hurt. Nothing hurt anymore. He must have been able to fix that last cut. Thunder and growling rippled through the air. He needed to sleep.

A smell brought him instantly to his senses: living Therian blood. Adrian forced his eyes open. Why was Perry here? He wasn't supposed to be here. But he was, and he was bleeding. Lachlan laughed again, but this time it was slower and deeper.

No one else was supposed to fucking die for him.

He pulled all the energy he could rally, until the effort alone seemed about to break him, and Adrian sealed the slash on his neck. No longer inverted, the trickle from his burn all but stopped. He felt light, like he no longer fit in his body.

"A natural born Therian in my lab." Lachlan's crooning came from somewhere behind him. "This smells familiar. Have I met your parents by chance?"

The sound that ripped from Perry was primal. It had the resonance of loss. It sounded like death. Shit! Not now. Not when he couldn't help protect him.

All at once, Siri filled his view. She'd crawled around the table to the sounds of violence. The skin on her face was still healing from a series of long jagged cuts.

"Adrian," she whispered. "Here. Take my life. We have to get out of here."

She sliced at her wrist with her teeth until the blood began to flow and held it to his lips. His dry mouth ached for it, begged him to swallow, told him he could do that much. If he did, he might have the strength to help Perry.

But he wouldn't remember who Perry was.

Adrian coughed it out.

"Don't you want to live?"

Hell, he actually didn't want to die.

The table he was strapped to was jostled.

She brought her wrist to his lips again. As he let the blood dribble out, a new voice joined the fray.

"He's mine, Perry! You get Adrian." Gran.

Siri looked up. Her black eyes narrowed to slits, and she threw herself over the table.

Blazing light seared through the room and made Adrian shut his eyes. Lach's screeching rent the air and then a metallic clang, and there was silence. Opening his eyes, Adrian saw Lachlan, his fair skin covered in red and black boils. A metal table leg protruded where his left eye should be. Pieces of skull and brain were strewn out across the wall behind his head.

Adrian exhaled. Perry was safe. He could sleep now.

Light steps were running away.

"I'll get her," Meg said.

"Adrian?"

He felt the table being moved, but it was far away, like when he *stretched*. Was he *stretching*?

"Adrian!"

The pain in the mutt's voice confused him. Perry didn't have to worry. Adrian was still there. He'd won this time.

Adrian felt Perry *stretch* to him across the distance.

"You're still there."

He was still here. He'd won.

"Hang on!"

He could feel the last threads to his anchor fray. Then, from across the void, a sensation touched him. Hot, sweet blood was filling his mouth. Flooding it.

"Come on! Swallow!"

It was so far, too far. He couldn't feel his anchor anymore.

Perry yelled like he was pulling on something heavy, and Adrian felt Perry's *stretch* grab on to him.

"Swallow, dammit!"

He did. The thread to his anchor solidified, and he drew in a ragged breath.

"Yes!"

Adrian felt his mouth being opened and more blood poured in. He swallowed. As Perry's wild strength began to eek into him, pain flamed in his body. His straps were being ripped off. Why did his skin feel like it was on fire? He felt himself eased to the ground. His bones. The fire was in his bones. More blood. Perry's blood. He swallowed. The blood seared all the way down, lighting him ablaze. He could hear a strangled sound escaping him. Finally, the pain receded to a faint prickle. He forced his eyes open.

Perry sat back on his hunches and ran blood-caked hands through his hair, relief on every line of his face.

"You bloody idiot!"

Adrian worked up a smile.

"Here. Your body... you need more." Perry held out his wrist again.

Not Perry's. He could feel his brow furrow.

"Don't even go there, asshole. Besides, you're not taking it. I'm giving it."

Adrian closed his eyes. Perry was right. It wasn't like with Paul.

He braced himself for fire as Perry brought his slashed wrist to his mouth again, but Adrian allowed himself to drink. There was no flame this time, but living Therian blood was more potent than anything he'd ever experienced. Perry's fierce, raucous life poured into him. It pushed, with joyous abandon, into his veins and injuries. Even the blood burn on his arm began to close. When a well of energy started to build in him, Adrian thrust Perry's arm away. The power felt intoxicating.

He pushed himself up as Perry closed his wrist. A slight sheen of sweat covered his friend's paled face.

"I took too much."

"Better?"

"*Coglione!* You should have stopped me!"

Perry shrugged. "I had to get you back for saving my hide the day we met."

"You're one insane son of a bitch."

"Watch it. Gran might take offense." Perry's lopsided grin faded into a quizzical look. "Your eyes—"

Motion caught the corner of Adrian's vision. A flash of metal. Perry jerked, eyes wide.

Lachlan was propped up behind them. His mutilated face stared with one eye, a hole displaying his partially damaged brain. His arm was extended. Adrian understood a moment too late.

They both looked down at Perry's chest. The wide end of the table leg protruded from it, covered in gore. Even if Lachlan's aim hadn't been true, Perry had given too much of himself away.

They locked eyes, and Perry croaked out, "Protect Mary and the pup."

The weight of his body fell limp on Adrian's shoulder. In a numb shock, he held on to him.

"Perry? *Perry!* Answer me you fucking bastard!"

Adrian stretched, but no *stretch* could reach his friend anymore. There was no light in his eyes, no excitement or curious wonder. All that was left of him coursed through Adrian. He laid his friend's empty anchor to the ground.

It had been for nothing. His brother was dead. Pain rose up like a mountainous wave.

And Adrian leaned into it.

He turned to face Lachlan. His foe was already launching himself but was slowed by his still gaping wound. Fueled with vibrant, savage life, Adrian ducked and thrust his hand up through Lachlan's mid-section. His fingers wrapped around the bastard's shriveled heart, and with a howl of grief, he tore it free of it's webbing.

Lachlan's body fell, and Adrian hurled the organ away. Covered in blood and screaming, he bent down and twisted the head from Lachlan's body.

A frenzy was upon him.

Only flashes entered the consciousness of the destroying angel. There was fire in the demolished lab, but he did not remember setting it. Flames neared Perry's body, and then he was carrying him up to the main level. There was another explosion. He was crouching over Perry, hemmed in and hissing. Debris and bodies littered the floor. The sprinkler system activated, and blood and water flowed.

Therians. There were Therians with the sound of their roars and snarls. Yellow eyes flashed at him, but he could not come and play. He only danced with death tonight. Every time he saw its black eyes, he wrought his retribution again. He remembered spinning and leaping and blood. Blood that spilled and poured and spurted. Blood that did not—could not—quench the crushing pain.

He reached the main entrance. Perry was in his arms again. The doors were splintered across the restaurant. The sounds of fighting were here too. Lights shone out in the darkness. The lights brought boils and screams. He strode through them.

A new sound began to wake Adrian. It sounded like the wrenching of his own heart.

Meg.

Meg was wailing and screaming over the burden in his arms. Time returned. He set Perry down, and Meg collapsed on top of him. Her body heaved and her fingers dug in as she gripped what remained of her grandson. Her cries were tortured.

The Therians, still torn and bleeding, encircled them, and Adrian was suddenly aware that the fighting had ceased. He looked around the circle, for a moment fearful—this was his fault—but one by one, they sent up a howl. And he added his voice to the dirge, bleeding his pain into the night air.

32

Surviving

Clare's Postscript: Don't just survive—Live

The sounds of battle were muffled: explosions, yelling, and screams diffused by distance and trees. Occasionally, there was the sound of footsteps fleeing through the woods. No one spoke. And then Jonathan dropped, his body falling like a marionette cut free. Clare and David both rushed to him.

She felt at his neck for a pulse before realizing how pointless that was.

"What happened," David asked. "Is he still alive?"

"I don't know." Clare ran her hand over his body, searching for some sort of injury. "I don't know." Then an idea surfaced. "Stay quiet. I'm going to see if I can find him."

"Find him?"

She just shook her head, laid her hands on Jonathan's body, and closed her eyes. Touching him made it easy to find the connection. She sank through his anchor, but his frozen mass of life was pulling away from it. She followed the pull, trying to grab hold of him. He was being drawn in toward a violently sputtering mass that was drawing others in and consuming them like a black hole.

Clare *stretched* harder, trying to reach him before the thing unraveled him and added his life to its own. She was never so glad for the icy pain that jarred through her, but the pull against them was so strong.

"You have to help me," she said to him as she tried to heft him back.

There was no response.

She pulled harder, but they were still going toward the cold blackness. Bits of him began to fray, and then fire bloomed around her.

"No! Not this one. Don't hurt him!"

The fire lashed out. Clare screamed, but it wrapped around her, warming and strengthening. Together, they held him against the flow. She could hear David talking far away. She must have screamed with her body as well as her soul.

"Clare! Are you all right?"

"Yes," was all she could push out. It was hard to talk, to do anything but hold on to Jonathan as the blackness fed and grew stronger.

She strained backward, her grip slipping, and then the pull disappeared with a suddenness that hurtled her into her anchor. Clare almost toppled over Jonathan's prone body. He still wasn't moving. Tears pricked at her eyes.

"Clare?" David put a hand on her shoulder.

"I had him. I could feel him. I think I lost my grip."

After everything else that had happened that night, she had nothing left. Clare rested her head in her hands and let the sobs come.

"Don't cry." It was quiet and shaky, but it was Jonathan.

"You're alive!" Clare struggled not to shout. Her relief came out in a flood of words. "I didn't know if it would work, and I was trying to hold on. Then I thought I lost you. What happened? Are you all right?"

As Jonathan pushed himself up into a seated position, his eyes caught the moonlight and reflected it. Beside her, David gasped, falling backward on his hands.

"It's okay." She reached out to steady him. After what David had been through, she couldn't fault him his panic. A few days ago, there would have been no convincing her that she'd ever willingly be near a vampire, let alone try to save one.

"He's a vampire! He's one of them!"

"He's one of *us*." She looked back at Jonathan who gave her a grateful smile. "What happened?" she repeated the question now that the drama was settling.

Jonathan grimaced, and when he spoke, his voice was gravelly. "Lachlan gave me life. Tonight, he needed it back."

"That pull?"

Jonathan nodded.

"Why did it stop?"

"He's gone."

"Dead?"

Jonathan nodded again.

"And you're okay?"

"I'm weak, but I'm alive. I wouldn't be if you hadn't come for me. But I won't be able protect you now if anything comes this way. I can't even regain human form." He pulled himself off the ground. "We should go."

Neither David nor Jonathan moved quickly, but they began to pick their way in the opposite direction of the mansion. Slowly, the sounds of war faded.

A single howl rang in the air, and then it was joined by innumerable others. "What is that?" Clare asked. "Did we win?"

"The Therians aren't fleeing," Jonathan said. "So we haven't lost, but *that* sounds like grief."

Clare made to move toward the sound, but he grabbed her arm.

"They're phased—dangerous—and wounded." She must not have looked convinced. "If you or I were ever in danger by them, it's now. Come on. The cars are parked this way."

They walked away from the dirge through the trees until they came to a service road. Without a word, Jonathan got in and started the last car in the convoy that lined the way. Clare grabbed the handle and looked at David across the car. Finally, he shrugged and got in the car with them. Jonathan drove them to a tall building in Richmond.

"I need to be here, in case any of the Solifugae come for refuge. I'll be able to let the Therians know what the damage is," Jonathan said. "Do you think you can find your way to the warehouse?"

"Yes." At least she thought so.

* * *

Very few Therians were left at the warehouse, and Clare had no answer for the anxious questions on their faces. A room was found for David, and she went to her own. She sat down on her bed to wait but must have drifted off. A caterwaul woke her. The hallway was filled with a blur of faces and murmuring, but she could pick out Kenyon who was supporting Miriam.

"NO!" Miriam wailed. "It's not real! He's not—he can't be!"

"I'm so sorry," Kenyon said, and Clare saw emotion on his face too.

Miriam began to keen again, and Clare knew. She didn't have to look to know she wouldn't see Perry. The crowd parted as Meg came faltering forward. Her eyes were yellow, and where whites should show through, there was only red. She held a trembling hand up to Miriam, and the women fell into each other's arms, their bodies heaving in sorrow. Clare turned away and slipped back to her room, face wet. She knew this pain, and there was nothing she could offer. Years might turn the agony to a dull ache, but nothing ever filled the loss.

She wasn't sure how long she'd sat on the bed with her knees drawn to her chest. The clock lay against the wall in pieces, but the sounds of mourning and motion had died away some time ago. At points, she drifted in and out of a dreamless sleep, but she lifted her head at the sound of her door opening, and her breath caught in her throat. Adrian, in all black, stood in the doorway.

"May I come in?" His voice was quiet.

She watched as he guided the door so that the latch held it ajar. A crack of light shone in from the corridor. He crossed over to the chair that sat by the nightstand. She sniffed at the air as he passed, remembering what Meg said about the smell when vampires had been healing themselves, but all she could smell was the strong scent of men's body wash. Clare turned her body to face him. He sat with his elbows on his knees and his head in his hands and did not move, did not look at her, for several minutes.

Finally, he folded his fingers, lifted his head above them, and said, "It's safe for you to go back to your father's house. You can't go back to your job or continue to use your pseudonym because some escaped. But they don't have the resources to track you back to your family now."

Relief rippled through her. She could go home. She was safe.

"Thank you."

He gave a harsh laugh, "I terrorized you, fucked up your whole world, and you thank me."

She ran her hand over her face and sighed. "I wasn't really living it. I was hiding from it, hiding from pain, from myself."

He looked at her with inscrutable brown eyes, and somehow she just found the words tumbling out.

"Now, I have to figure out how to live, and it's frightening in a way that you could never be. If it's me—if I'm not pretending to be a perfect daughter or worker—and I fail, then, *I* have failed. When you're a facade and something bad happens, it doesn't sink down to you, and you're still safe. Nobody knows you or loves you since all they can see is your mask, but you're safe. I don't have a mask anymore, and I'm afraid." Tears were escaping down her cheeks. "If you'd killed me, I would have died alone. I want to live, so that when I die, people can actually miss me and know what they're missing. I want to be brave, and I want to live... And I don't know why I'm telling you this." She laughed at herself through her tears.

He gave her a weak smile before his eyes grew distant.

"I'm... sorry about Perry."

She reached out and rested her hand on his shoulder. It was a gesture she'd found comforting in grief, but he jerked in surprise. He looked down at her hand and back at her, but then tentatively put his hand on top of hers. It felt warm.

"Thank you."

After a moment, he stood, and she let her hand slide away.

"I never thought winning would mean losing so damn much." Adrian headed for the door but paused as he reached it. "Therians don't often get to bury their dead. Between that and trying to connect with the team that was retrieving Jonathan's family, it may get hectic here, but Kenyon will take you home when you're ready." He slipped out and down the hall.

Clare followed after him. She was done running and hiding.

"What if I'm not ready for a while? Perry said there were more tests to run with my blood, and I could write, give the survivors a proper voice."

Adrian turned, dark hair falling across his cryptic gaze.

"That may abbreviate how much time you have for the living you want to do," he said.

"After this week, I think I have some idea of the risks involved."

He studied her for a moment. "Then, I think that would be welcomed. Last night's battle will ripple across our worlds, and the Therians could use the edge you might give them."

He started toward the door at the end of the corridor again, but the journalist had one more question.

"And you? What will you do?"

"Me?" Adrian asked, and Clare thought she saw a yellow glint in his eyes. "I've got some research of my own to do."

He gave her a sideways smile and stepped into the sunlight.

Epilogue

Jonathan felt strange being in Adrian's studio apartment. The older vampire's style and presence seemed embedded in the place. It was like Adrian might, at any moment, come around a corner and demand to know what he was doing here.

But Jonathan didn't know if Adrian was even alive or how long it would take the Therians to get a message to him. They certainly couldn't risk coming here. If any high ranking vampires had survived the attack, they were likely on their way now.

Hopefully, they had blood with them. Adrian's fridge was empty, and hunting was not something Jonathan was ever going to do again unless he absolutely had to. But he was so weak. Clare had managed to bring him back somehow, but not all of him. He needed to feed. He plopped down on the black leather couch to wait. Sunrise was soon. If any vampires were coming, they'd be here by then. If not, he could rest easy until nightfall.

He walked through the living room. Next to the sofa, there was a polished wood coffee table with a copy of *The Survivors' Handbook* and notepad. But not an electronic one—Adrian had nothing with a computer chip in his flat—just an old-style notepad. Adrian's angular handwriting stood out on the yellow paper.

It was a poem.

The House of Black and White

Here I am alone
   In the house of black and white
   I am chilled to the bone

With only myself tonight

I stare in the mirror
  My reflection's stare to see
  But it is not clear
  Which is image, which is me

Are we joined in a dance?
  Do we spin through the night?
  Or are we in a locked stance
  Of an untenable fight?

Who begets whom
  Does light chase the shadow?
  Am I me or am I you?
  What is real and what's hollow?
  A quiet invades
  With a single drop of red
  Black and white all fades
  For I am finally dead

Jonathan swallowed. Was Adrian dead?

He laid back on the couch, a stream of worries rolling across his mind until the rising sun sapped the last of his consciousness and he slept. He didn't know how long he was out, but access to a shallow pool of power told him it was night. And no one had come yet. Maybe they were all dead.

It was too much. He couldn't just sit and wait. Meg had instructed him not to access their computers once the attack had been executed. Said it was too risky, but Nidhi's computers were down. There shouldn't be any risk for days. He pulled the screen out of his pocket and unfolded it.

Kenyon had only allowed him into systems needed for the attack, but that wouldn't get him anywhere. He rooted around and found one message pinged to several other servers before being sent out. It didn't turn out to be what he was looking for, but it was from Clare, so he read it anyway.

To: JJones@youknowit.com

  Cc:

  Subject: My last assignment

  From: Clare@youknowit.com

  Janice,

Thank you for the opportunity to work at *You Know It*. I apologize for everything about the way I'm doing this, but I have to leave. I'm sure that you've read my submission for my article on the Helios, so whether you believe it or not, you know why. I was terrified when I wrote the first piece and have since seen almost all of those fears realized, which has led me to reflect on my tone. Please consider this as a replacement.

  I may be in touch.

  Clare

I was given a simple assignment, and it changed my life. I was asked to do a piece on the Heliophiles as a fashion trend and subculture. For those of you not acquainted with the term, it's the name taken by a group of people who are convinced of the existence of vampires. Many wear unusual clothing, have silver laced tattoos, and only operate during the day. They live by 31 rules set out in The Survivors' Handbook, *a collection of stories from the survivors of vampire attacks.*

I interviewed anyone who would talk to me, and while some seemed to have hopped on the train of the newest conspiracy theory, others were disturbingly rational about their beliefs. The Helios warned me repeatedly that, by writing this article, I would be drawing the vampires' attention to myself. I was told they kept surveillance on almost everything. As a purportedly sane person, it was a warning I disregarded.

I now find myself in the uncomfortable position of losing my job and my credibility because the Helios were right. I doubt that you, dear rational reader, will believe me when I tell you that I was attacked by a vampire anymore than I believed The Survivors' Handbook, *but I was.*

I originally wrote a piece to warn and advise, but I'm not going to tell you not to donate blood or to get a cologne designed to mask your scent from vampires. In the end, I think that they will do whatever they want to do.

What I want to tell you, what I am risking everything to tell you, is that life is much bigger than you think. Do not disregard the experience of another because you have not encountered it yet. And above all, live. Risk pain in order to love. Risk letting go in order to forgive. Risk rejection in order to be yourself.

I would like to set forth my own rule for the Handbook: *Rule # 32 Don't just survive - live! Maybe you will meet your end by a vampire. That's unlikely, but no matter how it comes, death comes to all of us. You may not have another day. So, whatever the cost, live today.*

Jonathan smiled. She'd made it back safely. She was going to be alright.

That still didn't tell him where to look for information on his family though. He'd been told the tactical team would cut the surveillance feed wires before going in, but that was the original plan, before things went sideways with Clare and Adrian getting captured. Jonathan backed out of the Therian systems and went to his feed access channel. It pulled up.

It was still live.

The house looked ransacked. There was broken glass, overturned furniture, and blood. He zoomed in on his son's room. It was empty, no blood. He panned over to the bedroom: empty of life, but it looked like a war zone. And he could just see something in the shadow of the open door to the master bath. He zoomed in and adjusted for low light. The screen dropped.

Tam's face stared out lifelessly from the bathroom floor.

Glossary of Italian

Italian is a creative language with creative swear words.

These are roughly translated:
   A fanabla: Go to hell
   Cazzo di merda: Fucking shit
   Caglione: Asshole
   Dio Santo: Oh God
   Figlio di puttana: Son of a bitch
   Madonna Santa: Mother of God
   Ma quanto sei coglione: You're such an asshole
   Merda: Shit
   Porca miseria: Dammit
   Porca troia: Fucking hell
   Troia: Whore
   Vaffanculo: Go fuck yourself

About the Author

J.E. Kraft wrote her first book, Kittens, when she was seven, and despite struggling with poverty, ADHA, and Dyslexia, she hasn't stopped writing since. She grew up into an awkward super geek; lover of animals, bugs, psychology, and science. She can be found in Tennessee with her husband, two kids, a cat, dog, lizard, frog, shrimp, and a variety of houseplants. When she's not busy writing, she advocates online for mental health awareness and crushes the hopes and dreams of her loved ones in board games.

More from City Limits Publishing

The year is 2363. The remnants of humanity are living on "Quest", a large space station that has housed the last members of the human race since its near-extinction hundreds of years ago. When the station is found to be on a collision course with a supernova, Captain William Scarborough and other members of the station scramble to survive in a deadly escape mission to a nearby planet. The only problem: the station's escape craft can't rescue everyone.

Concurrently, Jason Acker is not only struggling with the possible termination of his species, but with his own mind as well. The closer he and his family come to death, the closer Jason comes to going mad. He, along with his family, are led on an action-packed journey filled with sexual desire, deception and gore. Along the journey, Jason is confronted by a religious cult, his lustful spouse Fiona and the most horrifying decision of all; whether or not to give into his own demonic desires.

The clock is ticking for the Acker family and the rest of humanity and a decision must be made on what is more dangerous; the supernova or Jason himself.

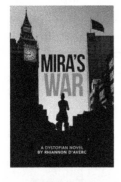

The EU is dead. The UK is gone. London's political climate is one of fear, death, and distrust. Into this comes Mira, a young punk with nothing left to lose. An ensemble cast of intertwining plotlines collide when Mira must choose to save herself - or an innocent boy.

Abigail Henderson was a slave in the Empire of Truth and Light; a fascist country that was as bad as Nazi Germany but followed Moses' instructions to the Israelites' in the Book of Numbers (31:17: Now, kill all the boys. And kill every woman who has slept with a man). After surviving a truly horrific processing, she was sold to an old man (Dr. Kurt Van Heflin) who intended her to be a companion to his blind granddaughter (Inga Van de Clerk), but, it wasn't long before she became more than just a slave; she became part of the family.

Once the Secret Police discover they've been helping the underground, they raid their home, not once but three times; each time subjecting them to more and more humiliation and torture. Finally they decide to escape. This is how they do it.